THE DATA COLLECTORS

DANIELLE PALLI

DEDICATION

Thank you to my husband, John Palli, my partner in love and life, and the technical advisor for this book (as well as in-house tech support and fixer of things that break). Thank you to my dear friend and colleague, Cindy Readnower, for production, marketing, and editing support (and your willingness to juggle many hats at once). Thank you, Mia Ruggiero, for your editorial eye. Thank you, Joan Peters, for designing the cover (and for your exceptional taste in wine. You are welcome to come to dinner any time). To the friends and family who make up my tribe, thank you for your never-ending love and support.

I am grateful.

CONTENTS

SECTION ONE

"If human laws are universal laws, then consider why anyone would kill another—fear, greed, power or hate. Often a combination of those traits. So, ask yourself who might exhibit those traits?"

DRAMATIS PERSONAE

R oman Aurelius: Human male (Section 0), wavy black hair, green eyes, tall and slender.

Cepheus Baruch: Royal male (Section 1, Section 3), stringy gray hair, yellow eyes, tall and lanky, shapeshifter (lizard/human).

Tanager Blackletter: Erde male (Section 1), curly blonde hair, brown eyes, average height and weight.

Drake Cushing: Human male (Section 0), black hair, blue eyes, medium height and stocky.

Bryce Cushing: Human male (Section 0), brown hair, blue eyes, medium height and build.

Dr. Archibald Ennis: Human male (Section 0), bald, brown eyes, tall and thin.

Fatima Fortunata: Human female (Section 0), purple hair, gray eyes, short and Rubenesque.

The Fortunata Family (Human): Keti (aunt), Tai (brother), Mama Fatima (mother), father, extended members, varied hair and eye colors.

Lucene ("Lucy") Jones: Earth-born female (Section 0), blonde or brown hair, hazel eyes, average height and weight, toned body.

Kunz Malaya: Male (Section 5), monarch, blue/gray fur and matching eyes, small, bulky stature, shapeshifter (wolf/human-like).

Reverend Isabella Simone: Human female (Section 0), spiritual advisor, white hair, violet eyes, tall and thin.

Jim Sparks: Erde male (Section 1), sandy hair, hazel eyes, short and slender.

Bagheera: Male cat (Section 0), black shorthair with yellow eyes, very handsome.

Fredo: Lesser Royal male (Section 3), red body and black eyes, large and thick, salamander-like with no noticeable shapeshifting abilities.

Ginny: Human female (Section 0), red hair and pale gray eyes, short and plump.

Hamish: Royal male (Section 3), brown hair and gold eyes, short and slightly overweight, shapeshifter (lizard/human-like).

Ivan (the Tinkerer): Human male (Section 0), red hair and green eyes, medium height and stocky.

Morphinae: Vitruvian (Section 2), shapeshifter, (varied gender, species, coloring), Balance-Keeper. Often prefers doll-like and butterfly-like lifeforms.

Odessa: Vitruvian (Section 2), shapeshifter (varied gender, species, coloring), prefers mermaid-like form the most.

Sabrina: Royal female (Section 3), black hair and yellow eyes, tall with average build, shapeshifter (lizard/human-like form).

Director Sutton: Human male (Section 0), light brown hair and hazel eyes, average height and slightly overweight.

LOCALES / SPECIAL GROUPS

The **Assembly:** Intergalactic gathering for the Intergalactic Peace Project (IPP).

Balance-Keepers: Special interest group in Section 2, Vitruvians. Will intervene to ensure all forces remain in balance.

Data Collector: Specialized team from Section 1, collecting data on Earth to save species.

Erde: Planet in Section 1, known for setting up preserves to rescue and protect humans.

Erdelings: Species from the Erde planet in Section 1.

Intergalactic Peace Project (IPP): Formed to create and maintain peace among intergalactic species.

International Registry of Alien Residency (IRAR): Created by the United Commonwealth (UC) to record and track aliens living on Earth.

Peace-Keepers: Nickname given to all inhabitants of Section 2, in particular, those living on Erde.

Royals: Nickname given to all inhabitants of Section 3, no specific planet-base, nomads.

Section 0: Earth and planets from common and neighboring galaxies.

Section 1: Erde and planets from common and neighboring galaxies.

Section 2: Vitruvia and planets from common and neighboring galaxies.

Section 3: Royal landscape and planets from common and neighboring galaxies. Galaxy boundaries change regularly.

Section 4: Limited communication with neighboring species, located in a section of the universe with multiple black holes.

Section 5: Silva and Trappist solar system as well as planets from common and nearby galaxies.

United Commonwealth (UC): Earth subdivision of the IPP to keep and maintain peace.

Terrestrial Academy of Research and Awareness (TARA): A leading university in Achel where the Data Collectors are trained.

Vitruvia: Planet in Section 2 known for its renegade band of Balance-Keepers.

Vitruvians: Species from the Vitruvia planet in Section 2.

PROLOGUE: THE STORM

25 YEARS AGO. 20 YEARS BEFORE THE ASSEMBLY.

"Forget the paddles, idiot!" Drake yelled to his younger brother above the wind and thunder as the downpour from the squall beat on them mercilessly. "Just hang on!"

The storm rolled in so quickly that the boys had no time to react. The waves were choppy, tossing their wooden fishing boat up and down as if it were a small coin that someone was flicking up in the air and then catching as it landed.

The sky was black, and visibility past the end of the boat near non-existent. With each toss of the boat more water splashed inside. The older boy tried to reach one hand to grab at a life jacket that slid past him, but he hadn't been quick enough, and it lodged itself under a downturned bucket at the front of the boat.

Bryce gripped the seat beneath him with both hands at his older brother's instructions. "What are you going to do?" He yelled over his shoulder as the sharp rain pelted him in the face.

"I'm going for the lifejackets!" Drake wiped the drenched hair from his eyes and tried to stand before the tossing of the boat landed him with a hard thud onto the wooden seat.

"Let me try! I'm closer." The younger boy lifted slightly out of his seat and cautiously reached an arm out in front, feeling around the wet floor until he touched what he thought must be the strap of one of the vests. "I've got it," he began to say, before the next wave overtook them, knocking him off the boat and into the frigid water. A loud thunderclap erupted, followed by an electrically-lit sky.

"Bryce!" the older boy screamed. The sky went black again. Moments after, the boat lurched onto its side, sending him into the lake before landing on top of him, cracking the side of his head in the process.

Bryce resurfaced, gasping for air and flailing his arms frantically. He circled his arms over the top of the downturned boat and hugged it for life. "Drake! Where the hell are you?"

A crack of lightning lit up the sky once more, just long enough for Bryce to see a head surface from the water. "Drake! Over here!" he yelled. "Swim this way!"

As instructed, the head began to move toward the boat, and it was only when it was several feet in front of him that the young boy could tell that this wasn't his brother.

Staring back at him was a blue face with black eyes that looked more like large buttons. Its skin had the texture of a crocheted plush toy, and its hair was stringy like indigo yarn. Just when the boy had convinced himself that it was the head of an abandoned toy that somehow ended up in the water…it blinked.

Bryce began to scream as the blue figure slowly drew itself out of the stormy seas, suspended in the air. It turned to look at him. The creature's chest was bare, and he wore ragged blue jeans that seemed like an afterthought. His body had the same pattern as his face. Otherwise, he had two arms and two legs and was almost human.

"I don't know what the fuck you are," the boy yelled at the figure, "but you gotta help me find my brother!"

The figure stared at the boy intently, as if doing mental calculations. Bryce fell silent, somehow understanding that his fate was at the mercy of this blue creature. From the scowl on the creature's face, Bryce feared that it would sooner kill him than help his brother.

The creature came to a decision, stretching one hand out over the water. Moments later, Drake's body floated to the surface. Bryce began to scream again, his words incoherent as tears flooded his face. The button eyes followed the scream as the boy's eyes grew wide in fear. The creature outstretched his other arm and Bryce found himself being lifted out of the water, hovering several feet above the waves.

As quickly as it had begun, the storm faded, and the night rolled in. Bryce felt himself being carried like a cat by the scruff of its neck, across the water alongside his brother, finally being deposited gently onto the nearest mangrove island. He struggled to balance among the meandering root system of the red mangroves that served as their floor. His brother lay limp along the small patch of wet sand. The creature stood over Drake, once again lost in thought. A moment later he flipped Drake on his back and touched a finger to his chest. With a jolt, the older brother's chest rose, his upper body lifted in midair, and then fell back to the ground. Water poured from his mouth as he choked air back into his lungs. He turned with eyes glazed over to look at his savior.

"Drake!" His brother called, stumbling toward him. At the sound of his name, Drake sat upright, shivering. Bryce knelt beside him, throwing his soggy arms around him in an embrace. "I thought you were dead!" he cried.

"He was," said the blue creature's deep voice.

"Who…what the hell are you?" Bryce croaked out as the creature turned his back on the boys and began to walk into the lake.

"Morphinae," the blue creature announced over his shoulder. "I am Vitruvian."

This meant nothing to Bryce, but as the creature began to descend into the lake, he remembered. "Thank you!" he called. Morphinae nodded slightly at the acknowledgement.

"Wait!" Drake found his voice. "You can't just leave us here, Blue-head! No one knows we're here, and we have no food or water."

"You should have known better," Morphinae chastised, his eyes growing dark. "Being at sea in weather such as this with no provisions." Once again, he began calculating thoughts. His button eyes turned momentarily to Bryce, and something in his heart softened. *But,* he thought, *the boy did say 'thank you.'* *Humans hardly ever did that.* Finally, he answered, "I will see that you have help." With that, he descended into the lake.

"CEPHEUS, PLEASE HELP US." Seven-year-old Lucene Jones concentrated as hard as she could, scrunching up her face until it hurt. She sat strapped into the back seat of her parent's green utility vehicle, hugging a plush, black, cat toy for comfort. The rain poured down violently, pelting the hard top, making it sound as if the rain and thunder were coming from inside the vehicle. Lucene's mother, Dora Jones, kept gripping the center armrest with both hands, twisting her body uncomfortably to check on Lucene in the back seat.

"I'm going to pull over at this next rest stop," her father, Xan, yelled above the storm, white-knuckled hands gripping the steering wheel. Dora nodded in agreement.

"Don't worry, Lucene," her mother comforted, "Daddy's going to pull the car over until the rain passes. It'll be okay." Her mother's words did not match her feelings. She, too, was afraid. Lucene could feel it. "Why don't you work on one of your meditations? It will help calm you down."

Lucene nodded. She had been doing that very thing. She imagined an open red door in front of her. Through it, was the storm. She watched the storm at a distance as she moved further and further from the door. With her mind's eye, she slammed it shut, drowning out the thunder and lightning trapped behind it. It was silent.

"Please, Cepheus," Lucene tried again, this time whispering aloud, "Could you please help us? We're really scared."

From lightyears away, Cepheus replied, "I will try."

Lucene took comfort in that and was just beginning to relax a little when she felt the car jolt. Her mother screamed as the SUV swerved off the road and began tumbling over and over, leaving Lucene hanging from her seat belt. She felt pieces of glass shatter around her, some of them embedding into her skin as the rain poured into the car. The last thing she remembered was a painful shock running through her before everything went black.

CEPHEUS FELT the energy of a lightning bolt shoot through him, awakening him from his meditation with a sudden start. He looked down at his arms in surprise but noticed no visible signs of any trauma. He tried once again to mentally connect with Lucene first, and then her parents, to no avail. He uncrossed his legs and stood clumsily, taking a moment to lean over and place his hands on his knees as if to both stretch his limbs and catch his breath. A tear rolled down his otherwise expressionless face.

He left the meditation room, softly closing the door behind him.

"Well?" Tanager asked eagerly, noticing his older friend and mentor's blank expression. "What happened?" The young man paused from the ornate wood sculpture he was carving.

"Nothing...nothing," Cepheus whispered, hanging his head. "They are gone. She is lost."

1

THE HOSPITAL ROOM

"Well, Ms. Fortunata, it appears that you were well-named," Dr. Archibald Ennis peered over his clipboard at the plump girl squirming in the hospital bed who was attempting in vain to unravel herself from an ill-fitting robe and a tangle of bedsheets. "We just let your parents know that you're going home today. Bet you're glad about that!"

Fatima Fortunata let out a giggle, "I sure am!"

Dr. Ennis smiled back, "They'll be up in a few minutes. You just sit tight."

Fatima wasn't sure she knew how to sit tight, or loose for that matter, her facial expression turning to one of deep contemplation as she gave it some thought.

Dr. Ennis passed by the second hospital bed and paused for a moment to look at the less fortunate Lucene. He tried to smile encouragingly during his quick retreat out the door.

Young Lucene let out a sigh. *When were her parents coming to get her?* she wondered, feeling a sudden bitterness in the pit of her stomach. She looked down at the strange, new fern patterns on her arms. According to the doctors, who were unaware of Lucene's keen sense of hearing while they were discussing her condition at the nurse's station with some Child Services something-or-other, she had been struck by lightning. They were watching for signs of numbness or tingling in her arms, dizziness, and headaches. So far, she exhibited none of these symptoms and the doctors were somewhat baffled.

"What happened to your arms?" Fatima asked, now standing at Lucene's bedside, barefoot.

"Lightning," Lucene answered. "It hit me and left these patterns on my arms."

"Does it hurt?" Fatima looked concerned.

"Nah," Lucene replied. "But I think it might be permanent."

"Cool!" Fatima squealed, enthusiastically. She thought about this some more. "I read in my comic book—not the one I have over there," she shook her head as she waved her hand at the book that lay face down on the end table beside her bed. "But the one I have at home, where this guy got struck by lightning and then had supernatural powers!"

"What are sup-ah-nat-ah powers?" Lucene wrinkled her nose, sitting up with interest.

"No, silly!" Fatima let out a giggle. "Sup-er-nat-ur-al…like, being able to fly, or super strength or the ability to read minds."

"Oh," Lucene was doubtful of this ability, but was willing to give it a try. "Okay, let's see…without actually *telling* me, think of your age, and I'll try to guess by reading your mind."

Fatima clapped her hands. "Oh, goody! You're fun! The last time I was in here, the girl didn't want to play or even talk to me." She furrowed her brows and thought of her age with all of her might.

Lucene closed her eyes and pretended her forehead was a movie screen, and she was watching it to see what would appear. She turned her head slightly to the left, and then right, and smiled.

"You'll be nine in a few days. Your birthday is Thursday," Lucene blurted out, not really sure where that information came from.

Fatima's eyes flew open wide. "Oh my gosh! You *are* supernatural. How did you *do* that?"

"I dunno," Lucene confessed. Though there was something familiar about the experiment, but her head felt a little fuzzy, and she was having trouble remembering much of anything. "I just saw you blowing out a cake with people standing around you...like a party or something. There were nine candles on the cake."

"That's amazing," Fatima gushed, "but where did Thursday come from?"

"I heard a song in my head, one I don't remember ever hearing. It was talking about Thursday's child, so I figured it had to be this Thursday."

Fatima's eyes grew wide with admiration. "Wow!" A nurse walked by the room, pushing a meal cart, pausing to scowl at Fatima. She pressed a finger to her lips to encourage Fatima to be quiet.

"Okay, let me try," Fatima whispered, checking to make sure that the nurse had passed. "You think of your age, K?" Without asking permission, Fatima climbed up on the edge of Lucene's bed. Lucene bent her knees, hugging them close to her to make extra room.

"Okay," Lucene thought of her age as clearly as she could.

"Eight?"

"No."

"Nine, like me?"

"No."

"You can't be ten. You're too little. You're not ten, are you?"

"I'm seven."

"That was my next guess." Fatima snapped her fingers.

"How come you're in here?" Lucene wanted to know.

"I have an arrhythmia," Fatima declared as a point of pride, dramatically waving her hands in the air for emphasis. "My heart beats funny, but not in the normal way that abnormal hearts beat. It's *mysterious* and very rare. My mom says it's because I'm so musical."

"You seem awfully happy about it," Lucene seemed doubtful.

"I'm always happy," Fatima answered with a shrug, as if that explained everything. And, in some way, it did.

"Fatima!" An older version of Fatima bounced in the room, bringing a boatload of energy and smiles with her.

"Hi, Mom!" Fatima climbed off the bed. Lucene watched as Fatima's mom wrapped her in a big hug. She wished her mom would hurry up and get here. Her heart sank a little. Something about the feeling told her that this was never going to happen. She choked back a tear as Fatima introduced her, "This is Lucene! She's my new friend. And, she's got superpowers!"

"Does she?" Fatima's mom played along, her eyes growing wide. "How wonderful!" She put out a hand and gently shook Lucene's. "It's nice to meet you, Lucene."

Lucene felt a warm glow rise from where the woman touched her hand to all the way up her arm. She smiled back. It was almost as if the woman had hugged her too.

Glancing down at the girl's arms, Fatima's mother became aware of the dark tree-like brown patterns on them but thought it impolite to mention them. To Fatima, she said, "Your father is pulling up the car and the nurse will be up in a minute so we can check out."

"Okay, lemme just get my stuff." Fatima went to grab her kid-sized, hot pink suitcase while her mother dashed to the nurse's station to confirm that someone would be along shortly. Fatima's suitcase rolled loudly across the white hospital floor as she passed Lucene's bed. "Here," Fatima paused and handed her a business card. "This is my calling card."

"You have a card?" Lucene seemed surprised. "I thought only grown-ups had those."

"I'm in the advanced classes," Fatima said matter-of-factly and without boast, as if this explained why a nearly nine-year-old would need a business card. "It has my full name on it, see?" She pointed. "If you ever end up in Florida, you can come visit me!" Fatima gave her new friend a hug. "See you soon, Lucene!" She waved as she met her mother at the door.

"Take care, Lucene," Fatima's mother called. "I'm sure your parents will be along in no time to collect you."

Perhaps Fatima was more supernatural than she realized, since Lucene was in New York and saw no reason why she would ever end up in Florida. She certainly did not expect to see her new friend anytime soon—at least not by her definition of "soon."

Lucene looked down at the calling card as if it carried with it some luck. *Fatima Fortunata,* the top line read. Beneath it: *Parrish, Florida.*

2

THE ASSEMBLY

FIVE YEARS AGO.

L ucene sat in the assembly room where more than 215 Earth representatives from the United States gathered for the Intergalactic Peace Project's (aka, the IPP) annual conference, sponsored this year by the United Commonwealth (aka, the UC). Above their heads, they were surrounded by a series of large flat screens, each one reflecting the representatives from Earth along with those of neighboring planets in their own gathering places. Some were in giant lecture halls, like the one Lucene was in, while others could be found in large outdoor coliseums. The agenda was lengthy and a solid four hours was planned for today's first meeting. From the look of it, there were nine planets in attendance, three fewer than last time. This was cause for concern.

She tugged nervously at the hem of her blouse. It scratched at her skin and felt almost as uncomfortable as her restrictive polyester pants and close-toed foot crushers, falsely advertised as shoes. Business attire never felt quite right to her. It was as if she were expected to wear a Halloween costume for 48 weeks of the year. *We can easily communicate with beings from other solar systems,* she thought, *but we can't seem to master 'business casual.'*

For the thousandth time, she fumbled with the translation headset wrapped tightly over the top of her head and snaking down the side of her face. It kept getting tangled in her blonde locks in spite of her repeated attempts to smooth her already abnormally straight hair. Somehow, she managed to set off a loud screech from the headset that had everyone in the assembly eyeing her with at least a minor level of annoyance. Lucene hated technology, more specifically, anything that she considered an unnatural wave-like connection to something else, such as wireless fidelity or virtual keyboards. In her mind, they were too easy to intercept and even corrupt. She got by with her headset by reminding herself that she could unplug it at any time.

"Sorry," she called, not realizing her microphone volume was still set on "max." A few executives jumped, tugging their headphones from their ears at the sudden vocal interruption. Lucene quickly set herself to "mute." Her boss, Drake Cushing, turned his head casually in her direction, grinned slightly out of one corner of his mouth, and then shook his head. Lucene let out an embarrassed sigh and slunk back in her seat. This was her first invitation to attend the conference and now she feared, it might be her last.

The other scribes around her did not seem to notice the eruption, too busy typing rapidly on the hologram keypads in front of them, their words projected onto the front of drop-screen visors that fell over their eyes. The visors, themselves, were attached to their translation headsets, making the group appear more android-like than human. Only they could see what they were typing. There were also a few archaic laptops, and a couple of daring early adopters of Mind-to-Text technology who sat in deep concentration as their thoughts were translated onto the visor in front of them. The latter was not yet perfected, and the scribes could be heard mumbling "delete" and "replace" under their breath.

Then there was Lucene, the only person in the room with a pad of paper and a pen. Recording and photographic devices were not permitted, except by an official member of the council, and Lucene was not, resigning herself to a mid-level government position. A few of the other scribes looked over her shoulder, perplexed. One young, sharp-nosed, auburn-haired woman leaned over and whispered into the ear of the man sitting beside her. She pointed at Lucene's notepad and stifled back a laugh.

"Who let Lucy, the teenage blogger, in?" she asked, reading Lucene's nametag as she spoke. The man beside her shifted uncomfortably in his seat and chuckled nervously. Lucene was tired of being mistaken for a teenager. She was, after all, 27. It's just that her body seemed to think she was still only 17. The woman eyed the tree-like lightning marks on Lucene's arms. Lucene pulled at the edges of her three-quarter-sleeve blouse in a futile attempt to cover them fully. Most of the time, she forgot they were there, except when someone paid special attention to them.

"Well," Lucene responded pleasantly, "Your information can be hacked from a million miles away. Mine, someone would have to physically take from me." The sharp-nosed woman looked surprised at being heard from such a distance. "And," Lucene continued, "It still wouldn't matter, because no one would be able to read my shorthand anyway."

"To each her own," the woman mumbled, sitting back with a complacent grin. She snapped her visor back in place and adjusted her headphones. Lucene choked back a response, secretly wishing the woman's virtual keyboard would suddenly display all the letters inside out, making her notes illegible.

"May I have your attention please," the facilitator on the central large monitor announced. "The gathering shall now commence. Please make yourself ready." There were short pauses between the facilitator's comments as the universal translator found the closest match to English or Spanish. During these meetings, Lucene occasionally liked to slip her headphones off and listen to whichever planet advisor was leading the session. Their native tongue, while mostly incomprehensible to her, was beautiful and fascinating. Though today, with the new headphones, she dared not, in case she accidentally caused another disturbance.

Today's speaker was from Trappist, a planet about 40 lightyears away. She watched as his bulky form projected outward from the screen, making it appear as if he were standing in the room with them. The likeness was so real he could have passed for a live person had he not been hovering in midair with a translucent glow around him.

While he had two eyes, a nose, two ears and two hands, that's where the similarities between he and Earthlings ended. Section 5 inhabitants moved on four limbs, two of which were retractable depending on whether the limb's owner opted to walk on two legs or run like a wolf on all four. Underneath his silver uniform, wrinkled gray-blue fur was the other obvious differentiator.

"For those who do not know me, my name is Kunz Malaya. I am the monarch of Silva, from the Western region of Trappist in Section 5. I am honored to be with all of you today. We will open with the setting of intentions."

For the next five minutes, Kunz read through the IPP creed to uphold peace at all costs, to be compassionate to brother and sister planets and to make open communication a priority—all things that sounded wonderful to Lucene when she first arrived. But, like others, the more she saw of war, hypocrisy, of planets fighting in the same way that countries on Earth fought, of death and disease, the less enthusiastic she became about her role recording and collecting all of this data. In fact, at this moment, she wanted nothing more than to go home, climb into bed, and bury her head under the covers.

"Today, we open our discussion with the most pressing cause for concern," Kunz frowned. "For this, we invite Cepheus Baruch of the planet Erde in Section 1 to take the floor."

One of the tall screens moved out from the wall as Cepheus's hologram stood in front of them, high in the air. He wore a plaid sweater vest over a long sleeved, cream-colored dress shirt and long black dress slacks, which told her that he was not only trying to appeal to the Earth audience, but more specifically, those in the Northern regions of the planet. "Thank you, Monarch. And, good morning, Assembly," he said. Chills ran through her when Cepheus began to speak. There was something familiar about his deep voice, though she couldn't determine why. The most human-like, those living in Section 1, had almost all of the same features with two exceptions. One, they had the capacity to heal from injury much more quickly, and two, their life expectancy was more than double that of a human. Consequently, they aged much more slowly than humans. It was rumored that Cepheus Baruch was born among the Royals in Section 3, giving him the unique ability to transform into lizard form in self-defense, and even grow back arms and legs if they were somehow removed. In her eight years working for the United Commonwealth, she'd never seen anything of the sort of those from Section 1 or 3, and thought the whole thing was a silly legend.

As she observed the speaker, Lucene felt a gentle warmth start at her heart and move outward toward her arms, legs and face, followed by a gentle buzzing through her entire being. She sat upright and began to smile, as if she had just re-discovered a long-lost friend, but caught herself. After all, she didn't know this man, did she? She'd only heard about him through past conferences. Lucene refocused her attention to the meeting at hand.

"What the heck?" the sharp-nosed woman behind her protested. "My keyboard is not projecting properly. It's like it's reflecting upside down and backwards. How can I possibly take notes on this?" Lucene withheld a smile. Really, she hadn't meant to do that…mostly not.

"Here, let me see," the man sitting beside her whispered. "Maybe it's something with the settings." She reluctantly unclipped her visor and handed it to him. He, in turn, temporarily replaced his visor with hers. "Hmm…looks fine to me." She snatched it back as he was still removing it.

"It is not fine, but I will have to type without looking and hope for the best." The man shrugged, returning his attention to the meeting.

"As most of you know," Cepheus began solemnly, "Erde has a special interest in supporting the inhabitants of Earth and their mission to re-create an environmentally sustainable world." Many nodded; others remained expressionless. "Unfortunately, there have been some disturbing patterns of late."

"Please share with us what you mean by 'disturbing,'" Kunz encouraged.

"We've noticed within the past 200 years, the depletion of Earth's natural resources, unusual weather patterns leaving disastrous conditions behind, the decreased availability of water, increased pollution, subjection to toxic elements—including damaging rays from the sun, and ill health of all species on Earth."

A murmur from the crowds ensued, mostly from Earth representatives, some present in the room and several others from their remote locations, their grim faces clearly visible on their screens.

"Order and dignity, please," Kunz addressed the crowd. "Cepheus, please continue."

"About 30 years ago, before the IPP was in existence, the people of Erde decided to try and intervene on the Earth's behalf by sending representatives to collect data on the existing conditions in an effort to discover a solution."

"Data Collectors who pretended to be humans, moving in secret among us," Drake Cushing interjected loudly from his seat.

"Please...Drake," Kunz intervened, reading Drake's nametag for reference. "Cepheus has the floor. We will hear responses momentarily."

"My apologies, Monarch." Drake slid his headset off in frustration and ran his hand through his thick, wavy hair, before putting his headphones back in place. He crossed one leg over the other, resting his ankle on his thigh. He tapped his upturned shoe with a stylus pen, in obvious annoyance. Lucene was surprised. Usually, her boss was exceptionally calm. She didn't understand this current state of agitation.

"It is true," Cepheus continued, "We did move in secret because we had no idea how humans would respond to our presence on their planet. And, as you well know, in the interest of, as you would say, 'transparency,' we informed the IPP of our Data Collectors as soon as a division was formed. They have since been entered into the International Registry of Alien Residency."

"And what happened after they were added to the IRAR?" the monarch asked, sympathetically.

"They began to die off. More specifically, someone or several people began to kill them off." Lucene could have sworn that Cepheus shot her a direct look of warning as he spoke. A wave of panic swallowed her.

You must protect yourself, Lucene. Cepheus's voice spoke to her, but not through the translation headphones. She heard his voice from inside her head. Lucene stared back at Cepheus's hologram, astonished. *How did he do that? More importantly, how did he know her birth name?* She'd been going by 'Lucy' since she was a child. Cepheus quickly averted his gaze.

The crowd erupted with holograms appearing all over the room as other realms tried to take the floor.

"Order and dignity, please!" Kunz exclaimed, and one by one began to mute both the audio and hologram visuals for the screens around the room. "Cepheus, please continue. You have about one minute to finish your presentation before I must give the floor to someone else."

"Thank you, Monarch. The fear is more than just the safety of Earth and the safety of our people, our Data Collectors. We believe that a group from one of the neighboring sections is involved in this slaughter, beings who do not wish to see Earth survive."

"Insanity!" Someone from Section 3 proclaimed. "To come here and be accused by the so-called Peace-keepers!"

"I'm not accusing any specific Sections or planets," Cepheus explained to no avail.

I didn't hear him accuse anyone; Lucene found herself defending this man she didn't know. She went through the filing system in her brain to try and remember. *Ah,* she thought, *the Royals.* The Royals were nomads—a very aggressive group that was constantly seeking to take over uninhabited planets to claim as their own. Many of the other Sections nicknamed them the "Royals" as an insult to their narcissistic and elitist ways. Somehow, they took it as a compliment. So, the name stuck. They had a tenuous relationship with the IPP, at best.

"Requesting the floor next, Monarch," Drake Cushing stood. Cepheus bowed and stepped back, his hologram fading as he did so.

The monarch acknowledged Drake's deference to the order of things and granted him the floor next. Drake stood and quickly made his way to the circular platform at the front of the room.

"Thank you, Monarch," Drake nodded to the facilitator, as was customary. To the crowd, he said, "Cepheus Baruch claims that the Data Collectors came here 30 years ago in the efforts of 'helping' the Earth by deceptively posing as humans to collect information about us." There was a murmur from the crowd. "But isn't it true that your planet has at least a dozen, quote, unquote, 'preservation' areas designed to support human life where you've absconded with members of the human race against their will?"

"No," Cepheus answered from his station on Erde, his hologram resurfacing above them. "Our preservation areas were set up by the Terrestrial Academy of Research and Awareness to provide a safe place for humans should the Earth prove unsustainable."

Lucene had heard of TARA, but she always thought it was more like an intergalactic university that welcomed many species to meet and study there. *Preservations?* This was new information to her.

"Ah, yes. TARA," Drake mocked, looking up at him. "Does TARA's 'research' include human experimentation in the interest of 'science'?"

"Absolutely not!" Cepheus was flustered. From behind Cepheus, other attendees in his group shook their heads in anger at the accusation. Over his shoulder, a younger man with a mop of curly hair peered at Lucene, curiously. She caught his gaze, momentarily, before averting her eyes. In a room of this size, she reasoned, and with so many neighboring planets in attendance, it's ridiculous to think that either of these men were looking directly at her. *Must be like a painting in a museum, where the eyes seem to follow you.*

"And, isn't it more accurate," Drake paused for emphasis, "that your Data Collectors were killed by humans in self-defense when they refused to return to your planet with you?"

"No, that is untrue."

"So, there are no humans currently living on Erde then?"

There was a pause. "There are…" Cepheus answered, honestly. "But they came with us of their own free will."

There was a loud uproar from all audiences and Cepheus's protests went unheard.

"Order and dignity, please!" Kunz protested, and the crowds slowly settled down.

"I don't recall anyone from Section 1 notifying the IPP of humans being relocated to another planet, do you?" Drake addressed the crowd, waving his arm and surveying the room for the answer he already knew. This was news. "You say you come in peace," Drake yelled above the crowd, which was getting louder by the minute. "But isn't it true that Erde is keenly interested in occupying Earth and moving the humans out…indefinitely?"

"No," Cepheus's eyes became flooded as if injected with a yellow die, and his nose began to shift, taking on an almost beak-like appearance. He closed his eyes and took a few deep breaths. Lucene felt herself become agitated on his behalf. She surveyed the growing unrest in the lecture hall, as many attendees were now on their feet and protesting upward at Cepheus's hologram. *Moving humans out? Was this related to the files Drake recently asked her to procure from the International Registry?* She was pulled back from her thoughts.

"For this reason, I move that Erde and all planets in Section 1 be banned from the IPP and be entered into investigation!" Drake demanded.

"Let us explain," the curly-haired man appearing behind Cepheus, jumped to his feet.

"You, sir," Drake addressed him. "Do not have the floor. Be silent!"

The commotion continued as Kunz Malaya tried in vain to calm the heated discussions in the forum. In all of his time as monarch and an IPP member, he'd never seen this level of contention before, and wondered what he was missing?

Lucene surveyed the scribes surrounding her, all feverishly typing their observations. She folded her notepad and tucked her pen away. "Excuse me," she said to the people who occupied the seats beside her. They leaned back into their chairs to let her pass. Once in the aisle, she made one final glance back at Cepheus's hologram who looked back at her with a nod, before returning to the chaos. She made her way out into the hallway and toward the building's exit.

"Excuse me, Lucy," a burly security guard stopped her. "Aren't you forgetting something?" Lucene looked down at her notepad.

"Ah, sorry. My brain doesn't seem to be working right today," she joked nervously.

"Happens to the best of us," the guard smiled.

No information of any kind left the building without permission. Written, audio and visual content was carefully curated and approved before any of it reached the media and the outside world. She'd have to leave her notes in her lock box in the resource room. Lucene quickly made her way down the hall past the IPP offices to the opaque glass doors at the end. She paused in front of them as a translucent red light passed over her form. "Welcome, Lucy," the computer greeted her, and the door automatically slid open. She slipped over the threshold and made her way to her lock box as the door closed behind her.

Lucene never did return to the IPP summit that day. In fact, she never returned to the United Commonwealth building ever again. After locking up her notes, she darted past security and out onto the streets of Manhattan. She breathed a sigh of relief as she exited the property, as if she had somehow been held prisoner there and someone might stop her at any time and prevent her from leaving. She began walking toward her apartment, mentally making her escape plan.

Escape from what? she asked herself. She didn't really know, but somehow Cepheus's warning echoed in her head. *You must protect yourself, Lucene.*

Moments later, she caught the unusual scent of sulfur. She jolted in panic as one might experience during a hypnagogic jerk, just before falling asleep. Then, an explosion shocked the ground. Lucene turned to see smoke billowing out of the Commonwealth building, followed by crowds of people fighting their way through the doors on the first floor. On the upper levels, government employees shuffled onto emergency escape hatches that sprang into place once the upper windows had been triggered, sliding one by one down toward the street below. Lucene stood motionless as sirens sounded and ambulances and military trucks pulled up to the scene.

"Stand back," a police officer waved an arm in front of her and the onlookers that had gathered around Lucene without her noticing. The police began roping off the area with many of Lucene's colleagues on one side, and her on the other. Through the smoke, she saw her boss rushing from the building, a handkerchief held over his face. Even from this distance, she could see that he was limping slightly.

Under normal circumstances, she would have stayed to make sure those she knew were safe, and to offer her testimony to investigators. But somehow, she knew that the best course of action was simply to blend in with the mounting crowds…and then disappear.

3

THE TERRESTRIAL ACADEMY OF RESEARCH AND AWARENESS (TARA)

ONE YEAR AGO. FOUR YEARS AFTER THE ASSEMBLY.

S tudents of the Terrestrial Academy of Research and Awareness, or TARA, as it was known, behaved much like students on Earth. And, save for a few refugees from neighboring planets, most looked like humans, as well.

The academy was founded as a way to educate students about Earth and other alien species and their cultures. One of its advanced training tracks was specifically targeted toward Earth studies and included those who would eventually work on one of the many Human preserves on Erde. They would be teaching humans the skills to evolve as a species in order to adapt to varied climates while protecting them until it could be determined if Earth would continue to be habitable for humans, or if other arrangements needed to be made. In return, humans living on preserves, shared as much as they could with TARA to ensure the success of the mission.

Other tracks included environmental research and development, in which TARA scientists examined collected data about the ecology and resource partitioning on Earth and created systems for the restoration of the Earth's natural balance...assuming they could convince key world leaders to adopt them.

Last, and arguably the most enviable track, was that of the Data Collectors—the ones who would make the yearlong journey to Earth on special assignment to collect information in their specialty, be it oceanic, freshwater, flora, fauna, substrate, human behavior, weather conditions and the like. Upon arrival, many Data Collectors opted to remain on Earth and report back throughout their lifespan.

But when the IPP was formed just over four years ago, Data Collectors began disappearing in large numbers. Many others had been found dead under questionable circumstances. Travels to Earth had been halted, but given the three-year commitment required for proper training, it was decided that classes should continue...for now.

A mild-mannered professor wandered through the long hallway toward Cepheus's office, passing dozens of students ranging from the very young to very old, and each dressed in a variety of garb...if at all. Not wanting to stifle anyone's free will, no major restrictions were put on dress code at the academy. That respect for personal choice had always been a distinguishing quality of those living on Erde and that culture was particularly evident at the school. The one complaint had been when several students decided to attend class garment-less, which disturbed the sensibilities of more conservative students and professors who were simply worried about hygiene. A compromise had been reached, and those students agreed to at least wear a bathrobe or a toga-like coverup while in class. Being a more empathic planet, conflicts were generally resolved quickly, and Erde enjoyed the distinction of having planet-wide peace for more than 100 years, so much so, that they became known as the Peace-Keepers to neighboring planets within the galaxy.

The professor knocked softly on the office door. "Cepheus, my friend, may I enter?" He pushed the door open just enough to peer around the corner at the tall man hunched over his work desk at the far end of the room. His features were shrouded by the black-hooded cape he'd taken to wearing.

"Yes, of course, Tanager," Cepheus replied, almost in a whisper. "Come in."

Cepheus's dimly lit office was something to behold, resembling a cross between an overstuffed library and an inventor's workshop. The room was filled wall-to-wall and ceiling-to-floor with books, electronic devices, blueprints, and scientific models. Contraptions hung from the ceilings and cluttered the tabletops. The windowsill above his desk housed an array of green plants, all competing for sunlight.

"Your students missed you today," Tanager offered, resting his brown, vegetable leather briefcase on top of a pile of books stacked haphazardly next to the desk where his mentor sat. "I'm afraid I'm not nearly as knowledgeable about Earth Agroecology as you are."

Cepheus turned his head, briefly regarding the younger man standing before him who was clad in a retro-style tan tweed jacket with matching slacks, and nodded. There was a glaze in Cepheus's eyes, as if he didn't understand what was being said, but preferred to be polite. His nimble fingers returned to their task of unraveling a series of tangled wires that were connected to an indeterminate metal contraption with wings that sat motionless on his desk.

"We received some news today," Tanager continued, "about Lucene."

Cepheus stopped working and looked over his shoulder. "Lucene?" he repeated, quickly sifting through the files of information in his mind, trying to match a memory to his immediate sadness at the sound of her name. "I thought she was dead...twice."

"No, my friend," Tanager continued, "she is very much alive, and she needs our help."

"Lucene needs our help," Cepheus repeated in a low voice. "What can we do?"

"According to one of our Data Collectors, she has resurfaced in Florida."

"Not dead?"

"No," Tanager confirmed.

"The car accident?"

"She survived."

"The assembly?"

"She survived."

"Then," Cepheus finally concluded. "We must go and retrieve her."

"I wish it were that simple." Tanager sat on the edge of the desk with one foot firmly on the floor. "With the Earth being such a hostile environment, I don't feel safe sending any of our new recruits under those conditions. Plus, it will take us two years round trip to bring her home, and we believe your parents…"

"My parents *are* dead," Cepheus interrupted, not without a hint of anger.

"I'm sorry, the *Royals*. We believe they already have a head start on the technology and are capable of travelling to Earth and back much more quickly than we do. If they find her before we get to her, I'm afraid…"

"They will torture her," Cepheus finished. "As they did the others…as they did me."

"Yes," Tanager was concerned. "They have no idea how her skills work, and may damage her in the process, or worse."

"I will go for her," Cepheus announced.

"Are you certain? I would go with you, of course, particularly since you are still under…Watch."

There was a long pause as Cepheus regarded a box of metal gears on his desk, presumably to operate a clock or similar mechanism. He stared at them intently. "If the universe operates like a clock, the planets being a system of gears all working together to keep the proper time, what will happen if one of those planets stop turning? How would the rest of the universe survive?" He began pulling the small gears out of the box, one by one, and lining them up on the floor at his feet—the only available space left in the room. "Cepheus?" The man did not respond to Tanager; he was busy frenetically rearranging the gears just so. Tanager let out a sigh. "I believe it's time for your medication." Without another word, Tanager put an air syringe up to Cepheus's ear and depressed the plunger, delivering an antipsychotic serum via a fast-paced puff. The slender man's eyes opened wide for a moment, in surprise, before his body began to topple forward. Tanager caught him and guided the man as carefully as he could, to the floor.

He could hear the sounds of students in the hallway just outside the office. Tanager quickly lunged for the door, closing it just as a few students passed by and looked in his direction. Revisiting the man lying on the floor, Tanager removed his own jacket, balled it up, and tucked it under Cepheus's head like a pillow.

4

THE MAN IN THE BLACK FEDORA

FRIDAY AFTERNOON. FIVE YEARS AFTER THE ASSEMBLY.

I t wasn't often that Lucene went grocery shopping in the middle of the day on a Friday. Come to think of it, it wasn't often that Lucene went grocery shopping at all. But there she was, loading up her green, box-shaped motor vehicle on a rainy afternoon, trying to unlatch the tailgate with one hand while attempting to balance her produce-filled cloth bags with the other. She wasn't having much luck.

"God, damn it!" She cursed as several apples, an orange and two Spanish onions rolled out of the bag she'd propped against her thigh that headed straight into a puddle. As she leaned down to retrieve them, her shopping cart began rolling away with her small leather backpack in tow.

Abandoning the fallen spoils, she ran after the cart, though not before the tailgate had a chance to coax her along by smacking her bottom. Lucene let out a few more expletives, cursing the rain, her matted wet pixie cut, and the melted hair mousse that burned her eyes as it ran down her forehead.

"May I be of some assistance?" Tanager asked, catching the shopping cart midflight and spinning it around with one hand. He was standing next to a lamppost holding a bright red umbrella with his other hand. She could barely make out his round features beneath the black hat he wore and the upturned collar of his gray trench coat.

"I'm okay, thanks." Lucene gave a gracious nod, snatched the cart, and proceeded to roll it back to her car. Hunching her shoulders as the rain grew heavier, it pummeled her neck and back. Water had now successfully soaked its way through her long-sleeved gray cotton t-shirt and jeans. For once, she was grateful that she'd remembered to wear a bra.

"At least allow me to shield you from the rain while you collect your groceries," he was persistent, sheltering her with the red umbrella as he fell into a quick step beside her. He wasn't much taller than Lucene and struggled not to accidentally poke her with the point of one of the umbrella's metal ribs. To his own discomfort, he endured the rain making a loud patter as it rudely smacked the rim of his fedora. He had a strange energy about him. Lucene could almost feel it, as if their skin were touching even though there was more than a foot of space between them.

"Um, okay, but I don't want to be a bother," she answered nervously, slinging her backpack over one shoulder and giving the cart a shove, watching as it sailed into the cart return, clanging against other carts in its path. She bent over the puddle and scooped up the fallen fruits and vegetables, decided they were still "good enough" and tossed them haphazardly into a cargo bin in the back of her car and slammed the tailgate shut. Tanager waited patiently as Lucene awkwardly fumbled with the tailgate lock. "Well, that's that. Thanks so much..." The man didn't respond. "Uh...good day to you, sir," she tried to dismiss him a second time.

"It was my pleasure," he tipped his soggy hat, and continued to cover her head with the umbrella until she was safely in the driver's seat. She felt her heart speed up, just a little. She sucked in a deep breath and held it, momentarily.

Lucene didn't like to think she was the kind of woman who thought the worst of people, but it wasn't every day that strange men went out of their way to help her. Other women, yes, but she never felt herself the sort who would warrant that kind of attention unless the intentions were bad ones. She kept a sidelong glance at the stranger standing outside of her car as she revved the engine. The green monster gave a pathetic shudder as the engine died. "Come on, Kermit," she pleaded with her car. "Not today." She revved it again...and again...nothing. "God, damn it," she hung her head with a sigh.

She watched as this strange man in the black fedora gave a slight knock on the driver's side window. She let out another deep sigh and strong-armed the window handle, rotating it just enough to produce a small opening between the top of the windowpane and the roof.

"If I may suggest," he offered, pressing his lips up toward the open space, as if it were a microphone. "My car is just over there." He pointed to a small blue compact car sitting in the otherwise empty lot. "Perhaps I could give you a lift? You can get your perishables home, and we could have a look at what's troubling your vehicle after the rain has stopped. What do you think?"

"While I appreciate the offer," Lucene bit the corner of her lip, "you should get out of the rain and quit worrying about me. I'll just phone my roommate and ask her to pop around the corner and pick me up." She fished through her backpack as if searching for something.

"Very well," Tanager conceded, mouthing the word 'pop' as if it confused him. She tried not to look too relieved. "I'll just wait in my car over there until you've made your call, just to make certain you have assistance on the way. You can," he paused a moment to think, "give me a wave as an all clear that help is on the way." He puffed his chest up and smiled, as if satisfied with his choice of words.

"Sounds like a plan," Lucene smiled, uncomfortably. He paused again, as if processing what she said, before flashing a smile and darting off to the warmth of his dry little car. Lucene picked up the closest item that looked like a phone, a small black notepad, and held it to her ear, pretending to have a conversation.

She glanced over at the man waiting patiently in his car, his fingers rhythmically tapping the wheel as if he were listening to music. From what she could see, he appeared to be clean-shaven with a small, nondescript nose and a medium complexion. His eyes were masked by the hat, but she could make out a tangle of curly blonde hair creeping down from the edge of it, the color hers used to be before she died it an unobtrusive brown and chopped it off. He looked relatively normal, but that didn't mean anything. It was then that she noticed his mouth was moving. *Was he singing?* She grinned in spite of herself.

A sudden flash of lightning, followed closely by a loud thunderclap, jolted her out of her momentary distraction. She dropped the notepad and tried to start Kermit, still dead. Lucene quickly weighed the options. She could run the 50 yards back into the grocery store and ask to use their phone, if only she could actually remember her home phone number. After all, she never phoned herself, or anyone, for that matter. She could ditch the groceries and walk four miles back home, or she could let the strange man in the black fedora give her a lift.

A wave of electrostatic flashes streaked across the sky overhead as lightning struck the ground in several places at once, the boom of thunder in her ears indicating that the storm was now directly overhead. The sky grew black, as if nightfall had arrived early. The lights of the supermarket went out in synchronicity. Such was par for the course in the "lightning capital of the world." Ironic that she chose to live in Florida, considering how much she hated thunderstorms. It was almost as much as she hated the cold. That was why she moved to Florida in the first place, wasn't it? She couldn't quite remember. No, that wasn't it. *You must protect yourself, Lucene.* The words came back to her as if she were hearing them for the first time. But, several years later, and she still couldn't figure out what exactly it was she was supposed to be protecting herself from, although, invisible forces seemed to loom over her in her mind's eye. Still, everything had been completely normal since her arrival in Florida. Well, almost normal.

The heavens picked that moment to finally open the floodgates, as a torrent of drops beat loudly on the top of her car. She shivered uncomfortably as fear overtook her, and that sinking feeling in the pit of her stomach returned. She gazed down at the brown patterns on her arm. Were they glowing? No, it couldn't be!

At that moment, she spotted a shadow out of the corner of her eye, and then it was gone. She tried to dismiss it as a side effect from the lightning strike, but if she had to be honest with herself, she suspected she was being followed. It happened many times, too, over the past few weeks to mean nothing. Of the two potential threats, at least she could see one of them. And what she could see, she reasoned, she could do something about.

Lucene reluctantly rolled down her window just enough to call over to Tanager, who was still sitting in his car singing to himself. He stopped singing abruptly at her beckoning. "Not having much luck, I'm afraid! If it wouldn't be a terrible bother, I'd like to take you up on the offer for a lift."

"It is not a bother at all," he called back. Moments later, the head-lights on his car came to life as he made a U-turn and pulled up beside her.

Lucene quickly jumped from her car and ran to unlock the tailgate.

"Please, allow me," he offered. Tanager opened the passenger seat of his car and motioned for her to climb inside. "I will retrieve your groceries, madam." Lucene somewhat reluctantly took a seat, allowing him to close the door after her. She glanced over her shoulder as he, one by one, snagged her grocery bags and settled them into the trunk. "Close," he commanded of her car, but the tail-gate remained open. "Close," he commanded again.

Curious, Lucene thought. She moved to roll down her window but couldn't find the controls. She motioned to him through the window, symbolically turning a key. He nodded in understanding, locking up her green monster, and snatching her keys from the latch.

"Here you are," he handed them to her as he sank into the driver's side. "I should have assumed it required a key turn."

Lucene forced a smile, taking the keys with one hand while keeping the other on the door handle, mentally making a plan in case she needed to make a hasty exit. *Weren't grocery stores the number one place where women got attacked by rapists?* Alarmingly, she wasn't entirely sure how to open this car door. There were no visible latches.

"You're very kind, Mr...." It was only then that Lucene noticed the rental sticker on the windshield. She felt the color draining from her face. *It's not even his car, registered in his name. He could be anyone, from anywhere.*

"Tanager," he smiled warmly, displaying a mouthful of perfectly aligned teeth. He put out his hand, cordially.

"It's nice to meet you, Mr. Tanager," Lucene reached across her chest with her right hand. He looked as if he were about to kiss it, so she quickly gave his hand an abrupt shake. She jumped slightly, as a static electric shock ran up her arm. She released his hand and returned to clutching the car door handle. "My name is Lucene." Even after five years, it felt strange using her given name: but for some reason, she no longer felt safe using the nickname she'd grown accustomed to for many years. Plus, changing her name gave her the illusion that she could somehow shed her past just as easily as she had discarded the name 'Lucy.'

"Loo-seen," he repeated the name slowly, as if saying it for the first time. "What a beautiful name," he declared, his brown eyes lighting up as if he were a small child who was just handed a big cone full of cotton candy. He tapped the steering wheel and started the engine. "Oh," he said as he released the break, "Tanager is my first name."

"Unusual," Lucene crinkled her eyebrows and pursed her lips as if trying to figure something out.

"I could say the same about 'Lucene.'" Tanager glanced in her direction as he left the near-empty lot and turned down the main strip that crossed in front of the deserted shopping center. "In my case, my family loved birds. My mother's name was Wren, and I suppose she thought she was being clever."

Lucene smiled (for real this time), letting her shoulders relax ever so slightly away from her ears. *He didn't feel like a rapist,* she thought.

"Where am I going," he asked.

"Just over there," she pointed. "Turn right at the next stop sign. I'm a few miles down."

She contemplated whether or not to point out someone else's neighborhood and walk the remainder of the way, but she already knew Tanager just well enough to suspect that he'd insist on helping her carry her bags inside. Besides, she didn't want to contend with the rain, or the lightning, or the strange shadows she kept seeing. Instead, she directed him down the small, winding street, past a series of horse and dairy farms and cottages surrounded by tangles of palmetto, magnolia, banyan and oak trees, some of which were at least a hundred years old.

Several turns later, they concluded their journey. "Make a left here and follow the dirt road to the little yellow house at the end," she instructed. "The one with the bright red door." When they arrived, the driveway was empty.

As anticipated, not only did Tanager insist on carrying her bags of groceries inside, but also in running around to the passenger's side in the rain and putting out his hand to assist her climbing out of the car. He handed Lucene his red umbrella. "Go on ahead," he told her. "I will catch you...I mean...catch up."

Just then, the rain stopped. Lucene folded the umbrella and shook it slightly before handing it back to him. "Thanks," she said. "I'll open the window for us. Give me a second."

Tanager mouthed the words, "Give me a second" to himself.

Odd, he thought, but assumed that he should simply wait a moment and then follow her through the window.

She darted across the cobblestone pathway, bypassing the front door and heading around to the side of the house. Tanager watched her, curious. Lucene fumbled with her keychain, and then inserted a small copper key into the window frame and slid it open. The window was just low enough where she could easily step over the ledge and plant a muddy shoe on the table that sat inside, just below the window.

"Hey, Chica," a short, Rubenesque, woman with wavy lavender hair that was long on one side and short on the other, greeted her from inside. "Why didn't you just ring the bell?" She instinctively reached for Lucene's coat as the soggy roommate took a seat on their living room couch and tugged at her muddy shoes. She'd attend to the man she'd left holding her groceries in a moment, not wanting to leave dirty footprints all over the floor.

"I didn't see your car in the drive and assumed you left for work early."

"Nah, Ivan's still trying to fix the compressor something-or-other for me. I swapped shifts with another cook and am not due in for another couple of hours. Agh!" She jumped, pointing wide-eyed at Tanager, who was skulking at the window.

"So sorry, madam," he said, apologetically. "Uh…where would you like your groceries?"

"Oh! Fatima," she explained to her roommate. "This is Tanager. Tanager, come around to the front door, and Fatima will let you in. Oh, wait…here, hand me those." She motioned to the bags of groceries still in his arms. Lucene took one and handed it to Fatima, and then grabbed the others and placed them on the nearby kitchen table. She once again motioned for him to go around to the front door. Tanager thought it best not to question why she had climbed through the side window in the first place.

"What happened?" her lavender-haired friend called as Lucene headed through the kitchen to the main entryway. "It looks like your hair was replaced by a clump of soggy beach grass. Didn't think it was even supposed to rain today!"

"It wasn't," Lucene mumbled at her luck as she began unpacking the groceries and laying them out on the counter. From outside, a second band of rain passed over the house and a thunderclap made them jump slightly.

Fatima peered over her shoulder. "Hey, where are the onions?"

"They'll be along in a moment," Lucene answered with a nod toward the door. Fatima obliged, flinging the door open, enthusiastically. Tanager had just enough time to run back to the car for the remaining goods, and now stood with cloth bags hanging on his arms like sandbags weighing down a boat. Fatima let out a high-pitched giggle that seemed to start out low, from the depths of her heart and gradually go up the scale as it made its way out and into the air.

"Here, let me help," Fatima relieved Tanager of the bags of produce he was attempting to juggle and laid them, one by one, on the table. She gave Lucene a wink. "I didn't know we were expecting visitors!" The man in the fedora paused to smile and tip his hat to her. Then, seeming to remember something, he pulled the hat from his head and held it to his heart, sending a small puddle of rainwater splashing to the floor. A tumble of curls fell around his face as he regarded the lavender-haired, gray-eyed woman who was only a few inches shorter than he, but considerably heavier.

At that moment, in the far end of the living room, an all-black cat peered its golden eyes around the corner of a doorway. Seeing a stranger, he quickly retreated back into the bedroom, his tail twitching nervously.

"Okay, formal introductions are in order. Tanager, this is my roommate, Fatima." To Fatima she offered, "Tanager rescued me from the grocery store when Kermit flaked out again." Lucene surveyed the pile of groceries on the table, bypassing the fruit in favor of a cinnamon roll she plucked from a pastry bag.

"Fah-tee-mah," Tanager emphasized the name as if committing it to memory and bowed his head slightly. "Another lovely name."

"Well, he certainly is quite the charmer, isn't he?" Fatima chortled, the laugh pulling up from her belly and resonating outward through her pursed, upturned lips.

"Oh no," Tanager answered seriously, "I don't practice magic, only science."

"I see," Fatima answered, shooting a wide-eyed glance at Lucene. "Well, kind sir, may I offer you some water or a cup of coffee while you're here?"

Lucene shook her head in caution, munching absentmindedly on a roll, as if on autopilot, but Fatima dismissed her. Tanager caught Lucene's glance and offered a practiced reply, "No, thank you. I'll just be on my way."

"Uh, thanks again for your help." Lucene started toward the kitchen door, stopping short of actually touching it.

"Surely, you will return to have dinner with us tomorrow night?" Fatima was persistent, ignoring a "what do you think you're doing, are you crazy?" glance from her friend and refusing to open the front door without an answer. "I'll be making..." she glanced with disdain at the Spanish onions, "something other than a red onion chutney and goat cheese tartlets, I guess."

"What? Didn't I get the right onions?" Lucene protested. This is why she rarely got grocery duty.

"No, these are Spanish onions. It's okay."

"What's the difference?"

Tanager interrupted the banter, "I beg your pardon. I must be going. As for dinner, I don't think I should..." He regarded Lucene's contorted face before she realized he was watching. She quickly replaced it with a smirk, leaning on the counter in what she hoped would appear to be a casual manner.

"You most certainly should. It's the least we can do for rescuing my friend from the grocery store. Ivan from next door is joining us, too," Fatima motioned toward their neighbor's house.

"Very well, then," he relented. "What shall I bring?"

"Just bring yourself and your scientific...disposition at 6 p.m."

Fatima hastened him along before Lucene could protest again. "You know your way out of the neighborhood, yes?"

"I believe I can manage," Tanager snatched his hat and quickly placed it on his head. "Now, about your car..."

"No worries, I'll call for a tow after the rain stops. Thanks." Tanager didn't know what a 'tow' was but nodded politely. "Until tomorrow night," he tipped his hat, and was gone. Fatima closed the door behind him.

"What the hell, Fatima?" Lucene slapped her leg in exasperation. "We don't know anything about him, and you invited him back into our home."

"Well, you trusted him enough to let him give you a ride in the first place," Fatima replied, as she dug through the grocery bag, unpacking an assortment of vegetables, lentils and other bulk food items. "Besides, you need to have a little more faith in people. He seems nice, and he certainly seems quite taken with you."

"I only let him give me a ride because I was low on options, and I saw this...never mind." Lucene was too frustrated to argue. "So, assuming Ivan the Tinkerer gets your car finished in time, is there any chance you can give me a quick ride back to the store before your shift tonight? Kermit seems to fix himself after a rest, and I'm hoping he'll do better once he's had a chance to dry out a bit."

"Sure, but I will never understand how a 35-year-old car will magically spring back to life, every time after it stops working. I swear that it somehow keeps running because it doesn't want you to *feel* bad." Fatima put the last of the groceries in the refrigerator while Lucene tossed the cloth bags into the adjacent laundry room. Lucene couldn't explain it either, but up until today, she'd been lucky, and the green monster hadn't left her stranded.

"Ya know, I could take a wee look at Kermit fer ya," a voice called from the window. Both ladies jumped at the unexpected voice behind them, remembering too late that the side window was still open with rainwater running across the sill and down the walls. On the other side, a red-haired bulky man with a mustache and goatee grinned, placing his oil-stained hands on the sill. He didn't seem to notice the rainwater.

"That's okay, Ivan, but thank you," Lucene declined.

"She doesn't trust anyone messing with her vehicle, and she won't buy a new one because she doesn't trust cars with computers in them."

"Ah," Ivan nodded in a way that really suggested that he had no idea at all what she meant, but was just being agreeable.

"That's not true, Ivan." Lucene explained. "I trust you. It's technology I don't trust."

"Wanna come in?" Fatima invited.

"Nah, I gotta git back to the shop. Just wanted to let ya know yer car's ready. I left it in the drive." Ivan was very proud of his work, and Fatima listened intently as he filled her in on the step-by-step process from diagnosis to completion. He clearly wasn't in that much of a hurry after all.

Lucene instinctively grabbed a small glass and spoon in order to mix herself an absinthe cocktail, before she remembered that she still had to go back and get her car that evening. She opted for soda instead.

Within the next hour, the rain let up and Fatima inched her petite yellow car up to Lucene's beat-up monster. Lucene hopped inside and revved the engine up, first try.

"Figures," Fatima called over the rumble of the engine. "Hey, listen. My shift doesn't end until 2 a.m., but I'll keep my phone on in case you have any more problems. I'll just have to call you when I'm on break. Do you remember how the landline works?"

Lucence wrinkled her nose and made a face. "Yes, I remember how phones work, smart-ass." She reached for the car door, neglecting to mention to Fatima that while she knew how to work a phone, she couldn't for the life of her remember where it was in the house. The kitchen? Living room? She never saw a use for it and wasn't always the most observant of people. "I'm heading home anyway," Lucene continued. "I can make dinner for us if you want and leave you a platter in the fridge."

"No thanks, Chica!" Fatima laughed, knowing full well Lucene's inability to find her way around the kitchen. "I'll get something at work. You just get home safe." Fatima waited just long enough to see that Lucene was safely on the road before taking off. As she looked in the rearview mirror, she commented to herself, "Her and her freaky car karma."

5

ROMAN MEETS FATIMA

FRIDAY EVENING. FIVE YEARS AFTER THE ASSEMBLY.

I t was 9:15 p.m. on a Friday evening, and Roman wasn't having any fun at all. He pushed his way past a crowd of twenty-something-year-olds congregating around the house band at the entranceway to the Crab Shack on the Pier bar and grill. It wasn't so much that he hated crowds as much as he abhorred what he would call a "lack of decorum." He detested it in himself as much as those around him. But then, his emotions were a little irregular as of late. By the time he'd elbowed his way up to the bar, he had decided that this night's research would likely be a bust. Not only that, but he was certain his blood sugar levels were dropping. Nothing he ever had to worry about where he came from.

"Gin and ginger beer," he told the bartender as he clumsily inserted himself between an awkward man and woman who were occupying two bar stools at the edge of the counter. He smiled apologetically at the woman for accidentally nudging her elbow. They were attempting to have an intimate conversation while yelling above the noise. From his best estimate, it was their first date, maybe not even a date. They likely met two hours earlier and were trying to determine where, if anywhere, their "relationship" might go. If

Roman had to venture a guess, it would have been nowhere. "And," Roman added. "A bar menu please, I'm famished."

"Excuse me," the overly confident and equally overweight man on the barstool snorted. "If you hadn't noticed, the lady and I are trying to have a conversation. Do you mind?"

The woman blushed. "It's okay," she told Roman in a nasal voice that was accompanied by a thick Northern accent. She twirled a lock of her bleached hair around one finger and smiled sheepishly. "It's crowded, and hard to get the bartender's attention."

The man glared impatiently at the interruption, the color in his face rising as he gripped his beer.

By then, the bartender laid Roman's drink down. He thanked her, plunked a twenty on the bar, tucked the menu under his arm, grabbed his drink, and started to walk away...but he couldn't quite bring himself to. This was just the sort of situation that would aid in his research. And, he was feeling much more brazen these days.

"Actually," he turned to the now-crimson man. "I did notice."

"What are you talkin' about?"

"I had noticed that you were trying to have a conversation."

"Yeah? So, you're just an asshole for no reason?" He laughed and nudged the pear-shaped woman who twirled her hair faster as she attempted to shrink into her stool.

"If you'd really like to know," Roman answered, matter-of-factly, "this woman has been politely trying to figure out how to get away from you for the past twenty minutes or so." The woman hunched her shoulders in a further attempt to condense herself. "She was trying to give you the benefit of the doubt, figuring you were nervous by the way you keep tapping your thick fingers on the bar and clearing your throat for no reason. But the truth of the matter is, you're just an unhappy man with anger issues, and when you get right down to it, she's not attracted to you at all. In fact, from what I've observed here tonight, she'd be much more interested in someone like me."

"You've got a lot of nerve!" He struggled to slide off his bar stool.

The woman perked up, holding back a smile as she looked up at Roman, hopefully.

"Oh, don't worry. I'm not the least bit interested in your lady friend." The woman looked crestfallen. "I just wanted to be straight with you to save you both an entirely uncomfortable evening."

The angry man clenched his fist, jerking his head in the blonde woman's direction, "Is that true?"

She snatched her purse and cradled it in her arms, uncomfortably. "Kinda," she admitted.

The man shot a spiteful glare at Roman.

"Sir, I can see that I've made you angry. However, I was just saving you both considerable time and unpleasantness."

"What are you, some kind of relationship expert?"

"Well, I do consider myself well educated when it comes to matters of the heart."

Without further comment, aside from a grunt, the angry man grabbed his sunglasses and pushed his way to the door, leaving his lady friend to close out the tab.

"Well," the woman offered, motioning to the bartender for a check, "thanks for saving me, anyway." Roman was about to walk away when she stopped him. "Hey, hang on a second. Uh, what's your name?"

"Roman," he paused as he quickly rotated through his mental rolodex of human behavior before offering his hand to shake hers, remembering that kissing someone's hand is generally frowned upon except in more personal settings. "And you?"

"Marcy," she answered before continuing. "Mind if I ask you something, Roman?" "I don't mind at all," he flashed a wide smile of perfect teeth.

"What's wrong with me?"

"Whatever do you mean?"

"Well, you seemed to size that guy up right away, and my lack of interest. So, I'm guessing you are pretty observant."

"Yes, very." He set down his drink and menu and leaned his tall frame casually into the side of the bar, resting an arm on the counter. He wasn't being conceited. Roman was matter of fact about most things. As the bartender plunked the woman's tab onto the counter, he took a moment to mouth the words, "The ahi tuna, please," as he pointed to the menu. She nodded and kept moving.

"Well, what I mean is..." Marcy tried again, "what's wrong with me that a jerk like that would like me, but someone like you wouldn't find me interesting? I'm a nice person, and I like to think I'm somewhat attractive."

"You're beautiful," he answered in earnest. A few passer-byes stopped to look at her, then him, trying to determine if he were making a joke. Roman was, after all, considered handsome by most cultural standards: black wavy hair that nearly reached his shoulders, bright green eyes and a pale complexion that only made his eyes more striking. Conversely, it wasn't that Marcy was entirely unattractive, but she certainly didn't fit the norm. She had large arms with little definition and equally large breasts that looked as if they'd pop out of her tank top at any moment. The rest of her frame seemed out of proportion. Her perfume and makeup were as extreme as her suntan, all of which appeared to have been quite heavily sprayed on.

"Well, thank you," she blushed. "But what is it about me that has me ending up with people who take me for granted, or someone – like that guy – who seems rude and angry all the time?"

Roman considered the question more carefully, noticing that a few people surrounding them were straining to hear his response. Marcy had a look on her face. *What was it?* Fear, he realized, and knew at that moment that he could either crush or raise her spirits. The first option, he also realized, would in no way be to her benefit. Even in his cranky state and with his newfound penchant for saying exactly what was on his mind he relented, sitting on the now unoccupied stool next to her.

"From what I have observed," he chose his words carefully, "you have a kind heart, so much so that you'd likely sit for hours listening to an unpleasant man talk at you rather than hurt his feelings." Marcy turned redder and gazed at the floor, crumbling her lips together, embarrassed. "However, I have also intuited that you attempt to dress and behave in ways that you think will make others happy with you instead of being the kind of person who you are happy with. Love yourself, and you will find love."

Her eyes lit up, as if suddenly struck by an idea. "You know, you're right!" Marcy quickly fumbled with her purse, slid off her bar stool and tugged at her bunched-up skirt until it untangled and hung just above her knees. At that moment, the bartender set a small plate of ahi tuna with avocado and wonton crisps in front of him. Marcy rested a hand on Roman's arm as he was about to take a bite of his food. "Thank you, Roman. What you've said makes a lot of sense, and I appreciate your honesty. Enjoy the rest of your evening." She slid a few bills under a coaster for the bartender before making her exit.

"You, as well, lovely Marcy."

By this time, Roman had drawn a crowd of female admirers along with a couple of men, each one asking him relationship questions.

Finally, he took a bite of his tuna appetizer. His eyes lit up, and he smiled brightly. Suddenly, his evening had gotten better.

"Excuse me!" He called to the woman behind the counter. "Who made this exquisite dish?"

"Uh, I dunno." She turned to a server who had stepped behind the bar. "Hey, Sally, who's working the line tonight?"

"Why?" Sally looked up from the ice maker suspiciously. "Something wrong?"

"Not at all," Roman gushed. By then, he'd already devoured half of his plate while a woman with her hair piled up on her head, held in place with several strategically placed pins, rested her hand impatiently on his arm.

"What about me?" She demanded, batting long eyelashes at him. This, Roman found annoying. He was through playing one-part counselor and one-part matchmaker. He was busy eating, after all.

"Okay, last one," he announced, gazing at his team of admirers. "One second," he told the woman. To the bartender, he asked, "May I have another order of this, please? Thank you." He pointed to his dish. "And, could you give my compliments to the chef? This is the most amazing food I've ever eaten." The bartender was too busy to roll her eyes, but her extended pause spoke volumes. But the more she brought him, the better the tips, so she nodded politely and grabbed a passing server to put the order in.

"Are you a food connoisseur?" A small-framed man with spiked salt and pepper hair asked with a smile.

"No," Roman admitted. "I just really like food." To the woman who refused to let go of his left arm, he said, "I would offer that it is in your best interest to develop a strong sense of independence." He promptly relieved his arm of her grip and turned back to his gin and ginger beverage.

"What's that supposed to mean?" She pouted. "I'll never find someone?"

Unlike Marcy, it was evident to Roman that anything short of a harsh dose of reality would not get past this woman's emotional wall. "It means that your need to find someone may be scaring off your potential prey. Ease up a little. I think I speak for most men when I say..." He leaned in flirtatiously, as if sharing a secret with her. "Confidence and an independent spirit are *very* attractive."

"Oh," her face became suddenly flushed. "Okay, thank you."

"No problem at all, and good luck."

He snagged his drink and shouldered his way to a small, unoccupied pub table in the far corner of the room, hating not being able to savor his food on account of the perpetual interruptions. "Ah, well," he thought. Another should be along shortly. He drained his drink. He assumed his height worked to his advantage, as he towered over the crowd; and yet, when he attempted to alert the bartender as to his new location, his flailing arms went unnoticed.

"I hear the sashimi is awesome," a voice from below Roman spoke. He turned, and dropped his gaze toward Fatima, who was holding up a second plate of the tuna sashimi. She set it down on his pub table.

For the first time this week, Roman was in love.

"Are you the chef?" he asked her.

"'Chef' is such a strong word for a place like this," Fatima snickered. "How about 'cook'?"

"I would call you 'amazing'."

For the second time that evening, several onlookers dressed in designer garb and purses worth more than the average person's monthly rent seemed perplexed, horrified even. But when they gazed at Roman lovingly, it was clear to see that he wasn't telling a woman what she wanted to hear; he was speaking from his heart. Perhaps that's what made him so attractive.

Fatima let out a full-bellied laugh.

"What a delightful laugh," Roman leaned an elbow on the pub table and rested his head in his hand.

"Another charmer!" She smiled until her cheeks hurt. Unlike Tanager, Roman was completely versed in Earth culture, in addition to his vast studies in psychology, anthropology and sociology, he was fully equipped with metaphors and terminology across many continents. So much so, that he was contemplating writing a book about it when he got back home and entitling it, *How to Behave Like a Human in 30 Days or Less,* as a guide for his fellow Erdelings.

"I have been told I am charming, yes." He answered without the slightest hint of modesty. "What is your name, amazing cook."

"Fatima," she, once again, let out that infectious laugh that rolled up her toes in a wave.

Fatima? He was astonished but tried not to show it. Could this be *his* Fatima? The one he had been searching for?

"Hey, hang on a sec," she broke the awkward pause. Fatima disappeared through the crowd, navigating her large frame effortlessly as Roman attempted to follow her with his eyes, hoping she hadn't gotten too far and was planning on coming back.

A moment later, he saw a bottle of wine floating high in the air as Fatima reemerged carrying the bottle and a glass.

"Try this," she instructed. "It's a limited-edition chardonnay and I know you'll like it with this particular dish." She poured Roman a glass and waited for him to take a sip, followed by a taste of the tuna and avocado.

"Even better than the last order," he complimented, trying to memorize her face.

Fatima's cheeks blushed crimson as she kicked the base of the pub table nervously with her toe. She was not generally shy, but it wasn't often she was given such high praise from such an attractive admirer.

"Well, I gotta get back to the kitchen," she motioned a thumb over her shoulder. "I just had to meet the man who gave my food such rave reviews."

As she turned to leave, Roman touched her arm lightly. "I'm Roman, by the way," he told her hastily.

"Well, it was very nice to meet you, Roman."

With that, Roman watched as his lavender-haired beauty with the mesmerizing gray eyes darted through the swinging door that led to the kitchen. He savored the wine and sashimi for the next half hour with a stupid grin plastered on his face. He was oblivious to the loud music, dancing and noise from the bar goers around him. Someone might have accidentally elbowed him in the ribs a couple of times, but he couldn't be sure, and he certainly didn't care.

Roman was confused. TARA had placed him in charge of studying love and the reproduction habits of the human population several years ago. Yet, today he admitted to himself that his emotions have been getting the better of him, and he didn't know why. Had he been human for too long? Was his genetic coding changing, or is this just a result of conditioning? He'd have to make a note of this in his report and have himself screened on his next TARA medical check-in.

Surely, what he was currently feeling could be labeled "infatuation," couldn't it? This was an emotion he was becoming all too familiar with lately. Consequently, he had outlined the timeline of emotions that proved to be fairly consistent: the initial stages of "puppy love," infatuation, and "crushes" only lasted about two or three months, longer for the unrequited. After the hormonal rush wore off, love sometimes developed, but only after that initial grace period. He was certain that "love at first sight" was a myth. Even more implausible is that he began to feel love before he'd even met Fatima. He picked up the loving energy she put in her food. He knew from his research that emotions are vibrations, and it made sense that he'd feel love...but *in love*? Impossible.

For the first time, he did what he swore he'd never do. He took a pen from his shirt pocket and scribbled his first name and number on a paper coaster. So, there was no confusion, he wrote at the top, *For the cook called Fatima*. He took his place by the swinging door that led to the kitchen as a classic country band took the stage, opening with their local hit, "Love Hit Me Like a Truck."

The best way to describe Roman's behavior at that moment was to say that he was doing a great job of skulking. As he skulked by the kitchen door, occasionally peering through the tiny circular window, a few of the servers became nervous.

"Can I help you?" A beefy man who matched Roman's height but outweighed him by about 80 pounds of pure muscle, asked in a low voice, resting a meaty hand on his shoulder. Roman glanced at the security badge attached to his black t-shirt.

"Yes," Roman answered, gratefully, completely missing the obvious. "Would you mind delivering this note to the cook who calls herself Fatima?" He pushed the note into the beefy man's chest.

"If I pass this on, will you be on your way?" The beefy man enquired.

"Oh, definitely. And, I would be most grateful..."

The man snatched the note from him. "Goodnight then." He made his way into the kitchen, stopping once through the doors to shoot a warning glance through the window on the off-chance

Roman decided to follow. Roman reluctantly pulled himself away from the door, and after giving himself a harsh talking to, decided to call it a night.

He meandered quickly through the bustling crowd, keeping his head low to avoid eye contact, particularly with anyone he'd met earlier in the evening. Once outside, the unusually thick air enveloped him in a shroud of sticky heat. He spotted a few couples hastily making their way to their cars. He paused beside his small, black electric vehicle and glanced back at the restaurant, where people were packed in like sardines in a can. Not a single person wanted to sit out by the dock with the temperatures rising, not falling, as the sun went down. "And still they're denying that climate change is real," he muttered angrily to himself as he got into his car. Instead, the "Powers That Be" blamed the abnormal weather patterns on the Urban Island Affect and, of course, an act of God. He drove home in silence.

Once Roman had reached his small condo, he kicked his shoes off by the door. He then stopped at the small efficiency kitchen and pulled a single ice cube from the freezer, walked across the room to the adjacent living room, and deposited it in the planter of a Moth orchid that was blooming beside the window. "Sorry," he apologized to the orchid, closing the shade that remained partially open while he was gone. "I should have done that this morning."

The room resembled a minimalistic hotel room with stain resistant gray upholstery covering a small couch and chaise lounge. Against the wall, sat an espresso-colored TV stand and 32" flatscreen that the stand seemed to swallow.

He flopped on the couch and reached into the drawer of a small coffee table that was wedged between the chaise and the couch. Roman pulled out a notepad and pen. He wanted to get his notes from the evening down before he forgot anything. Instead, he started sketching aimlessly on the page. It wasn't until he got to the eyes that he realized what he'd done. He held the notepad away from him and smiled at the round face and lopsided hair...Fatima.

It was only then that he noticed the phone in his shirt pocket was vibrating: one missed call.

"Hi," he listened to Fatima's voicemail message. "I hope this won't sound too forward, but I'm having a couple of friends over for dinner tomorrow night at 6ish. Wanna come? Here's the address..."

Roman snatched his pen and scribbled down the address. Perhaps the evening wasn't so bad after all.

6

IVAN THE TINKERER

FRIDAY EVENING. FIVE YEARS AFTER THE ASSEMBLY.

To Ivan's credit, he never asked a lot of questions. It wasn't that he didn't care, as much as he thought it best he did not know. If he didn't know, then he couldn't be held responsible for sharing. He liked to dance a fine line that few can manage—that of being morally neutral. Less inclined to label anything as inherently good or bad, he preferred to make decisions based on practicality, and its benefit to the whole.

Somewhat reclusive, his neighbors had taken to referring to him as "Ivan the Tinkerer," as he spent most of his time in a small commercial garage behind his house, rumored to have more inventions in the works than Da Vinci or Edison ever had.

As with many inventors, it all started quite by accident. As a teenager, he noticed he had un-customarily thick auburn hair that coiled tightly and grew faster than a kudzu plant, an unfortunate reality that required he shave almost daily. His first invention was his home-crafted laser hair removal system that left a noticeable scar under his chin. He now alternates between a goatee and a beard because it's easier than explaining. After a series of fails: an electro-magnetic weight reducer that provided first-degree burns, a voice-activated drone equipped with a flashlight and miniature toolkit that mistakenly propelled a ratchet handle whenever he said, "screwdriver, flat head," and a gas, spring-foot propeller intended for home use that would eliminate the need for a footstool that was largely functional, but required a considerable amount of balance. He finally made it big at the age of 37 when he introduced the world's first portable, 3-D printed, micro-tool car repair kit. Sale of said invention to people who could actually market it, netted him a comfortable retirement and the luxury of spending his days doing what he liked best—creating tools to make the world a safer and more efficient place.

Late into the evening, Ivan was busy working on an engine that didn't really exist. Hunched over a laptop that rested precariously on the edge of a table saw, he typed in a code with his two meaty index fingers. The computer would beep, he'd scratch his head and wipe his fingers on his hole-ridden t-shirt as if he were cleaning his hands of the formula, hit delete and try again. Meanwhile, a car engine—a real one—sat helplessly on the garage floor awaiting its fate. A hollow knock on one of the doors brought him out of his quandary. Remembering their agreement, he retreated to the back of the garage, opening a small side door to greet his guests.

"Good evening," Tanager smiled in his affable way. "You must be Ivan."

"I am at that," Ivan bellowed. "Cepheus! Good to finally meet ya. Come on in!"

"Thank you, but I am Tanager. I believe my friend, Cepheus, said that you were expecting us?"

Ivan's intellectual capacities made it difficult for him to connect to the average person, particularly in social settings. As a result, two years ago he'd taken to posting to a private inventor's blog where likeminded tinkerers could share ideas and ask for advice without, he had hoped, giving away too many trade secrets. Maker197 showed up in their invitation-only chatroom one day, and a friendship was formed. It was only when Cepheus requested room and board for a few days that the two learned one another's names, and this was after more than a year of online communication.

Cepheus and a colleague would be in Ivan's neck of the woods and both needed a place to stay. They could pay handsomely for room and board if Ivan could be counted on for discretion, as Cepheus claimed to be working on a special project and didn't want competitors to know he was in town. To Cepheus's surprise, Ivan offered to put them up for a few days in the two spare guest rooms in his home, but he didn't want money. He wanted mathematics.

"Ah, yeah." Ivan shook Tanager's hand heartily. "Good to meet ya, friend of Cepheus."

Tanager waited for Ivan to ask where Cepheus was, and a long awkward silence ensued while one person waited for the other to speak. Ivan leaned against a wooden table, looped his thumbs in the belt buckles of his jeans, and stared expectantly. Finally, Tanager broke the silence.

"So…Cepheus is just getting a few things out of the car and will be along momentarily."

"Ah good, I have the rooms all ready for ya both."

"Thank you…" Tanager paused cautiously, "there's just one thing I should tell you first, so that you're not caught off guard…"

Cepheus didn't wait for the invitation, he peered his head around the door like a tentative cat, as if to gauge the safety of his arrival. Even in his relatively normal state, he still had sharp, vampire-like features: a pointy chin and ears, and sallow eyes. The gray patch of hair on his head was thin at best. He blinked nervously at Ivan like a frightened animal.

Tanager cautiously waited for Ivan's reaction, but Ivan seemed oblivious. "Cepheus, old boy! Nice to finally meet ya. Git over here!" Cepheus floated over to his friend who gave him a bear hug and slapped him on the back. He returned the sentiment with a soft pat on Ivan's back. "Let me get ya situated. I'll help ya with yer bags."

"Thank you, my friend," Cepheus answered in his deep, resonant voice that didn't seem to match his lanky frame. "We have traveled light."

Tanager was puzzled. It had only been a few years since non-humans had been allowed to freely travel to the United States, and only those representing foreign relations were permitted to live here as temporary residents. And yet, Ivan showed no visible reaction to Cepheus's rather unique appearance. Perhaps he was premature in asking Cepheus to wait in the vessel until Tanager thought it appropriate that he could be present.

"I have some news for you," Cepheus whispered excitedly to Ivan, as the tinkerer hoisted a bag from the back of their vehicle before Cepheus could protest.

"I cannah wait to hear it," Ivan smiled back.

"I think I may have the solution to your battery algorithm quandary." Cepheus's eyes lit up.

"God bless ya, I've been fighting with the voltage and timing all evening. If yev got a solution, I swear I'll build ye yer own damn guesthouse next time ya visit."

Tanager followed soundlessly behind the two men who were busy chattering in hushed voices like schoolchildren sharing secrets. While he was happy to see Cepheus returning to his normal self, he questioned their anonymity, his trust in a virtual stranger, and Lucene's safety. The thoughts weighed heavily on his mind as he allowed Ivan to escort them into his home. How much had Cepheus actually shared with this human? He turned pale as he soon found out.

"Just one question, if ya don't mind," Ivan asked Cepheus as he put the bags down in the hallway. "Did ya manage to conceal yer spacecraft at the preserve properly, or do I need to do recon?"

7

SABRINA AND HAMISH

FRIDAY EVENING. FIVE YEARS AFTER THE ASSEMBLY.

S abrina was used to getting her way—always. And Hamish secretly worried about the consequences the first time that did not happen. When she was sweet—which wasn't very often—she was very sweet. But when she was angry, venom poured out of her eyes. Literally. Still, after 58 years of marriage, he felt an odd sense of duty to her. It wasn't love, exactly, was it? No...maybe? He wasn't sure.

Sabrina felt out of place in her surroundings and he knew she hated that. She often wore ill-fitting pantsuits or black dresses and red lipstick, along with equally red nails in an attempt to pass as more human-like. However, her flat nose and gray-toned skin were difficult to cover up with makeup. She contemplated cosmetic surgery and pigment injections for the trip, but decided against it, since she found herself to be exceptionally gorgeous under normal circumstances. None dared to disagree with her.

"Ham!" His wife's voice jolted him to attention, rattling his nerves.

"Yes, my love?"

"We're going to need to have another baby."

"If you say so, my love."

"Right away!" She pulled him into the bedroom suite. "Twice as evolved and it's a shame we still have to do things the primitive way." Hamish and Sabrina were among the last of the Royals. Somehow, they evolved slightly faster than almost any other species in the universe, while aging approximately 68% more slowly than Earthlings and 18% more slowly than the rest of the known multiverse. It was no myth that they could regrow organs and limbs if not mortally wounded or suffering an incurable disease (there weren't many), and they could adopt their lizard features to protect their outer form when under attack. This included rugged leathery skin and venom that flowed from their nails at will, if they scratched you. They weren't always particularly fond of this form, mind you, but it was functional during wartime, and…unfortunately…involuntary when under duress.

Sabrina pulled Hamish close to her in a tight embrace.

Hamish gave her an obligatory peck on the lips. Hamish was much shorter and wider than his wife, looking more like a plump iguana stuffed into a three-piece suit.

"Why did you kiss me?" she demanded. "I didn't tell you to do that."

"I was being affectionate," Hamish explained. "I thought you'd like it."

"My dear stupid husband, this isn't about affection. It's about survival. Haven't you noticed that of all the species across the universe, humans are the only ones who have *devolved*?"

"And yet their populations are three times that of our Royals, in spite of our evolution."

"So are fruit flies, but what's the value in them? I can't wait until we can clean the slate and try again."

"We've tried before. What makes you think it will work this time?"

"Because this time, we'll have a genetically born Data Collector to help us."

"And why would she be inclined to do that?"

"You saw what happened to Cepheus," she reasoned. Hamish nodded, solemnly. "Then you know how persuasive I can be."

Not forty-five minutes later, the Royals were ready for the evening's dinner party in the hotel's banquet hall. Sabrina surrounded herself with fellow Royals, along with neighboring species that she deemed acceptable, running the only five-star casino hotel she knew of in the area that was both maintained by, and catered to, Royals. The general population was unaware, as it was managed by humans who were paid exceptionally well to keep their mouths closed. It only took one leaker to the local paper to mysteriously die by accidentally getting run through a commercial dishwasher, several times, before, even more unwittingly, becoming locked in the walk-in freezer overnight, for the rest of the staff to catch on.

Yes, employees were carefully vetted and often included underground aliens doing their best to blend with the human population in the event they needed to act as the public face of the casino to answer any odd rumors that might be floating about. Rumors, for instance, that thanks to illusive architecture, the hotel was sectioned off so that Earth guests stayed on one side, and aliens on the other - the two sides never to meet. The outside world must never know that the aliens who frequented the place were as illegal as the money they gambled.

The currency at the Royal casino was the Earth dollar. While Sabrina detested humans, she still loved their money. It was considered of special value in the universal marketplace because once humans went extinct, their money would cease production and become valuable antiques. She already had plans to create a money-lined room in her palace when she returned home.

Sabrina and Hamish waltzed through an alien banquet hall, followed by Fredo, their personal bodyguard. Fredo was a formidable beast with a bright red salamander-shaped body and arms and legs as large as tree trunks. He wore what could only be described as a form-fitting black wetsuit that kept his skin moist and his body cool.

Guests looked up from their one-armed bandits, roulette wheels and card tables as they passed, most choosing to wear cocktail dresses and suits from the world they were visiting, though many were noticeably from the wrong time period.

A chestnut-haired woman, donning what could best be described as a black and white gothic cocktail uniform, carried a large box filled with candies and cigarettes. She presented it to Hamish as he passed, who politely declined. Fredo intercepted, not so politely, telling her to kneel before her sovereign.

"That won't be necessary..." Hamish began, but it was too late. She'd already kneeled, dramatically balancing the box of goodies on her thigh, uncomfortably.

"You don't approach the sovereigns, and you don't speak unless spoken to," Fredo spat, swiping his arm and tossing the remnants of her box all over the floor.

Sabrina smirked at first, until she noticed a few disapproving glances from her guests. "Fredo! That was uncalled for." She leaned over the woman, taking her by the chin and lifting upward until the maiden had no choice but to stand. "Forgive me, my dear. My serf is often protective of his ambassadors. I would love a box of your delightful cigarettes." The girl, along with several staff members who heard the commotion, rushed to her side, helping to gather up the contents of her box before she sheepishly presented it to the queen. Sabrina selected one.

"Matches?" the girl inquired and winced in Fredo's direction.

"Not necessary, thank you," Sabrina announced, swiping a nail across the tip of the cigarette. A small ember quickly began. She puffed for a moment. "Most acceptable." They continued down the aisle as a quiet sign that guests should collect their things and follow the procession. Dinner would begin shortly.

LUCENE MEETS CEPHEUS

FRIDAY AT MIDNIGHT, OR THEREABOUTS. FIVE YEARS AFTER
THE ASSEMBLY.

Something that went bump in the night startled Lucene from an incredibly unproductive nightmare about being kidnapped by aliens for special powers she did not possess. She sat up quickly as her eyes struggled to adjust to the blackness, vaguely aware that the nightlight was offering no assistance. She threw the blankets off and planted her feet on the carpet. She tugged at her pinstriped pajama top, adjusting her matching pants as she stood.

"Bagheera," Lucene called out to their black house cat. "Whatcha doin', kitty?"

The room went silent as she fumbled for the light switch. As the bulb flickered to life, she let out a scream.

A cloaked figure the size of a full-grown man crouched atop her dresser. His face was partially shielded by the black cape, and he peered over his shoulder with lizard-yellow eyes and an Ibis-beaked nose. His skin was a pale yellow with a green hue.

"Mrow?" A sound murmured from under his cape.

Lucene's heart was pounding loudly in her ears as she put a

downturned palm out in front of her. "Please, do not hurt my cat," she implored the beast.

The beaked figure glanced down at his cloak. As it fell away from his arm, Bagheera could be seen cradled in the beast's arm as the figure pet him gently with his opposite hand. "I want the cat," Cepheus answered simply. The beast leapt gracefully to the floor and headed toward the bedroom door, Bagheera still nestled in one arm.

"No!" Lucene spoke firmly, picking up the nearest weapon she could find: a weighted brass hand mirror. The beast looked at his reflection in the mirror as if mesmerized by his own image.

"But I want the cat," he paused. "And I want that reflective glass, too." He moved toward her.

"Stop!" Lucene commanded. The beast obeyed, shrinking backward like a chastised animal. "I don't know who you are..."

"Cepheus."

"I'm sorry, what?" Lucene asked.

"I am called Cepheus, and I want the c—"

"Yes, I understand...uh...Cepheus. You want the cat; but you may not have the cat." He crinkled his face in discontent. "However," she held out the brass mirror, "you may have the mirror."

Bagheera wiggled out of his captor's arm and leapt to the ground just as Cepheus snatched the mirror from Lucene's grasp, but instead of running to safety, as was his typical behavior around strangers, Bagheera stood by the man's dirty leather boots, grooming.

Cepheus gazed at his reflection and murmured, "I would never hurt the cat."

The intruder blocked the entrance to Lucene's bedroom, and she had little confidence in her ability to pry the window open in a timely enough manner to leap to her escape.

"Cepheus," her voice crackled, nervously. "Who are you and why are you in my house?"

The beaked man's eyes rolled slightly, and he swayed his head back and forth as if he were trying to sift through files in his brain and remember something. In her own way, Lucene was doing the same. *Why was that name so familiar?* She tapped the side of her head with her palm as if to knock things in her brain back into place. A sudden knock at the door made Lucene jump. Under normal circumstances, she would have screamed for help at the top of her voice, but as she looked down, she noticed Bagheera was purring as he rubbed up against the man's boot.

Instead she asked, "May I answer the door, please?"

Cepheus seemed confused. "The door did not ask you a question." The knock repeated, more insistent.

"Lucene," a voice called from outside.

"Tanager?" She answered carefully, afraid to make a sudden move. "I will be right there!" To Cepheus, she asked, "Would you please let me through to open the door?"

"Let you through what?" he asked, leaning over to show Bagheera his reflection in the mirror, smiling broadly, revealing a row of saw-like teeth.

"Cepheus," she tried again, calmly. "Please walk forward three steps." He took exactly three steps forward and Bagheera followed him. The mirror caught light from the lamp and reflected a bright beam on the carpet. The cat began chasing the light, pawing at it in vain. Cepheus let out a gleeful snort, baring sharp teeth once again.

Lucene took the opportunity to rush through the bedroom door. A soft light from a lamp in the living room left on when Fatima was working late partially filled the room, giving more light-bouncing opportunities for her cat. "Bagheera," she called as she ran to the kitchen door, in an ineffective attempt to get her cat to follow her. She didn't expect that he would, as he never had in the past.

She stood in front of the red door, reaching her hand out, but unable to open it.

Tanager could feel her energy on the other side of the door. "Lucene, please let me in."

"I can't," she answered helplessly. "The door's locked and I have to get out." She ran to the window and quickly unlatched it. She had one leg on the side table, and the other over the sill, when Tanager came around the corner and stopped her.

"I can help," he reassured.

"Let me out, there's a strange...being..."

"Cepheus, I know," he answered. "Let me in."

Lucene pulled her leg back, glancing nervously over her shoulder toward her bedroom. Cepheus was still playing with Bagheera, waving the mirror around as the cat pounced on stray light beams. Tanager gently nudged his way past her as he climbed through the window, tipping his hat in an apologetic gesture for his brashness. He glanced momentarily at her very thin pajama set, which did little to hide the details of her form. He tried not to notice. Lucene leapt from the table and followed him.

"Cepheus," he commanded. "Please stop whatever it is you are doing and come out here, please."

Lucene pulled her shoulders back, trying to make sense of what was happening.

Cepheus peered around the bedroom door, grinning sheepishly like a small child. He walked out of the bedroom, clenching the new beloved mirror to his chest with Bagheera right at his heels. He smiled down at the black feline.

"I want the cat," he explained to Tanager.

"Yes, I know you do, my friend," Tanager answered calmly as he removed his fedora and placed it on the dining room table. He began peeling his brown leather gloves off. "But please be careful. If her cat were injured in some way, Lucene would be very upset." Cepheus recoiled as Tanager came closer.

"I would never hurt the cat," Cepheus dropped his gaze in shame, "or Lucene."

Lucene was startled at the sound of her name as it passed his lips. There was something familiar about his voice. *Where had she heard it before?*

"I know you would never intentionally hurt anyone," Tanager set the gloves on the table beside the fedora, walked around the dining area until he was within arm's reach of Cepheus. "Now, as I was saying…" Before Cepheus could react, he placed a small cylindrical tube inside one of his ears and released a puff of air from a vacuum seal. Cepheus's eyes rolled backward, and his lean body lurched forward. Tanager put out an arm to catch him, struggling slightly with Cepheus's tall frame. Lucene jumped at his side, helping as Tanager guided Cepheus over to the couch where the faint beast promptly collapsed in a heap. Tanager did his best to adjust the beast's limbs so that his arms and legs weren't sprawled in every direction. "He'll come round in a few minutes, you'll see."

"Well, that's reassuring." Lucene threw her hands in the air. "What the hell is going on?" she demanded. "And who are you people, really?"

"Are you sure you don't already know?" Tanager stood up, looking intently into her eyes. His gaze made her uncomfortable, but there was something soothing about it too. She still felt anxious about tonight's activities, but no longer threatened by either of the men. *What kind of weird hypnosis is this?*

"Know what? You're not making any sense." As if on autopilot, Lucene made her way into the kitchen and pulled a bag of pork rinds from the pantry. Among her many eccentricities, Lucene was also a nervous eater. She began munching on a rind as Tanager looked at the bag distastefully. "Life was completely normal until you showed up yesterday, and now…him!" She pointed at the slumped over Cepheus before licking her fingertips. Bagheera now sat at his feet, watching expectantly.

"Normal?" he questioned. "I am curious as to your definition of normal."

"What's that supposed to mean?" Lucene demanded.

"For example," Tanager offered. "Is it normal that you have the worst diet of anyone I have ever seen and yet, you have the body mass of an athlete?"

"My diet is just fine. Besides, I exercise. And, how would you even know what my diet is like, or my body mass, for that matter? I don't even know what my body mass is!"

"No? Fatima exercises...daily...and she's still a good 20 pounds heavier than you. She eats better, too."

"Again, how would you know that? Have you been stalking us? Is that what you were doing outside the grocery store the other day?" Now thirsty from munching on the pork rinds, she reached in the refrigerator for a can of ginger beer, annoyed at what she perceived as a distinct invasion of privacy.

"Well, no," Tanager answered calmly. "Stalking implies that I am obsessed with you and am a threat."

"Aren't you?" Lucene squinted her eyes at him, not really believing it herself.

"No. It might be better if you sat down," Tanager suggested, pulling a chair out from under the dining room table. Lucene sat, taking the pork rinds and ginger beer with her. Tanager took a seat across the table. "We've been watching you for several weeks now, trying to find the right time, and the best way to make our introductions."

"'We'...meaning you and the lurking vampire over there," Lucene gestured toward Cepheus before snatching a napkin from the dispenser on the table, resulting in several sticking together with orange pork rind smudges. She fought to no avail with the napkin holder.

"I really wanted to reveal this in a more delicate way...," he paused, with minor annoyance, as he helped steady the dispenser for her, "but we appear to be short on time."

"You're going to tell me that you and Cepheus aren't from this planet." Tanager was surprised. "Yeah, that much I figured out." Lucene let out a snort and took a sip of her soda. "And you came all this way to give me nutritional guidance." Lucene's snarky side was always unleashed when she felt defensive or misunderstood in some way.

"Yes, and we knew your parents. Do you remember?"

Lucene's breath caught in her chest. "What do you know about my parents?"

A moan from the couch interrupted their conversation. Cepheus sat upright, rubbing his head. "How long have I been in the other state?" he asked Tanager.

"Oh, about 30 minutes or so. I came looking for you as soon as you disappeared."

"Oy," Lucene jumped at the sound of a resonant voice coming from the window. "Everything okay in here?" Ivan popped his head through the open window.

"Yes, my friend," Cepheus answered, struggling to his feet. "I apologize for my episode. I'm okay now."

"Wait," Lucene looked at Ivan. "You know these two?"

"Er, well, yes and no," Ivan struggled for the right words, and then decided that answer was sufficient.

"Ivan agreed to help us solve a problem with our vessel. He is quite brilliant," Tanager offered.

"Right," Lucene squinted her eyes again. Something in her brain connected with something in Tanager's brain. "Because you need to leave Earth and return to Erde." She took a sip of her drink, absent-mindedly.

Tanager paused. "What makes you think we are from Erde?"

"What?" She looked up, as if distracted. "I have no idea where you are from," Lucene answered, with no recollection as to what she had just blurted out. "What I want to know, is what you know about my parents." Tanager gave her a sideways, confused-puppy stare before exchanging questioning glances with Cepheus.

"What?" Lucene demanded. "Why the looks?"

"Um...beggin' your pardon," Ivan called from the window, but can someone open the door so I can join you? Unless this is a private conversation."

"It's not," Lucene answered. "But these gentlemen were just leaving." Tanager started to protest. "You cannot be here when Fatima gets home from work," she told him. "And furthermore, you cannot tell her anything about this."

"Aye," Ivan agreed. "Don't know what all happened here, but her heart is weak, and she should nah be stressed. Why don't ye two come back to my place and leave the ladies be." With that, Ivan vanished from the window.

"Okay," Tanager reluctantly agreed. "But we need to continue this conversation...very soon."

Cepheus leaned over to give Bagheera a final scratch behind the ear. To Lucene, he said, "My memory is foggy, but I hope I didn't do anything...inappropriate." Lucene could feel the sorrow in his heart. He continued to stare at her as if she were a long-lost daughter that he hadn't seen in a very long time. He wanted to hug her and tell her everything, but he knew the timing wasn't right. Instead, he smiled at her with a sense of pride. In spite of everything, here she was...alive and well. She was resilient, just like her parents.

"Not at all," she replied gently, shaking him from his reverie. "And if it makes you feel any better, my memory is a little foggy too."

"I don't understand how that would make me feel better," he answered in earnest, fumbling between clarity and confusion. Lucene was too tired to explain the expression.

Tanager unlocked the door and Cepheus made his exit, Ivan on the other side, carefully taking his arm as an assist. To Lucene, Tanager asked, "Are you okay to..."

"Lock up?" she answered, somewhat embarrassed. "Er. Would it be a horrible bother to ask you to bolt the door from the inside and..." She motioned toward the window.

"Of course not, I mean, no bother at all." He tried to focus on her face, not the rest of her. She felt a strange buzzing across her skin as he passed in close proximity to her. She noticed it briefly in the car ride the day prior, but now, it seemed to be getting stronger.

It was only after he'd climbed through the window and she'd secured the latch, that she realized he'd left his hat and gloves behind. The sound of an unhappy car motor could be heard coming from down the street. Fatima. Lucene quickly snatched the gloves, stuffing them into the hat and tucking them under her arm. She then grabbed the rinds and soda before retreating into her bedroom and shutting the door. After depositing everything she held onto her dresser, she quickly shut off the light and felt her way to her bed. It was only after she was snuggled beneath the covers that she realized she'd forgotten something.

From behind the door, she could hear Fatima fumbling with the lock. Once inside, she heard her friend say, "Oh, Bagheera? Did your mom forget to take you into her room before bed?"

Damn it! Lucene thought.

"That's okay, kitty," Fatima cooed. "You can come sleep in my room tonight."

9

THE INTERNATIONAL REGISTRY OF ALIEN RESIDENCY

FIVE YEARS AGO. SEVERAL WEEKS BEFORE THE ASSEMBLY.

"Lucy Jones, come in," Drake Cushing invited Lucene into his office. "Shut the door behind you, if you wouldn't mind." He looked her over from head to toe, admiring the shape of her legs and the way her flared, knee-length skirt moved when she walked. Her white blouse, however, was buttoned up to the neck...disappointing.

Lucene blushed at the attention, not considering the possibility that his gaze was borderline inappropriate. In fact, in her mind, this was the beginning of a recurring fantasy she had in her head about her boss.

"Don't just stand there like a lemming, sit down," he directed her toward a chair across from the desk where he sat.

And the fantasy was gone.

She sat, crossing her legs modestly at the ankles and resting a notepad in her lap, tapping her pen nervously against it. He smiled his usual toothy grin. Standing up, he moved over to the front of the desk, sitting on the edge of it with his legs extended and hands supporting his weight by grasping the top of the desk on each side of his hips. His new authoritative position was unnervingly close to

Lucene, who was forced to look up at him to meet his gaze. After what seemed like an uncomfortably long silence, he spoke. "I have a new assignment for you," he announced, suddenly.

"Oh," Lucene was surprised. The past three years had been tedious, to say the least. She was beginning to think she'd be stuck in the file room forever if she didn't do something about it.

"I don't think we've been utilizing you to your full potential. I admit, part of that was my fault. I always thought you received special treatment because of your *situation*," he glanced at her arms. She crossed them, nervously covering up the burnt-in scars. By "special treatment," Drake was referring to the fact that she went to college with a partial need-based scholarship. When added on to a modest academic scholarship, she had enough to get through her undergraduate degree but just barely. As an orphan being shuffled from one house to another, she took it upon herself to move out on her own by special government permission, as soon as she'd turned 17. The following year, she'd applied to a state university and qualified for assistance.

"But I went back and looked at your file."

"Why?" Lucene was legitimately curious.

"No particular reason," he cleared his throat, and stood up, doing a three-quarter turn before changing his mind about something and sitting back down. "Well, that's not exactly true. I happened to notice other newer employees moving out of that file room, but not you. I confess, I thought it was a competence issue, but then..." He moved to his desk drawer, pulling out a file that had about four pages in it, at best. "I looked at your resume. Top of your class, you then worked your way through grad school, and in the past three years you haven't taken a single sick day and have received nothing but stellar performance reviews. Which makes me wonder, why on Earth did you never ask for a promotion or to be moved to a department with opportunity for growth?"

Lucene gave the question some serious consideration. "I don't know," she answered quietly. It was the truth.

"Well, I noticed," he dropped the file on his desk with a sense of smug satisfaction. "And, if you're willing, of course, I'd like to give you a test assignment."

Lucene nodded with a sense of excitement and apprehension. She was flattered to have received the attention of her department's director, but the thought of leaving the file room suddenly felt rather terrifying. "Of course," she practically whispered.

"Good," he answered. "I should warn you that you'll be dealing with some sensitive information. I trust you will keep it to yourself?"

Lucene nodded. *Who would she tell?*

"Is that a 'yes,' " he paused impatiently.

She nodded again before adding, "Yes."

"Good, that's what I thought." He went back to his desk. "First, I need you to retrieve some files for me. The file numbers are..." Lucene opened her notepad, ready to take down the numbers. "No, don't write them down, just remember them."

He has a lot of unwarranted faith in my memory, she thought.

"IRAR4—"

"Wait," Lucene interrupted. "I don't have clearance to access files from the International Registry."

"I know," he leaned uncomfortably close, looking into the distance as if making a decision before turning his gaze back toward her. "Neither do I." Lucene returned a questioning expression. "There are forces at work here that require us to break the rules for the greater good. I need someone I can trust. I trust you, Lucy." He smiled broadly. He could tell from her facial expression that that trust was not shared.

He walked back to his desk and took a seat opposite her, planting his forearms on his desk and leaning in as if letting her in on a special secret. "I have a story to tell you," he spoke quietly, forcing her to sit on the edge of her seat and lean in to hear him.

"When I was a young boy, I almost drowned during a storm."

"Really?" Lucene was intrigued.

"It's true. My younger brother, Bryce, you may remember him

from the office holiday party last year..." Lucene remembered. Bryce was the complete opposite of his older brother. Where Drake oozed confidence, and always showed up for every special occasion dressing in a tailored suit with an attractive, well-proportioned fashion model on his arm, Bryce preferred to live in his brother's shadow. He wore understated brown dress slacks and an ivory shirt to every company event. If there were more than a dozen people in the room, he became nervous, and would hug the least occupied corner. With a watered-down drink in his hand, his equally under-stated wife of six years always stood beside him. Drake got him a job in the cyber-security department several years back, and he was likely to remain there for the foreseeable future.

"Well, we were foolish enough to plan a fishing excursion despite all warnings against it due to inclement weather," Drake continued, raising his voice slightly when he noticed Lucene's mind wandering, as if visualizing the entire event. He snapped his fingers in front of her eyes, jolting her back into the room. "Our parents were out of town and we thought we knew everything." Drake went on to share his story about the storm, and how an alien being named Morphinae flew up from the waters to rescue him. Lucene's eyes widened. "I know, it sounds preposterous," he laughed, gauging her reaction.

"I believe you," Lucene responded, astonished that she, unequiv-ocally, did.

"Well, I was supposed to die that day, but didn't. And I was saved by an alien being. Who would have thought it?" He didn't wait for an answer. "Soon after that I realized my purpose in life. There are beings on this Earth, some who are here to help us, like Morphinae, and others who mean to harm us. It is my mission to help navigate the murky waters of intergalactic negotiations to create unity, while also protecting Earth from being exploited. Doing that requires that we sometimes break the rules. Do you understand what I'm saying?"

Lucene nodded, although she wasn't completely certain that she did. All she knew is that at that moment, she wanted to both prove to herself her value and not let her boss down. For some reason, she needed his approval. Still, something felt very wrong about this. "I'm just not sure..." she began.

"You can't spend the rest of your life hiding behind the safety of books and file cabinets, Lucy." *That hurt,* she thought. "Now, I know you'll find a way. Those numbers are..."

Lucene watched the numbers scroll across her mind as she committed them to memory. She nodded, and quietly left the room.

10

CLASS

FOUR YEARS AGO. ONE YEAR AFTER THE ASSEMBLY.

"I'd like you to take a deep inhale through your nose. Feel the air as it moves to the back of your throat, and then down into your belly, to about two inches below your navel," the meditation instructor said, in a flowing, melodic voice. "Pause your breath, and then exhale slowly." The instructor sat tall, her neck long and back straight. She wore a pair of brightly colored palazzo pants and a short-sleeved yellow tunic, accenting her dark skin and elegant white hair wrapped in box braids. If you looked closely, you would notice a serene smile on her face.

Fatima shifted uncomfortably on her meditation bolster and squeezed her eyelids tightly together, taking uneven breaths.

It was all Fatima's idea. She was convinced that Lucene was bottling up unwanted emotions and was certain that trying a meditation class would help slough all that stuff off. And, it was her turn to pick a class.

In an effort to expand their horizons, also at Fatima's suggestion, the two friends embarked on a monthly ritual of trying something new for the month and then seeing what would stick. They had already attempted sailing lessons, stand up paddle boarding, bocce ball on the beach and lute making classes. So far, bocce ball was winning.

Lucene sank into meditation easily, somehow. All of this felt familiar. She could hear the instructor's voice in the distance as she continued, "For this meditation, we are seeking to explore a situation from the past that may be preventing us from moving forward into the future."

It was a small class, only nine people in attendance. They were meeting in a small temple that turned out to be a short distance from Fatima's cottage, the class led by the church's priestess, Reverend Isabella. One man started to drift off to sleep but caught himself as he began to slump forward. He snorted slightly, looking around to make sure no one had noticed, and resumed his practice. Another woman sat with clenched fists, slowly releasing them as the meditation continued.

"You are walking down a long hallway, and at the end of it, is a door," Isabella continued. "Walk slowly toward it." Lucene felt uneasy but made her way toward the door. It was a Rembrandt-style, rustic, red arched door. "Behind that door, is the past stressor that we will work with today." The instructor reminded everyone to approach whatever arose from the perspective of an outside observer. Lucene's face became flushed. "Put your hand on the knob or handle…and slowly open it."

The door swung open and Lucene let out a scream.

"Oh my gosh, what happened?" Fatima tried to rush to her friend's aid, only to realize that her right leg had fallen asleep and she couldn't stand up. She pounded on her leg and winced through the feeling of pins and needles. There was a murmur from the class, as Isabella knelt down beside Lucene and took her by the shoulders, rubbing them gently to bring her back to the present. "It's okay," she told her. "You are safe." Lucene nodded, embarrassed.

Isabella called for a five-minute break. The class stood, stretched and moved about the room whispering, with occasional glances in Lucene's direction. Lucene stood, doing a forward bend and wrapping her arms around the back of her legs to stretch, then rolled up to a standing position and rotated her head from side to side to loosen up her neck. "I'm okay now," she told the teacher with a confidence she didn't really feel. "But I think I will step outside for a moment." Isabella nodded slowly, understanding, but said nothing.

"I'm fine," Lucene reiterated, even though she hadn't been asked a question. She stepped out into the parking lot. The sun shone brightly on her face.

"Wait up," Fatima called, limping slightly after her friend. "What the heck happened back there?"

Lucene wasn't entirely sure herself. "I don't know. I got to the door, and it was red."

"Red!" Fatima interrupted. "Couldn't you have imagined a green door or a blue door?"

"I couldn't help it. It wanted to be red. Anyway, I opened it, and suddenly I was flooded with images, and sounds and emotions...so much emotion...that I just couldn't take it," Lucene began trembling. Fatima wrapped her arms around her friend in a sideways bear hug, pinning the top of her arms to her side. "I could feel all the pain and joy in the world, at the same time. It was just too much," she explained, feebly attempting to hug her friend back, but managing only to tap Fatima's forearms with her free hands. "Sorry to embarrass you."

Fatima let out a giggle that made her entire body quiver like a Jell-O Jiggler. "Oh my gosh," she laughed. "As if that were possible. Don't worry, my friend," she released her bear hug and looked Lucene in the eyes. "I have no shame."

Lucene wiped a tear from her cheek.

"Excuse me," Isabella approached, her palazzo pants swaying gently in the breeze. "I'm sorry to interrupt, but I feel compelled to speak with you." Lucene and Fatima stepped back to allow her to join their circle. "As you know, I am priestess of this sanctuary." Lucene and Fatima introduced themselves in return, waiting for the pitch inviting them to become a member of her church. They both hated being recruited, as neither of them considered themselves to be particularly religious.

She handed Lucene her card. "I am in need of an assistant to help me manage the sanctuary. If you are seeking a job, please contact me, or just stop in. The door is always open *for you.*"

"You don't even know me, and you're offering me a job?" Lucene was surprised, partially because she had just made quite the spectacle of herself, and even more so because she happened to be in need of some type of income.

"Anyone with that much empathy is clearly called for a higher purpose." With that, she went back into class. "We'll be continuing class in a moment, perhaps just a simple breathing meditation instead, I hope you both will join us."

"Sure," Lucene answered, "we'll be right there."

"You sure?" Fatima asked.

"Yeah, as long as there are no more red doors, I'll be fine."

"I was right about one thing," Fatima bragged as she followed Lucene back inside.

"Yeah, what's that?"

"You sure do have a lot of pent up emotions to slough off."

11

JOURNEY TO EARTH

ONE YEAR AGO. FOUR YEARS AFTER THE ASSEMBLY.

"We will be entering the Deep Zone soon," Cepheus informed Tanager, who was in the fitness room running—no, more like taking a brisk jog—on the moving belt. He loathed exercise, in spite of knowing its necessity for health, and was constantly measuring exactly how much of it he needed to be at peak performance without going above that ratio at all. "Make yourself ready."

"Thanks," Tanager replied, working on his colloquialisms as much as possible before their visit to Earth. "I'll suit up." He slowed his pace and stepped down, the belt crawling to a stop as soon as he did so. "Do I have time to hit the showers?"

"Hit the—" Cepheus paused for a moment, and then nodded, "yes."

Within a short time, Tanager had changed and was strapping himself into a navigation chair beside Cepheus.

The Deep Zone was an ocean-like pocket in space where extreme pressure could prove hazardous to both themselves and their vessel. To compensate, the vessel had collapsible external walls that were vented to add an extra layer of protection, while still letting interstellar gases pass through without harming the ship. As an added precaution, travelers wore more traditional suits with built-in oxygen masks that were fastened into their seats. Fortunately, this was a small zone, which meant they would be able to resume normal flight functions within the hour.

"Are you nervous?" Tanager asked his colleague. His voice sounded like a faraway broadcast as the sound traveled from the intercom in his suit to the headset in Cepheus's.

"Why should I be nervous?" He sucked in a deep breath.

"About meeting Lucene. She'll be about 31."

"32," Cepheus corrected.

"Yes, 32. She'll be about 32 when we get there, and you haven't spoken with her in more than 25 years."

"That's not entirely true. You're forgetting the assembly."

"Ah, yes," Tanager remembered.

"She may not have remembered because of the lightning strike, but I know a part of her recognized me."

The two traveled in silence for the next ten minutes, each routinely running monitor checks to make certain that all of the contractable sections of the ship remained intact. "But, yes," Cepheus said.

"What?"

"Yes, I am nervous." They continued in silence for a few minutes more. "What about you?"

"What about me?" Tanager asked.

"Are you nervous?"

"Why should *I* be nervous?"

"Because we learned at an early age that you were both of the same vibration, and that it was very likely that you'd make a good pair."

"Don't be nonsensical."

"Silly."

"What?"

"I believe the word you were looking for was 'silly.' Don't be silly."

"Exactly, *thanks* you…I mean, thank you." Tanager pointed toward a clear window view of an approaching ringed planet. Cepheus nodded and smiled. "I have no reason to be nervous," Tanager finally answered. "Firstly, she's many years younger than I."

"What does that matter?"

"Nothing where we come from. I recognize that we typically live twice as long as Earthlings, but it will matter to her."

"Why should it? If you don't tell her your age, she'd never know."

"Well, that would be misleading, wouldn't it?"

"Perhaps so," Cepheus agreed.

"Secondly, we're from two different planets—two vastly different experiences."

"That might change."

"And thirdly," Tanager persisted. "Who is to say we'd even feel that way about one another?"

"Same vibration," Cepheus pointed out.

"All that means is that we're inclined to have similar interests and values. That doesn't mean anything. And fourthly…"

"There's a fourthly?" Cepheus was surprised. Tanager nodded.

"And fourthly, our biggest concern is getting her to safety. That needs to be our focus."

"This is true," Cepheus acknowledged somberly. The two continued on their journey, taking a moment to admire the surplus of stars popping up as they neared the Deep Zone's end. A good half hour passed before Tanager spoke again.

"Yes."

"Yes, what?" Cepheus asked. "I've forgotten the question."

"I am a little nervous."

12

THE GATHERING

SATURDAY EVENING. FIVE YEARS AFTER THE ASSEMBLY.

F atima buzzed through the kitchen like a hummingbird, singing to herself. How she managed to move with such ease while wearing an ankle-length brown corset dress, high-heeled boots and with clock charm bracelets running up and down her arms, Lucene had no idea. If Lucene was not mistaken, the tune was "Some Enchanted Evening." She watched as her friend swiftly diced up onions on the cutting board, Fatima's lavender hair pulled back on one side in a tight bun as she gazed softly at the board in front of her and smiled, not really seeing it. Lucene had witnessed this look many times before, and it could only mean one thing—Fatima was in love— again.

"You seem extra cheerful today," Lucene commented, casually pushing the dining room chairs in so they lined up neatly around the table, all while doing a cursory check to make sure there was no evidence of last night's encounter. Fatima smiled softly and nodded but did not reply. "Anything I can do to help?" Lucene offered, uncertainly, peering down at her rather loose-fitting teal maxi dress, wondering if she were over or underdressed. Having no sense of style, she really wasn't sure.

The two did not entertain very often, and when they did, it was usually when Fatima's very large family descended on them unannounced. In those instances, Lucene had nothing to do but watch in wonder as both men and women coordinated a large-scale meal with minimal bickering as to whether the soup needed more garlic, or the rice could use a pinch more saffron.

"Hmm..." Fatima thought for a moment. "You could set the table. We need five places. Oh, and maybe put on some music, something fun."

After a quick mental headcount, Lucene came up with only four names: Fatima, Ivan, Tanager, and, of course, herself. She knew that Cepheus's appearance would inspire too many questions and he would not be in attendance. "Fatima?" Lucene adopted *that* tone of voice. "Why do we need *five* places?"

"Oh," Fatima waved her hand as if the matter were of small consequence. "Because I met someone." She let out a twitter and, quite literally, jiggled up and down like a small child who just learned that she was going to Disney World.

"Fatima, you *didn't*, once again, invite a total stranger into our home!"

"I did!" She twittered again, grabbing Lucene's shoulders for emphasis. "And, he's *wonderful*. Don't worry."

But Lucene did worry. Still, she bit her tongue. She knew better than to try to reason with her friend. And yet, she cringed every time Fatima met someone new, or rather, every time she fell in love, which was pretty much the same thing. She hated having these confrontations with Fatima. Voicing her opinion in the past would always result in an argument. It was the only time Fatima would lift her nose like a dog sniffing the air, reminding Lucene just who the house really belonged to. Still, her concern escalated. Fatima didn't typically invite them home until they had been around for a while, which didn't happen often. Perhaps it had been unwise of her to allow Tanager to give her a ride home. It sent the wrong message that it was okay to trust strangers.

"So..." Fatima coaxed. "How about that music?"

"Oh, right." Lucene scurried to the living room and inspected their growing music collection. Fatima's music was mainly housed on a digital sound bar about the size of a small brick that sat inconspicuously beneath a television, which was, admittedly, not much bigger. Beneath the TV lived a vintage portable DVD/CD player, amplifier, and a cabinet which held Lucene's outdated CD collection. She flipped through them haphazardly, as they were in no particular order, before settling on one with minimal scratches and adding it to their media player. Cole Porter's "Begin the Beguine" filled the room.

"Ooh, I love this one," Fatima cooed. "Can you turn it up?" She hummed along gently from the kitchen.

The two friends may not have had much in common, but they both shared an eclectic taste in music, which included a particular fondness for songs ranging from the 1920s through the 1940s. Fatima preferred to stream her music online, but knowing Lucene's distrust for computers and advanced technology, she humored her friend's insistence on playing only CDs, drawing the line at cassettes and vinyl records.

The doorbell let out a bird-like tweet signaling an arrival. Fatima quickly wiped her hands on her apron. "Here!" She held a wooden spoon over a large pot of homemade curry lentil soup. "Stir!" She commanded. Lucene quickly obeyed, grabbing the spoon dutifully while Fatima answered the door.

There stood Ivan and Tanager. Tanager was dressed in a double-breasted gray suit, button-down vest, and crisp white shirt that looked more in line with the time period of the music they were listening to than with today's era. He carried with him a bottle of a 15-year-old tawny port. Ivan, on the other hand, wore a black Earth Day t-shirt and the only pair of jeans he owned without holes in them. He polished the look off with penny loafers, placing flat washers where the pennies should have been.

"We happened to arrive at the same time," Ivan explained

awkwardly after seeing the laser-eyed warning Lucene shot from her place at the stove. He understood enough to know that it was best to keep Cepheus hidden and pretend that he and Tanager hadn't met before this evening. It wasn't much of a stretch, as the gentleman had really only known each other for the past 24 hours.

"Well, since you two have already met," Fatima smiled graciously, " come on in. It's nice to see you both again."

Tanager offered up the port. "I wasn't sure what to bring," he apologized, but I thought this might be a good digestif? The woman working at the store recommended it." Fatima accepted the gift, eyeing the bottle approvingly.

"Perfect," she whispered, and meant it wholeheartedly. Still smiling, she set it on the counter. "Please, make yourselves comfortable." Fatima relieved Lucene of the spoon at just the right time, as Lucene began stirring the pot so fast, they would have been eating pureed lentil baby food in a few more minutes.

"Yes," Lucene jumped in. "Nice to see you again. Can I take your jacket for you?" While Lucene helped Tanager with his suit jacket, Ivan followed Fatima to the kitchen, scratching nervously behind his ear.

"So, uh...while not exactly a dinner gift, I did bring something fer ya." Ivan reached into his back pocket and pulled out a tiny plastic case and popped it open. Inside, was what looked like a phone memory chip. He held it up for her to see. Fatima politely moved in for a closer look.

"I see," she replied politely…but she really didn't. "Thank you."

"Aww, ye don't even know what it is yet, cuz I have nah told ya." He smiled sheepishly, well, more like a bearded goat, actually.

"What is it?" Fatima asked. Having finished with the soup, she moved to the Spanish onion tortes in the oven. She shooed Ivan away from the oven door, and he backed up to the refrigerator, still holding the tiny black disk between his meaty thumb and forefinger.

"Well, let's say your car was a homing pigeon…"

"Interesting," Fatima offered, engrossed in removing the torte from the oven and testing for doneness. "Would you mind putting down a trivet for me?" She motioned an eye toward the still unset table. Ivan rushed to comply, putting the small device back in its case, and tucking it into his pocket.

Lucene wrapped Tanager's jacket around the back of one of the dining room chairs, and then darted around Ivan in a quest for dinner plates.

"May I be of assistance?" Tanager offered, helpfully.

"Sure," Lucene answered, pausing to look him in the eyes as if searching for information. She still needed to ask him what he knew about her parents, but had to find the right time.

"No," Fatima jumped in. Lucene took a step back, jarred from her thoughts. "You're our guest. Just be comfortable and Ivan can help Lucene set the table for the five of us." Ivan tilted his head slightly, unsure whether to be offended at not being considered a guest or flattered that she was comfortable enough with him to put him to work. He decided on the latter. After all, he did know where the silverware was kept, and had the table set for five in no time. He had just begun to wonder who the fifth-place setting was for, when the doorbell rang.

"Salad!" Fatima exclaimed as she ran for the door. Both men looked like confused puppies, but to Lucene, it was perfectly clear. When Fatima cooked, she went into militant mode.

"Excuse me," Lucene nudged Ivan out of the way. As expected, an Asian kale salad with peanut dressing sat inside the refrigerator, waiting for its debut. Lucene grabbed the covered glass bowl, quickly setting it on the table before rummaging for tongs in the utensil drawer. According to her best estimation, dinner would be in exactly five to seven minutes, just enough time to greet the final guest, make sure everyone had a beverage, and then serve the torte, soup and salad together. Not one to believe in serving courses, as that just complicated things, Fatima preferred to set the feast out all at once. Ivan had learned the hard way that it was best to start with the hot foods while they were still hot, then move on to what was already cold, lest he receive an icy stare from the chef.

"My lovely Fatima!" Roman stood in the doorway, dressed in a button-down black poplin shirt with white buttons and a pair of black jeans and matching shoes. His wavy black hair was tied back. Fatima's smile matched Roman's and then some, revealing two deep-set dimples and blushing cheeks. Her gaze fell on the carnations in his hand. They were frosted purple! "These are for you," he offered. "They match the highlights in your hair."

"Who's that?" Ivan asked Lucene, with visible uncertainty from the kitchen.

"Not sure," Lucene answered honestly. "She's only just met him."

"I don't like him," Ivan decided. "There's something about him that rubs me the wrong way."

"Rubs you *how*?" Tanager was confused.

"It's an expression." Ivan and Lucene answered in unison.

Fatima seemed to have momentarily forgotten all about dinner, and everyone else in the room, for that matter. "Thank you," she answered, attempting to tuck a strand of hair behind her ear nervously, only to remember that it was rolled up in a bun. "They're beautiful. Please, come in." Fatima stepped aside. "Roman, this is my friend and roommate, Lucene." Lucene offered a hand politely. Roman outstretched a pale, thin hand and took it, hesitantly. "Nice to meet you," she said.

"Any friend of Fatima's is, no doubt, a friend of mine," he gushed, kissing Lucene's hand in a grand gesture. Fatima blushed once more. Lucene smiled politely, and then retreated to the kitchen sink to wash her hands.

"This is my neighbor, Ivan," Fatima continued, ignoring Lucene's departure. Ivan scowled momentarily, before conceding to offer his hand. "Aye," he added. "And longtime friend and Praetorian. Don't kiss me hand," he advised. Roman shook it, cautiously. Ivan noted the softness of Roman's palm and handshake, adding it to his mental list of why he did not trust him. Fatima did not seem to notice. "And this is Lucene's friend, Tanager from..."

"Out of town," he offered.

"I am pleased to make your acquaintance," Tanager followed suit by presenting an outstretched hand in friendship. Relieved, Roman shook it without incident.

"Drinks!" Fatima launched back into military mode and softly added, "While I just go and put these in some water."

"Please," Lucene suggested. "Have a seat while I get the wine and water." As expected, Tanager insisted on helping, and was tasked with setting out five water glasses, and filling them with cooled lemon water from the refrigerator while Lucene opened a Rioja Reserve that Fatima had settled on just for this evening. "I'll get the wine glasses," Ivan declared before adding, as he glanced toward Roman, "since I know where they are."

Lucene was only two minutes off, as dinner was served exactly nine minutes after the arrival of the last guest. It was mostly uneventful, with a few praises to the chef and compliments on the wine. Lucene sat at one end of the table, Roman at the other, with Tanager seated to her right, Ivan to her left, and Fatima sandwiched between her two admirers, across from Tanager.

"So, how is it that you two met?" Roman inquired, eyeing Lucene and Tanager back and forth.

"Tanager rescued me from the grocery after my car broke down in the rain," Lucene answered, simply.

"The Fates are amazing women, aren't they?" Roman remarked, shooting an admiring glance at Fatima. "And, how long ago was that?"

Tanager retrieved his pocket watch. "About 29 hours ago," he answered, snapping it closed, and placing it back in his pocket.

"Really?" Roman was taken aback. "I would have guessed that you'd known each other for years. Interesting."

"And how did ye two meet?" Ivan rested his elbow on the table, motioning toward Fatima before she nudged him to remove the offending elbow.

"I was at the bar at the restaurant where Fatima works." He paused to take a forkful of the torte before continuing. "I wasn't having any fun at all until I tried the most exquisite ahi tuna made by this lovely lady."

Ivan sat back and shot Fatima a self-explanatory look. *Really?* the glance said. *At the bar where you work?*

"The Fates," Fatima shrugged her shoulder and sipped her soup.

"And what brought ye to the Crab Shack that fateful evening," Ivan inquired. "Searching for a soulmate, were ya?"

"Not at all," Roman answered, turning his gaze back to Fatima and clasping her hand gently at the table. Fatima did not chastise him for putting *his* elbow on the table, and shyly clasped his hand in return. "It just worked out that way." Ivan swallowed a bit of salad with some difficulty. Lucene was beginning to share Ivan's sentiment, but not out of jealousy. It was due more to his over-the-top overtures to someone he met just the evening prior. It was as if he were a child in a man's body, experiencing puppy love for the first time. Tanager sipped his wine in silence, observing with as little judgement as possible.

"If you must know," Roman continued, as if relenting to divulge private information under duress, "I was there for my research."

"Research?" Tanager's eyes perked up, intrigued.

"Yes," Roman continued. "While I can't go into detail at this juncture, I can tell you that I am an anthropology professor currently conducting research for a white paper I'm writing on relationships in the modern era."

"How fascinating," Fatima all but batted her eyes at Roman. "Let us know how we can help with that research," she fawned. Realizing that her statement may have been interpreted more seductively than she had intended, her cheeks returned to a flushed crimson.

Ivan's also flared red, but for a very different reason.

At that moment, "It's Time to Say Goodnight" began playing from the sound bar. It was unclear whether Tanager found it to be the perfect diversion in order to diffuse a potentially volatile situation, or whether he simply liked dancing. Whichever the case, he quickly turned to Fatima and asked, "As host of this evening, would you honor me with the first dance?"

"Well, sir," she answered, brushing her napkin to the side. "I would be delighted." Fatima took the hand he offered and accompanied him to the living room, where they began waltzing in the small open area in front of the couch. Fatima, among her other talents, was an enormously good dancer, and followed easily as Tanager led her around the floor.

"Can I ask you a question?" He whispered, leaning in.

"Sure," she smiled warmly. "Ask me anything."

"I couldn't help but notice that Lucene seems to have an aversion to doors. Any idea why?"

"Oh, only red doors," Fatima answered matter-of-factly. "That's why she goes through the window and avoids the front door," she motioned toward the kitchen.

"I see. Actually, no, no, I don't see. Why red doors?"

"She won't tell me. I've offered to paint the front door a dark blue, but she would have none of it."

"Why not?"

"Because she said she would always know that it was a red door posing as a blue door." Tanager simply nodded, as if this logic made perfect sense, and the two continued their dance.

"There's more," Fatima whispered. "She doesn't like computers or things with computers in them."

"Really?" Tanager was curious. "Did she say why?"

"I dunno," Fatima shook her head. "But I suspect that she thinks someone is trying to follow her. She's been weird like that since she moved in with me five years ago. I try not to pry."

Tanager's expression changed, as if a lightbulb just went off in his head. He pushed the thought away and replaced his look of surprise with a warm smile. Fatima smiled in return.

Roman admired Fatima from the kitchen, resting his chin in his hand on the table, with a half-upturned smile plastered across his face. "I wonder what they're talking about," he mused. "Me, I hope." It was only then that he noticed Lucene awkwardly pushing a stray piece of kale around her plate. "Um, Lucene, would you care to dance?"

"I would, except that I really don't know how to do...that," she motioned toward Fatima and Tanager, who were floating around the room like Fred and Ginger.

"Not to worry," Roman answered, "I have a solution. Follow me."

Lucene reluctantly followed Roman to the makeshift dance floor while Ivan decided it might be a good time to pop open the port.

"Now," Roman instructed, circling an arm around her waist. "Step on my toes."

"Excuse me?" Lucene gave Roman a sideways look. A good deal taller than Lucene, she ended up peering at his nostrils.

"Step on my toes," he tried again. "Then you don't have to worry about a misstep. Don't worry," he reassured. "I don't mind."

Lucene stepped carefully on his feet. He winced. "Sorry," she moved away.

"No, it's...fine."

Lucene wasn't so sure it was fine. He awkwardly lifted one weighted foot at a time as they hobbled in a misshapen square pattern.

From the kitchen, Ivan noticed a carpetbag sitting at the end of the long countertop, the one Fatima carried with her everywhere. He glanced at the two couples on the dance floor, but each seemed preoccupied. He once again removed the tiny case from his pocket, and reached into Fatima's bag, poking around until he'd found what he was looking for.

Moments later, the song ended, and another began, "Moonlight in Vermont."

Fatima smiled as she crossed paths with the other couple, stopping abruptly. "Lucene, let me show you how it's done. May I cut in?" Lucene gratefully stepped down from Roman's toes and allowed her friend to cut in. Roman circled his arm around her thick waist, and the two moved with surprising ease. His lean frame stood more than a foot above her. As far as couples go, many tend to resemble each other, but these two were like watching a plantain and an acorn squash dance.

"May I teach you?" Tanager spoke softly over Lucene's shoulder. She shivered.

"Well, you can try, but I've got no rhythm," Lucene laughed awkwardly as she turned to face him.

"I don't believe that's true," Tanager answered, thoughtfully. She expected verbal instruction, but instead, he simple began stepping and she followed. It was as if there were a magnet between them and she naturally followed where he led. Before she knew it, she too was moving with ease around the room. They kept dancing, long after the music stopped.

Lucene glanced up to see Roman, Fatima and Ivan off to the side of the room, watching the two in earnest.

"Well," Fatima offered. "One, I didn't know you could dance, Lucene. You've been holding out on me. And two, you both realize this isn't the 18th century and you're allowed to actually hold hands when you dance?"

It was only then that Lucene realized that Tanager had not actually had his arm around her waist, nor did they have their arms up in a traditional couple's dance. But the energy between them was so strong that she was sure they had been touching. Tanager searched Lucene's face for some sign of recognition but found none. Instead, she pulled away and headed back to the kitchen. She glanced down at her arms, noticing that the branch-like lightning patterns had a glow about them. Lucene quickly crossed her arms awkwardly in front of her. "How about pouring me some of that port, Ivan?"

Roman arrived home with an ear-to-ear grin that he just couldn't shake. It wasn't often that one found the woman of their dreams, and yet, he had. Nothing could spoil this moment.

He stopped abruptly when he reached his bedroom, eyeing all the pictures on the wall. There was a brief swirling in his head—like when you awaken from a dream and it takes you a moment to remember who and where you are.

"Stupid man," Roman hit himself in the forehead. He had been so distracted by love that he forgot all about his mission—Lucene. There were pictures of her, and others, tacked up all over the walls. He'd followed her from New York to Florida. Yes, his research for TARA was important, but Lucene's safety was supposed to be his primary concern.

What's more, is that he was almost fooled by this Tanager… almost. *Why hadn't he realized it sooner? He's got to be working for them.*

He slipped the lapel camera from his shirt, pulled a portable computer out from the bedroom dresser drawer and set it on the carpet. Plugging it in, he then retrieved photos—mostly of Tanager and Lucene dancing, but also of the entire evening. The camera had been set to auto-capture regularly. From another drawer, he drew out a mini-printer, hooking the cable to the computer and laying them side-by-side on the floor.

After he'd printed what he felt were the most relevant photos, he searched for pins or sticky putty to post them to the wall. *Where did he put them?* He searched the bathroom, catching a glimpse of himself in the mirror. He paused; it was almost as if he were looking at a stranger. He didn't recognize himself.

Roman opened a drawer and found it filled with prescription bottles. "I see what's happening here," he looked up and told his reflection. "The Royals know I'm here, and they're trying to torture me too."

13

ALL MEN ARE CRAZY

"**H**e told you what?"
"That he's an alien," Fatima grinned gleefully from the corner of the couch, where she sat nestled, hugging a throw pillow to her chest.

"When did he have time to tell you that?" Lucene stood behind the couch, before being summoned back to the kitchen by a teakettle whistling on the stove. "Sometime between the 'let's have port' and 'pass the creme brûlée?'"

"Relax," Fatima called after her. "It was at the end of the evening, after the boys had left and you were clearing the dishes. Hee! How fun is that?"

"I'm not sure why you find this so amusing." Lucene returned to the living room, handing Fatima a cup of tea. While cooking was not her thing, tea, she could manage.

"What? It's not like it's the first time I dated someone who claimed to be from another planet," Fatima reflected. "Besides, you of all people should know that there are some aliens taking up residence on Earth."

"Yeah," Lucene agreed, "but there's so much controversy around them that most keep a low profile and don't advertise it, particularly beings who look so much like us that we wouldn't know the difference without checking the International Registry. Why would he be that open about it?" Lucene thought back to her recent encounter with Cepheus. Previously, her only interaction with other life forms, to her knowledge, was when she was working with the UC, and that was merely as an observer. And even then, they were tuning in from their home planet, not Earth. Somewhere, in the corners of her brain, a memory surfaced. It had something to do with Cepheus and his connection to the IPP.

"Look, I'm not saying I believe him," Fatima interrupted the thought and it vanished as quickly as it arose. "Just that I don't care if he *thinks* he is. He's sweet." Fatima sighed, wistfully.

"But, that's crazy."

"All men are crazy," Fatima reasoned. "At least this one's not suicidal. I once had a boyfriend, this was way before you moved here, who threatened to chain himself to the underside of a delivery truck and let himself get dragged to death if I didn't go back to him after we broke up."

"What did you do?"

"I felt bad, so we dated for another year."

"Oh, Fatima." Lucene shook her head, taking a seat beside her friend.

"The way I see it," Fatima paused to take a sip of the tea, nodding with approval at its preparation. "We all choose our life experience, our reality, if you will. If he chooses a life experience where he's an alien, then who am I to argue?"

"But what if *his* life experience can potentially cause harm to *your* reality?

"Oh, he's harmless," Fatima waved her hand in the air, "even if he is a bit paranoid."

"Paranoid? What do you mean 'paranoid'?"

"Well...he thinks he's one of the last Data Collectors left on the planet."

"What?" Lucene's eyes widened. Synapses in her brain began to reconfigure and connect as memories from five years ago began to flash like camera bulbs behind her eyes.

"You know, the story that was in the news a couple years back about aliens from Erde hiding among us collecting information about us to report back."

"No, I know who they're supposed to be. I'm just surprised he claimed to *be* one." *A little odd that he would surface at the same time as Cepheus and Tanager. Did the men secretly know each_other, but pretend not to for some reason?*

"What's wrong?" Fatima looked concerned. "Your face just turned white as a ghost. Does this have something to do with your time in New York? I know you don't like to talk about it but..."

"I just want you to be careful."

"Awww, that's why I love you, my friend. I will be careful."

"So, what's he collecting data on?" Lucene asked. "Don't they have a specific area of expertise?"

Fatima giggled, settling back on the couch. "Oh, you're going to love this, he's studying the nuances of romantic relationships. He wasn't lying when he said he was writing a white paper last night at dinner. And, get this, he told me he didn't believe in love at first sight until he saw me."

"That's very...sweet," Lucene was unconvinced. "And where's lover boy today?"

"Said he had to meet another of his friends from back home today, some guy named Jim, Jim Sparks. What a funny name. He lives on a boat."

"Another Data Collector. So, there's two of them?"

"Yeah, but they have to be careful since they tend to be a target for hate groups. Come to think of it, maybe I shouldn't have told you?" Fatima looked concerned.

"Fatima, who would I tell? I'm practically a hermit."

"Reverend Isabella or, I dunno, maybe your new boyfriend, Tanager?" she teased.

"He's not my...oh, never mind." Lucene stood. "Speaking of Reverend Isabella, I've got to run some errands and get to work. I promised I'd get there early to help set up for the new moon celebration she's having tonight."

"I don't understand you, Lucene." Fatima eyed her friend curiously. "You have a master's degree and had a great job with the UC that had tremendous potential for growth. Why on Earth, no pun intended given our recent conversation, would you take on an entry level administrative job at a local church that pays minimum wage and offers no hope of advancement? I don't get it."

"No, you don't," Lucene answered. "And, I'm afraid I can't explain it to you. I'm sorry."

"Hmmm...maybe it's not just limited to men. Maybe we're all crazy."

"Perhaps," Lucene acknowledged, as she made her way back to her bedroom to grab a pair of shoes. "But not everyone's brain got fried by lightning, either. I can't explain to you what I can't remember."

"True," Fatima acknowledged. "But you remembered me." She smiled as Lucene resurfaced from her bedroom, moments later.

"How could I forget?" Lucene pinched her friend's cheek, playfully.

"Hey, don't wait up. I'm heading to a family reunion today and won't be back until late. If you change your mind and want to join us, the number is on the fridge."

"Thanks," Lucene answered awkwardly. To say that Fatima's family was fun loving was an understatement, and yet she still couldn't handle the energy of being around that many people in one location. "I will." In the meantime, she made a mental note to ask Tanager about Roman and investigate this Jim Sparks.

She couldn't explain it to Fatima because she couldn't quite understand it herself. Lucene looked down at her arms. People viewed them with odd fascination, as if she had intricate henna work tattooed on her arms. But to her, their patterns unlocked a secret somehow. Except that ever since she got them, she couldn't remember what it was. She barely remembered the car accident that killed her parents. Nor did she remember the lightning strike or much that happened in the first seven years of her life. But she did remember meeting Fatima in the hospital room as a child and was grateful for the only true friendship she'd had for most of her adult life.

Lucene pulled Kermit into a new age shop and pulled out her list. Reverend Isabella had sent her in to pick up Peruvian resin and a hand drum she was having repaired. The woman behind the counter greeted her with a smile. "Hi, Lucy," she beamed. In spite of Lucene's many requests to be called by her complete name, the shop owner never seemed to remember. Lucene cringed, but said nothing. She gave a polite smile back. "I've got Reverend Isabella's drum right here," she pulled it out from underneath the counter.

"Thanks." Lucene picked up a bag of resin from a wall display and placed it on the counter. "We need this, too."

"So weird," the woman continued, carefully unwrapping the drum that she had rolled in cloth for protection "You can see that it's smooth again." She ran her hand over it for emphasis. "But how on Earth did it get punctured like that? It's like someone jabbed a knife through it."

"I couldn't say," Lucene answered. "How much do I owe you?" After completing the transaction, Lucene left the store and climbed into her vehicle with the resin and drum placed carefully in the passenger's seat.

It wasn't as if she didn't like people, but she didn't trust inquisitive ones who can't remember your name even after you've been a customer for more than four years. The less she knew, Lucene reasoned, the better.

She had no idea how the drum got damaged in the first place, but since Reverend Isabella didn't ask her a lot of questions, she gave her boss and mentor the same respect. In truth, Reverend Isabella had been the one person who had been able to help her with her "glitches," like the one she'd experienced the first day in her meditation class. Since then, her mentor had made a point of inviting her to every meditation, yoga and tai chi class held at the sanctuary. She periodically suggested things for Lucene to be mindful of, encouraging her to practice this while tending to her tasks of gardening, cleaning or providing info to attendees.

Things like, "When trimming the shrubs in the garden, be sure to thank them for providing oxygen to the air we breathe and for protecting us from the harsh sun. Let them know that you are trimming them so they may continue being a source of health and beauty to all who visit us." Or when a Northern Mockingbird randomly flew through an open window into the main hall, she'd say, "Ask them what message they have for you, and be sure to thank them. Guide them to the window if they've gotten lost and give them space to leave unharmed."

And when that backfired, like when the shrubs and birds became too chatty, instead of calling her crazy, Reverend Isabella taught her to mentally separate herself from the chatter. Since she quickly learned that red doors were a source of stress, Lucene was taught to shut the red door, leaving the sounds behind it until she was ready to address them. Lucene didn't understand her phobia, or the flashes of insight that would hit her like a thousand radio waves tuning in to different channels—all at the same time, but she was grateful to have someone treat it as a gift to be trained instead of a mental illness to be eradicated.

So, while she may have been making only minimum wage at a

little sanctuary in Parrish, the benefits she received working there were profound. Plus, she felt safe being hidden away from normal day-to-day interactions. This is why she stayed, but she couldn't quite articulate this to Fatima. She wasn't sure if she would ever be able to.

14

FAMILY

"Tanager!" Two small boys, spouting a mess of curly orange hair on their heads, ran up, each wrapping their arms around one of his legs as Tanager pretended to struggle as he walked through the door.

"Boys," a tall woman with bright auburn hair called, cradling a small child as she reached the door. "Let him be," she laughed.

"Tanager! Tanager!" One of the boys tugged at his pant leg. "Guess what I'm going to be when I am as big as you are?" he asked. Without waiting for an answer, he spat out, "a Data Collector!" He smiled a wide, crooked smile.

Tanager mussed his hair. "Well, that is a noble occupation." The other boy would not be overshadowed by his twin.

"And I'm going to be a professor, just like you and my dad," he proclaimed proudly.

"That's enough, boys," the red-haired woman intervened. "Go and help your dad with the samphire stew." She leaned over to touch her forehead to Tanager's in a warm greeting. "So nice to see you again, friend."

"You as well, Petrichor. And this must be the lovely Tallulah." He went to stroke the baby's fine hair with his hand, but the child caught one of his fingers and held on with pure fascination, giggling gleefully. "The grip of a tigress," he complimented, "what a strong soul." "She takes after her mother," Cepheus's wife smiled. "Come in. Dinner will be ready in just a moment." Tanager followed Petrichor through their living room. While he'd been in their home a number of times, he was still in awe of it. There were two built-in waterfalls on each side of the room that flowed gently into a pond that poured under the walkway where he now stood. Live vines hung from the ceilings with bright yellow, orange and red flowers growing from them. "Be careful of the Walleyes," she warned, glancing at her feet. "They appear to be agitated today." As if on cue, several fish leapt across Tanager's feet before disappearing under the water.

Dinner was held at a small round table in their kitchen. Unlike the living room, the kitchen was simple with stations for growing hydroponic herbs and vegetables, a station for prepping food, one for cooking and another for assembly. Behind the stations were walk-in units with foods stored at varied temperatures. The assembly line ended, and the kitchen table began, making the layout as efficient as possible. Adjacent to the kitchen was a formal dining area used to entertain dignitaries, colleagues, friends and distant relatives. But Tanager wasn't considered merely a friend and colleague. He was an honorary member of their immediate family, and despite a considerable age gap, Cepheus regarded Tanager as his brother. And so, he sat at the informal table in their kitchen, as a sign of high respect.

One of the boys ran around the table, laying out platters while the other filled glasses with water. This boy had a tentacled creature stuck to his shoulder, its suction arms wrapped around the boy's arm and a bulbous one-eyed head peering at Tanager curiously. It tapped the edge of its tentacle like a dog wagging its tail.

"Cephi," his mother scolded. "Get Merla out of the kitchen and back in the water. She has no business being at the dinner table!" The boy reluctantly took his five-legged pet into the living room and released her into the pond. "Wash your hands," she commanded, once he'd returned.

As was custom, everyone took their place once dinner was ready. Cepheus went around the table with a stew cart, passing out food and bread to the boys, then his wife, then Tanager. Baby Tallulah sat in a safety chair next to Petrichor, being bottle-fed by a mechanical system attached to the chair. Once everyone's plate was filled, he filled his own and took a seat. Petrichor reached for a bottle of home-made pomegranate and blackberry wine, pouring it into an empty cup and passing it to Tanager who accepted with a smile, before doing the same for herself and her husband. Pretrichor was the best wine maker in their village. During one particularly poor growing season, her vineyard thrived while many others failed to produce a single crop. It was Cepheus's belief that his wife had literally loved the vineyard back to life.

They held hands in a moment of silence, each giving thanks to the spirit of their choice before the boys dug into their food with gusto.

"I have news," Cepheus proclaimed, eagerly.

Tanager quickly swallowed a mouthful of stew before answering, "What news?"

"Dora and Xan have finally made contact."

"Really?" Tanager seemed surprised. "After hearing nothing for two years, I was worried something had happened to them."

"As was I," Cepheus nodded. "And something did happen, something wonderful!"

"Well, don't keep me in suspense."

"They had a baby, a girl," Petrichor announced, reaching over and touching Tallulah's cheek and smiling.

"On Earth? That is good news!"

"There's more," Cepheus said.

"What?"

"The child has abilities."

"Abilities?" Tanager questioned.

"Without any genetic altering, she was inherently born with all of the same abilities as our Data Collectors."

"Astonishing! A natural empath born of two genetically enhanced Data Collectors."

"Her skills have to be developed, of course," Cepheus explained in-between sips of wine. "But now that Dora and Xan have resumed communication, I can begin mentoring her remotely."

"Wonderful news. But did they say why they dropped communication?"

"Let's just say it was unsafe for them for a time," he sent a knowing glance in his boys' direction, and Tanager understood.

Tanager redirected the conversation, "This calls for a tribute." He raised his glass in a toast, and Cepheus and Petrichor joined in. "We send blessings to the beautiful family that is Dora, Xan and…what is the child's name?"

"Lucene," Cepheus supplied. Tanager suddenly got chills down his spine but didn't know why the name had significance. He shook it off and smiled.

The children had all been put to bed, and Cepheus, Tanager and Petrichor were sitting in the living room watching the Walleyes jump as they sipped an after-dinner cocktail. Merla was acting strangely, Petrichor noted, as their octopus-like pet climbed the vines of one of the walls.

"Strange," Petrichor noted to Cepheus. "She's never done that before."

Moments later, there was a loud explosion as the walls of the living room caved in, sending water, debris and bloody Walleyes flying mid-air, smacking down on what was left of the stone walkway that had bisected the living room.

Petrichor had barely yelled, "The children!" when there was a second explosion at the back of the house. Her face contorted in horror. Royal soldiers poured in, several grabbing Cepheus before he could react and dragging him outside. He called to his wife, peering over his shoulder just seconds before witnessing a soldier grab Petrichor and break her neck with a single twist. Her head lying limply to one side, he tossed her body into the pond as easily as one might throw pellets to a fish. Cepheus began screaming, only to be silenced by another soldier striking him on the back of the head with his fist.

For Tanager, everything appeared in slow motion as he watched Cepheus being dragged away, unconscious with blood running down his face. Petrichor floated, face down, to the surface of the pond. The rooms where the children slept were now piles of rubble and smoke, and with the roof of the house now gone, he could see the dark sky and stars above. It was a humid night, and the air was sticky. Instinctively, he sought to run after his friend, only to feel a soldier grab and slam his body to the ground, wrapping his arms behind his back and tying them together. His face was pressed into what was left of the stone floor. Moments later, he was being dragged, semi-conscious, across the ground, rolling over grass, dirt and rubble, cutting his body and the side of his face. He felt pain and was no longer able to open one eye. Tanager was about to lose consciousness before he was suddenly flipped over and a bright light blinded him.

Fredo loomed over him, dressed in a soldier's uniform that appeared two sizes too small. "Sovereign Sabrina and Sovereign Hamish did not appreciate the Peace-Keeper's interference with their son decades ago, any more than they appreciate them ruining trade negotiations now." He kicked Tanager in the ribs. Tanager let out a groan but could not react beyond that. "Take a message back to the Peace-Keepers in charge of TARA. Tell them that if they do not pull their Data Collectors from Earth immediately, the Royals will react swiftly and families of Erde will meet the same fate as this one experienced here tonight."

The lights faded and Tanager lost consciousness.

15

THE VESSEL

SUNDAY MORNING. FIVE YEARS AFTER THE ASSEMBLY.

Not long after Fatima left to visit her relatives, there was a knock at the window. Tanager stood peering in from outside. Curious, Lucene unlocked it and slid the glass panel open.

"Can I show you something?" Tanager asked, tipping his hat to her. Lucene didn't know whether the hat was a disguise or if he had an old-fashioned notion that men should always wear a hat when outdoors and remove it when inside.

"That depends. Is it obscene?" She answered, flatly.

"No, why would it be?" Said Tanager, missing the joke.

"No reason. What did you want me to see?"

"Please, follow me." He held out his hand to help Lucene through the window.

"I'm good," she waved away his hand. "I'm a pro at this." Tanager stepped aside, giving her space to climb down. He continued to be confused by her choice in words. Lucene closed the window, locking it behind her and tucking the little key in her pocket. "Okay, I'm ready."

Tanager led the way silently, heading toward Ivan's house. But, instead of going to the front of the house, as Lucene had expected, he took her the back way, where Fatima's cottage and Ivan's shed shared a connected lawn shrouded by oak and red cedar trees.

She'd never seen the inside of Ivan's workshop, but having heard strange sounds emanating from it at all hours of the night, Lucene was curious. Tanager gave a knock on the door. After hearing a few odd whirs and clicks, the door slid open.

Cepheus's eyes lit up in both surprise and joy at Lucene's arrival. "Lucene," he smiled. "It's nice to see you." Lucene beamed back, noticing a gentle warmth in the center of her chest. "He is a genius," Cepheus continued, nodding toward Ivan, as if he'd waited all morning to share this information with her.

Cepheus motioned toward the workbench with what looked like a small compressor connected to an even smaller computer. Behind them, the computer projected what appeared to be the engine room of a large craft. Had it been real, it would have engulfed the entire shed. The workshop, itself, was filled from wall to wall and ceiling to floor with tools and gadgets—the larger items mounted neatly to the wall, the smaller bits of hardware stored in stackable containers on shelves.

Ivan was too engrossed in problem-solving to do more than grunt at Lucene before returning to work. "Cepheus, you've got thinner fingers than me. See if you can thread this wire."

"Of course," Cepheus's eyes grew wide, half in acknowledgement of suddenly realizing Ivan's solution and half to indicate his support. Everyone watched curiously as Cepheus delicately threaded the wire, reconnecting it to an adaptor.

"Ivan is helping us get home faster," Tanager whispered over Lucene's shoulder. She shuddered ever so slightly at his close proximity but did not back away. "Perhaps you will decide to come with us," he said in a manner that was half-joking and half-serious.

Ivan briefly glanced up from his project, but said nothing.

"And, why would I do that?"

Cepheus nodded at Tanager and resumed working with Ivan. It was almost time to begin welding.

"Why don't you and I take a short walk?" Tanager suggested.

"Probably safer," Ivan agreed, handing Cepheus a spare welding mask.

Lucene nodded. She'd witnessed the after-effects of Ivan's experiments gone wrong numerous times and was happy to keep her distance. "There's a short trail behind the house. That do?"

There was a pause as Tanager translated the meaning of 'that do.'

"That will be perfect."

They walked in silence for several minutes before Tanager offered, carefully, "I'm trying to share this info with you as gently as possible."

"Well, spit it out," Lucene replied, somewhat impatiently, after a long pause. "I'm sure it will be fine." *There it was again, that stupid energy between them. What was that?*

"Spit it o—," Tanager paused. "Oh, speak quickly and hold nothing back. I see."

"First time to Earth?" Lucene chided.

"First time to any planet, actually."

"Well, you've got me beat."

He eyed her curiously. "The way you speak is fascinating." She felt her cheeks getting warm and quickly diverted her eyes. He fought back a small grin. "I think I understand contractions now, but my slang is obviously outdated. You would be excellent if you ever decided to teach a class on Earth communication back home."

"Let's not get ahead of ourselves," Lucene said. *Damn it! There I go again.* Before now, she hadn't realized that nearly everything that came out of her mouth was an idiom. Tanager interrupted her thoughts.

"I don't think it's wise for me to 'spit it out.' It may be too much all at once."

"Well, what can you tell me? Maybe you could start by telling me what you know about my parents?"

Tanager paused. "Do you not remember them at all?"

"Did *your* parents never tell you that it's rude to answer a question with a question?"

Tanager let out a sigh. She was proving more challenging than he expected. "It was Cepheus who met your parents first…a very long time ago…on Erde."

There was a long pause while Lucene struggled to connect the dots. "Are you suggesting that they were not born on Earth, or that they were on Erde…for some reason?"

"Your parents were born on Erde. Cepheus met them at the Terrestrial Academy of Research and Awareness…where your parents were training to become Data Collectors." He paused for the information to sink in. "Are you familiar with what that means?"

She and Fatima had just discussed this. "I remember…What was their assignment?" She vaguely remembered that her dad loved plants and thought it might have something to do with horticulture.

"Well, it…changed after you were born."

"Oh," Lucene frowned, thinking she'd interrupted their work.

"No," he touched her shoulder. "You were…are…a good interruption." He smiled. "Your parents," he reminisced, "were the kindest people, and they adored you."

"Wait," Lucene commanded. Tanager stopped in his tracks. "No, not literally." 'Literally' didn't help much, but he was beginning to understand the communication patterns in her mind the more time he spent with her. "How could you know them? You've got to be at least five years younger than I…maybe more. Were you a baby?"

"Actually, I knew them very well. As it so happens, I'm actually older than you."

"Really, how old are you?"

"I'm about 56 years in your timeline."

"But you look half that. How is that possible?"

"It's just that our environment is more ideal than Earth's. Our physical systems are more evolved than yours. Therefore, we heal faster and do not age pre-maturely."

"Pre-maturely? So, we should be living longer?"

"Under the right conditions, both in the internal physiological environment and the external environment, your average lifespan would be double what is currently is. Were it not for your medical breakthroughs, some of which we contributed to, your species would definitely not have fared as well."

"I see. I mean," Lucene clarified, "I understand."

"Thank you," he laughed. "I've started a list of common expressions and am cataloging them. It's a long list."

"I'll bet," Lucene answered. "Oh, there's another!"

Lucene wanted to know more about her parents and was about to ask.

"I would love to tell you lots of stories about your parents, perhaps on the long journey back home?"

"You are a tease…there's another. I'm afraid I can't stop myself."

What the hell is wrong with you, Lucene? she thought to herself. He was making her nervous in a *he's much more attractive and interesting than I first thought* kind of way.

"It is okay. That's how I learn. 'I'll bet,'" he smiled at picking up the term. "Cepheus knew at least 99% of all Earth expressions, regardless of culture. Unfortunately, he lost much of it after the…incident."

Her attention was suddenly brought back to the present in an abrupt, and sorrowful, way. For this, she didn't need to ask. While Lucene couldn't make out the details, she could feel that Cepheus had suffered extreme physical and emotional pain…and betrayal. She could also feel how sorrowful that made Tanager, and now, her as well.

"They will hurt you, too," Tanager read her thoughts.

"Hey, stay out of my head," Lucene whined. "I mean, is that it?" She pointed to the side of her head. "Could you actually read what I'm thinking if you wanted to?"

"I'm sorry," he apologized. "We are on a similar wavelength. I pick up mostly emotions, but occasionally, words and phrases too. But, don't worry, your brain puts out natural blockers for anything private. It would be very difficult for me to see anything you didn't want me to."

"But not impossible."

"No, not impossible. Though, if I sense resistance, I will try to be polite."

"Well, that's reassuring," she answered, for once without sarcasm. *Did he know he was making her nervous? Stop it brain. Stop it!* "So, who's trying to hurt me and why?"

Tanager paused for a moment before answering. "In addition to rigorous training at the Terrestrial Academy of Research and Awareness, TARA for short, Data Collectors voluntarily participated in a DNA splicing program. When given certain biological attributes, they were 90% more likely to respond to intuitive training. Each Data Collector on Earth was paired with one of the trainers on Erde. Instead of transmitting information over the air waves, they could do so telepathically."

"Neat trick," Lucene admired.

"No trick," Tanager replied. "It had to be the right combination of biology, training and emotional predisposition toward compassion."

"In other words, soulless jerks need not apply." Tanager looked at her, quizzically. "Never mind," she said. "So, my parents had the right combination. But I've never been sliced and diced, nor given any special genes. I've never trained at your academy, and I'm not known for being the most touchy-feely of people."

"No," he agreed solemnly. "You are probably the last person anyone would mistake as having special skills."

"Gee, thanks."

"That is a good thing. It is probably what kept you safe for this long."

"Not helping."

"My concern is…" He took her by the shoulders and looked into her eyes. She shivered slightly but didn't resist. "Your parents discovered early on that you had all the signs of someone who had received the DNA splicing, except that you hadn't, but you were born to two people who had. You are the only natural born Data Collector, and from that, we can hypothesize that there exists within you the potential for great power, with training...of course. Some dangerous people can't seem to decide if they should fear you or use you."

By this time, they had looped the nature trail and were back at the shed in time for Ivan to say, happily, "I think we're on to something!"

Cepheus curled his long-nailed fingers lovingly around the compressor they had been working with. "Ivan has figured out a way to get us home in half the time it has taken us to get here."

"How?" Tanager asked, skeptically.

"Well," Ivan scratched his head. "Are ye familiar with virtual machines?"

"Yes."

"And machine learning?"

"Yes!" Tanager grew increasingly more excited.

"So, let's pretend the vessel has one engine with hardware abstractions that convince it that it really has two engines. It will do the trial and error all on its own until it actually figures out the engine efficiencies to make it react as if there are actually two engines at work instead of just one."

Tanager's eyes lit up. Cepheus began to bounce up and down like an excited cat.

"Ahem," Lucene interrupted. "Can you explain this to those of us who haven't a clue what you're talking about?" She could feel their excitement but understood little else.

"Aye," Ivan said. "We won't know fer sure until we actually install this contraption in the physical vessel. But, if it works, it means they'll have enough power to get back to Erde in six months instead of a year."

"Six months?" Lucene muttered. She couldn't even manage six hours on a plane without getting claustrophobic. She couldn't imagine committing to a journey that took that long. Besides, she wasn't entirely convinced that Tanager and Cepheus could be trusted yet. It took more than two days to get to know someone. It had taken her a good four and a half years before she learned to trust Ivan. And then there was a faded memory that wanted to come out, like an itch that she just couldn't seem to scratch.

"You don't have to decide tonight," Tanager reassured her, feeling her apprehension.

"But, very soon," Cepheus added.

Lucene started to turn away, the doors to the shed about to close behind her before she doubled back. The sensor on the doors triggered and they slid back open. Tanager was the only one who looked up while the other men re-focused their attention on their experiment.

"I am helping out at the local sanctuary. There's a new moon celebration tonight. I don't suppose you'd care to join me?"

"I would be delighted," Tanager replied, nodding a head toward the two hard at work behind him. "I am useless to these gents anyway. It is best if I'm out of the way."

"Okay," Lucene answered. "So, I can come pick you up in Kermit."

"Kermit?"

"My car," she explained.

"Your car has a name?"

"Why wouldn't it have a name?"

"Didn't you say it was rude to answer a question with a question," he teased.

Lucene rolled her eyes. "As I was saying, I can pick you up. Where are you staying?"

"Just over there," he pointed to the house.

"You're staying with Ivan? Both of you?" *How had she not noticed that?* "Never mind, in that case, can you meet me by the window. Say, 6 p.m."

"Certainly," he smiled. "By the window at six." Lucene began to walk away. "Wait...please." Lucene turned around. "You feel far more emotionally stable than one would expect considering the information I just gave you. Why?"

"Maybe once you've spent more time in my head, you'll understand," Lucene smirked. "It all makes perfect sense to me. I've never felt like I belonged on this Earth. Never!"

16

THE UNDESIRABLES

FIVE YEARS AGO. TWO MONTHS AFTER THE ASSEMBLY.

"Roman Aurelius," the imposing man formed his question more like a statement. "I'm Director Sutton and in charge of the American division of the International Peace Project." Director Sutton stood over Roman who was seated in a straight-backed chair that was too low to the ground for his long legs. His knees knocked the bottom of the folding table in front of him. The room was painted a dull gray and mostly bare except for two chairs, a desk and a "Peace for All" Assembly poster advertising the next IPP event in Dubai next year. Somehow, Roman wasn't feeling the love that the IPP claimed to espouse. After an indignant body scan and rude questioning, they had yet to offer him so much as a glass of water…and he was parched.

"It's nice to meet you, Director Sutton." Roman folded his arms and tilted his head in a way that would suggest otherwise. "What can I answer for the IPP today that I wasn't able to answer last week, or two weeks before that?"

Director Sutton waved away the two men who were standing at the door. The last to exit closed the door behind him. Sutton pulled up a chair and sat across from Roman, removing the rather thick

Manila envelope that he had tucked under his arm. He laid it on the desk. Roman let out a deep sigh as the bulky man opened it to page one, eyeing the director's unsavory wardrobe —a pinstriped shirt so tight that the buttons threatened to pop at any moment, with gaps between them that revealed a yellowing undershirt from too many washes without bleach to cover up the sweat stains. There was no doubt in Roman's mind that Director Sutton was a bachelor, and likely to remain so for quite a while.

"Roman Aurelius," he said again. "That your real name?"

"Yes, no relation to Marcus," Roman smiled. Director Sutton didn't get the joke.

"It says here you were a high school anthropology teacher until a year ago when you were let go."

"No, not let go," he corrected. "I am currently on a sabbatical."

"That's not what it says here."

"Well, your report is wrong. Likely someone at the administrative office at school clicked the wrong box on the computer screen. I can phone the principal if you like?"

"That won't be necessary," Director Sutton nodded as he read further, as if whatever followed in the report explained what he needed to know.

"You seem to have an insatiable interest in aliens," he continued, flipping through the pages of his report.

"Well, as I've stated many times before, it is part of my research. And that is the definition of a sabbatical: to take a year to continue studies in one's field of expertise in order to remain current on developing trends."

"I know what a sabbatical means, Mr. Aurelius. But, why aliens?"

"What could be more interesting to an anthropologist than learning how humans will adapt to the integration of beings from other planets coming to live on Earth?"

"Integration may be a strong word," Director Sutton sucked at his teeth, distastefully.

"You don't like the idea of non-humans populating the Earth?" Roman asked.

"We're not here to talk about me, Mr. Aurelius. We're here to talk about the fact that you have an entire collection of photos, documents, and in some cases, interviews of aliens who are voluntarily listed in our International Registry. How did you even find these aliens, Mr. Aurelius?"

"Behavior patterns," he answered simply.

"Behavior patterns," Director Sutton repeated.

"Exactly."

"Care to share what those might be?"

"Actually, I'd rather not."

"Why not?"

"I don't know if you are aware of this, Director Sutton, but non-humans aren't exactly safe in our world. If you look at what happened with the Data Collectors ever since they alerted us to their presence decades ago..."

"I'm glad you brought them up," Director Sutton pulled a series of photos from his file and began tossing them on the table. "Recognize any of these 'non-humans,' as you like to call them?"

Roman turned white. They weren't just any photos of Data Collectors, they were photos of deceased Data Collectors, ones he's spoken with and they had been murdered in various graphic ways.

"What's the matter, Mr. Aurelius?" Director Sutton appeared suspicious.

"What do you mean, what's the matter?" Roman coughed back a gag reaction and fought off tears. "Why would you show me these? That's horrible!" He pushed his chair back and hugged his knees to his chest, heels resting on the edge of his seat.

"Take it easy, Mr. Aurelius," Director Sutton patted the table. "Can I get you a glass of water? Maybe some coffee?"

"Water would be nice," Roman brushed back a tear, slightly embarrassed. The director opened the interview room and poked his head out, motioning to one of his assistants and mouthing the word 'water.' A moment later, a cup of cold water arrived. Roman unfolded himself and accepted the cup of water, sipping it slowly. Finally, he asked, "Do I need a lawyer?"

"As of right now, Mr. Aurelius, we have no reason to suspect that you are actually involved in their deaths. However, you seem to have a knack for finding them. Are there any more aliens out there that we should be aware of?"

"No, the IPP confiscated all of my research—a year's worth of information that I painstakingly gathered, I might add."

"I'm sorry about that, Mr. Aurelius." He didn't really seem sorry. "But it doesn't reflect well on the American division of the IPP that beings from other planets are showing up dead in remarkably high numbers. If you can help us locate any remaining Data Collectors or have any insight as to who is killing them off, we would be very appreciative."

Roman paused for a moment before answering, "Director Sutton, I am unaware of any other Data Collectors or alien beings in our midst."

"Well, just answer me this. You're an expert in human behavior. Who would want them dead?"

"That's just it, Director Sutton, we're not dealing with strictly human behavior."

"Any theories?"

"If human laws are universal laws, then consider why anyone would kill another—fear, greed, power or hate. Often a combination of those traits. So, ask yourself who might exhibit those traits?"

"Why don't you just tell me?" Director Sutton tilted his head impatiently.

"Well, from an everyday human perspective, if aliens inhabit our Earth, humans may fear that aliens will overthrow us. Or, at the very least, take our jobs, use up our resources, create overcrowding and try to change our culture. For religious zealots, aliens go against every belief 75% of the world has held dear for centuries, the fact that there is life on other planets. Furthermore, the existence of alien life on other planets where they are thriving, means that they are likely much more advanced that we are."

"So, you think humans are targeting aliens. But you just said we were dealing with 'universal laws.' That suggests to me that you also think aliens are involved." Director Sutton leaned back in his chair and smirked, proud of his deduction.

"Yes," Roman nodded. "I also believe that aliens will target both humans and non-humans if it is to their benefit."

"Why?" Sutton leaned so far forward that Roman could smell his breath. Coffee and bologna were not a pleasant combination. "In this case, what's their motive?"

"This has been going on for nearly 30 years now, probably even much longer than that. Why are you asking me questions you already know the answers to, Director Sutton?"

"You just let me ask the questions." The Director shifted, visibly annoyed. "What reason would one alien group have for killing another?"

Roman rubbed his forehead with one hand in an attempt to stave off a mounting headache. "Let's pretend that Earth is a well-sought-after tropical island that several people want to buy. One bidder might simply wait in the hopes that the owner can no longer afford it and buy it out from under him when the owner is ready to give up. Another bidder might make life difficult for the owner, perhaps even making threats if he refuses to sell. Meanwhile, you have a special interest, a close relative, who would much rather lend the owner money and teach him how to sustain his island and rebuild it to its former glory. That's what we are, also, most likely dealing with here."

"So, assuming these bidders are actually aliens from different planets who want to take over Earth, are you suggesting that one of these bidders is trying to snuff out the competition?"

"In a manner of speaking."

"And what about the fact that humans are still very much living here?"

"A necessary casualty in their mind, I'm afraid." Roman placed his fingers on the table and began drumming them rhythmically. "But you knew all this, Director Sutton."

"But I needed to know how much you knew."

"That's everything. You may kill me or arrest me now."

"I have no interest in harming you, Mr. Aurelius," Director Sutton replied. "But I can't promise we won't be watching you. It's easiest if you willingly share any information you come across from now on. Understood?" Director Sutton stood.

"I understand."

Roman left the IPP satellite station more rattled than he had in the past. Some of the people in those photos he had spoken to recently, and he had a gnawing feeling in his belly. What if he had led someone directly to them and gotten them killed? As he walked into a local bodega, he had another fear: What if he were in danger too?

He surveyed the market with caution, noting a security mirror in the upper corner of one wall, and a camera on the other just next to the TV situated behind the checkout counter. What if they were filming him at this very moment? Roman grabbed a bottle of kombucha and a bag of green bean chips and stood impatiently in line while some woman rifled through her oversized backpack looking for exact change. He eyed her purchases in disgust—beef sticks, potato chips, donuts and a large bottle of lemonade. *What is it with Earthlings? They put the worst foods in their bodies and wonder why they become ill?* Although, he thought, she seemed to be awfully fit for someone who indulged in high calorie foods. He wondered...

"We accept credit cards, too," the cashier offered helpfully.

"No, thanks. Don't trust them," Lucene answered. Roman tilted his head. *What a peculiar thing to say,* he thought. "Aha," she proclaimed, proudly producing a nickel. By then, a long line had formed behind Roman. The cashier sighed, accepting the coin.

Just then, a news report came on, and everyone paused to look up at the TV screen.

"Think you'd recognize an alien? Think again. Our latest report uncovers the truth. There may be more foreign visitors on Earth than you believe. Moira Sugg brings us this developing story after this..."

"Damn undesirables," an overweight man behind Roman sputtered. "They should all go back to where they came from." There were a few mutters from people behind him, some nodding in agreement, while others folded their arms and looked around uncomfortably. "Hell," he continued, "they don't even speak English."

Lucene turned to look past Roman, at the man standing behind them. "Has it ever occurred to you that less than 20% of the Earth speaks English? And, it's commonly thought that Earth languages are considered primitive in the multiverse, with our planet being one of the few remaining whose linguistics haven't evolved over time."

The man paused for a moment. "Alien lover," he mumbled and turned his gaze toward the ground.

Lucene completed her purchase, regretting having called attention to herself, and made a hasty exit. Roman quickly laid his cash on the counter. "Keep the change," he told the cashier, gathering up his purchase and following Lucene out the door. He watched as she hopped into her old utility vehicle, annoyed that he couldn't trigger his lapel camera. The tiny camera kept beeping at him, needing a firmware update. He would have to return in the hopes that she would pass this way again.

SECTION TWO

"Stay calm and remember, you are in control of what experiences you let in."

17

THE FORTUNATA FAMILY

THREE YEARS AGO. TWO YEARS AFTER THE ASSEMBLY.

L ucene wandered into the kitchen still wearing a baby blue bathrobe and white comfy slippers. Her hair was a short, disheveled dust mop on her head. As she reached into the refrigerator for a morning ginger beer and a pastry, she could hear Fatima snoring from the room next door. She smiled to herself, as Fatima's nasal sounds were as boisterous as she was—they would make an elephant-like "ah" sound on the inhale and an enthusiastic cockatiel-like whistle on the exhale. She was her own one-woman zoo.

She was just about to settle on the couch with the morning paper when she heard a commotion at the door. "Shit," she muttered to herself. "Not today."

"Hullo-oh!" one of Fatima's aunts rapped on the door. There was a sound of chattering people behind her. "We're heee-rr-e!"

As Lucene ran to Fatima's room and began banging on her bedroom door, she witnessed Fatima's younger brother Tai peering through the side window with a wave and a wide-eyed grin. Other faces soon followed, smiling broadly and clearly oblivious to the fact that Lucene was still in her night clothes. She waved back, weakly, as Fatima threw open her door still in a long white nightgown with earplugs in and an eye mask drawn upward and hanging awkwardly on her forehead.

Fatima's reaction was distinctly different. Her face grew into a wide smile.

"Hi!" She waved enthusiastically at her brother and extended family through the window, motioning them to come to the front door.

Lucene took it as her opportunity to retreat into her room.

"Don't hide in there forever," Fatima ordered to Lucene as she threw open the door for her family.

Inside her bedroom, Lucene closed the door and stared at Bagheera. "I know, right?" She gave the cat a scratch behind the ear before he retreated under the bed. "You got extra room under there?" she joked.

Had she actually been paying the kind of rent she should be paying for room and board, instead of the meager amount that Fatima requested to cover monthly utilities, she would have complained a long time ago about boundaries. It wasn't that she didn't like them, per say, she just couldn't manage that much energy from that many people at once, particularly without so much as a phone call warning that they were coming.

Lucene threw on a white t-shirt and blue jeans while mentally preparing herself for the onslaught of smiles and questions. "One hour," she repeated to her image in the mirror as she brushed her teeth. "We agreed to one hour." That was deal she made with Fatima for events such as this one.

"You're my best friend," Fatima would tell her. "I want them to get to know you." When she saw Lucene's reluctance, she would add. "Okay, how about this? One hour. If you can socialize and mingle for just one hour, then you can make some excuse about having to get ready for work or something, and you won't hear a peep out of me."

Lucene plastered a smile on her face as she threw open the door.

"Ah, there she is!" Fatima's mother gushed, running toward the young woman and wrapping her in a tight, bear-like embrace. She had to admit, Mama Fatima had an unconditionally loving energy. She hugged her back, and actually kinda liked it. After an eternity, she finally released her grip.

"Hey, hey" Fatima's brother Tai gave her a one-armed bro hug, backpack slung over his opposite shoulder. She suspected Tai might actually have a small crush on her and overcompensated by being aloof. "Whassup, Lucene?" *Oh, you know, Tai,* Lucene thought to herself, *the usual. I hate crowds. Computers are tracking us. Red doors give me the willies, and I'm certain I'm being watched. Other than that, just dandy."*

"Not much," Lucene answered. "How about you?"

"Same," he nodded his head and punched her playfully in the arm. "Wanna see the new virtual keyboard I bought? It's so cool. Nobody has these yet...but I know a guy." He reached into his back-pack. *No, no, no,* Lucene thought, followed by, *they've been around for years, just not to the public.*

"Sure," she forced a smile. *One hour...*

The loudness and banter continued as one-by-one, each family member took turns hugging her. Some part of Lucene enjoyed the inclusion and appreciated that none of them seemed to be remotely mean-spirited or judgmental. The worst that could be said about them was that they lacked boundaries, both physically and culturally.

"Seeing anyone yet?" Fatima's very large, heavily made-up Aunt Keti nudged Lucene in the arm.

"Not yet," she answered. It had been the same answer for as long as she'd known them, and she suspected they thought this was strange.

"Yeah, neither is Fatima at the moment," Aunt Keti frowned, as if this was news to Lucene. Then, she had a thought. "Hey, you two aren't a couple, are you? I mean, we don't care if you are. I was just wondering."

"No, Auntie Keti," Lucene replied. "We are not."

She leaned in closer. "You would tell me if you were, right?"

"You'd be the first to know," Lucene whispered back.

"Good." Keti was satisfied. Then she noticed Lucene's lightning-scarred arms. Her face fell, sympathetically. "That doesn't hurt, right?"

"Not at all," Lucene answered, not for the first time since her meeting Aunt Keti nearly two years ago.

"Ah, well," she grabbed Lucene's chin with her hand and squeezed, her nails leaving an imprint on Lucene's jaw. "You're still beautiful."

"Thank you," Lucene attempted to reply, fish faced. *For the record, the lightning marks don't hurt, but your eagle grasp does!*

"Quit hogging Lucene's attention, Auntie," Tai complained. "I wanna show her my cool new tech."

Keti pinched his cheek and wrinkled her nose at him. "Such a smart boy," she praised her nephew.

One hour...

"Hey, Fatima, where do you keep the turmeric?" Fatima's father rifled through the kitchen pantry. "I always forget."

"I don't have powder, only fresh. Check the veggie drawer in the fridge," Fatima called back, turning the oven on before they'd even decided on what they were making.

*One...two...three...*Lucene counted twelve people, including herself, spread out between the living room and kitchen area. This was ten more people than was comfortable.

"Okay, so then, where's the grater?" her dad yelled back.

"Check this out," Tai tried to put the visor over her head so she could try the virtual keyboard herself.

"No!" She said so loudly, pushing it away, that Tai turned pale and the family all stopped talking. The room was suddenly silent.

"I'm super clumsy," Lucene offered. "It looks expensive and I don't want to break it."

"Aww," Tai smiled, knowingly. "It's okay, you won't." The entire family let out a relaxed sigh and went back to their chattering.

"Hey, Lucy?" Fatima came to her rescue. "It's getting late. Don't you have to feed Bagheera and get to work?"

"Oh, geez," Lucene looked at the clock in mock surprise. "Thanks for reminding me."

"You have to work on a Sunday," Aunt Keti lamented. "That doesn't seem right."

"Lucy is the assistant director at our local sanctuary, very important spiritual work."

"Ohhhh," their eyes grew wide in admiration.

"We understand," Mama Fatima said. The family nodded in approval. "It was nice to get to see you, if only for a little bit."

Fatima shot her friend a wink before Lucene escaped to the sanctity of her bedroom. Bagheera eyeballed her quizzically from under the bed.

"I made it, Bagheera," she reached down and rubbed his ear. "One hour."

18

MR. CUSHING AND THE ROYALS

SUNDAY AFTERNOON. FIVE YEARS AFTER THE ASSEMBLY.

"What do you have for us?" Sabrina demanded. Fredo gripped Drake's shoulders and squeezed until the man winced and began slumping to one side.

"Easy boy," Drake spat through clenched teeth. Fredo's grip remained fast.

"Fredo, let him go," Hamish ordered, sounding more ambivalent about the whole ordeal than usual.

A look of disgust crossed Sabrina's face. She enjoyed watching someone else's pain, even more so if she was watching someone else inflict it. She rubbed her belly, instinctively. Hamish used to be fun, she remembered. Now, he was a bore.

The four stood in the enormous abandoned warehouse, completely out of place in the surroundings. The sovereigns were dressed to the nines, while the rotted reinforcements that held the ceiling in place threatened to cave at any moment. Sounds of water slapping the dock could be heard outside.

"I encourage you to be...uuughh...nice to me, Sovereign," Drake groaned. There's a good chance I have access to something you want." By now, Lucene's former boss was hunched over to the point where he could almost rest his head on one knee.

"You found her?" She nodded to Fredo. "Release him!" Fredo obeyed, disappointed.

Hamish raised an eyebrow as the two—Royal and serf—exchanged glances but said nothing.

"I believe I have found her," Drake rubbed his shoulder. "But I have to be sure."

"Well, where is she?" Sabrina demanded.

"Somewhere safe," Drake lied. "Somewhere secret."

"I see," Sabrina began circling him like a shark. "You're not going to try and change the nature of our deal, are you?" The veins on her back turned a murky green as her skin began yellowing. She momentarily cursed him in her native tongue. Drake's pain turned to amusement.

"Now, my sovereign. Why would I change our deal when you have been so…hospitable?" He glanced over his shoulder at the large salamander who was busy picking at his teeth with a nail.

Fredo hoped he could soon expire this human in a slow and painful way. He didn't like him. He was fake, and he didn't like fake. He could appreciate his female master's power and danger because it was true to who she was. He could even stomach the fact that his male master was weak and somewhat feeble. It was who *he* was. But he had a difficult time with anyone who pretended to be something they were not. He would call him a chameleon, and chameleons were so afraid of their world that they always changed color to fit their surroundings. Fredo did not doubt that this human would turn on his masters anytime it suited him.

They had enlisted Drake Cushing's help long before that fateful Assembly explosion. Or, rather, Drake solicited his services as a negotiator between the Royals and the Vitruvians. The proposed plan was to help them divide Earth up between the two species. On the surface, it was a fair deal that would only be enacted if and when Earth was no longer habitable by humans. He'd be well paid for his time and, with any luck, he'd have long since died of old age before the deal could be actualized. At least, this was what the Royals and the Vitruvians were told in negotiations. In truth, he had no qualms about selling Earth out to the highest bidder as long as he was offered protection and a comfortable life. Thus far, the Royals were taking the lead, and his side deal included the delivery of one woman with very special skills who could help ensure the Royals gain control of the planet sooner, rather than later.

"The plan is the same as it has always been, Sovereign." He took a seat on an old whiskey crate, careful to make certain it could support his weight.

Sabrina leaned against a wooden beam. "I just need to be sure you'll keep your end of the bargain."

As instructed, Drake met Fredo back at the abandoned warehouse at the designated time. It was a half a mile from the Sovereign Casino. Fredo opened the limo door for Drake and motioned for him to get in. Fredo didn't even try to hide the contemptuous sneer on his face, slamming the passenger door a split second before Drake managed to pull his leg safely inside. In spite of Fredo's actions, Drake's expression remained calm.

"Thank you, Fredo," Drake smiled politely after the salamander stuffed himself, rather uncomfortably, behind the driver's seat. Fredo adjusted the mirrors so that he wouldn't have to look at the annoying Earthling in the back seat, and the two road to the casino in silence.

Fredo pulled up alongside another two-dozen identically designed limos lined up at the service entrance to the casino. There were no service trucks that evening. The 54 IPP representatives popped out from their limos. They were all that remained of the original 215 representatives, just five years prior. Following the assembly explosion, many retired, some disappeared, others resigned, and a large number fell victim to mysterious onsets of heart attacks, strokes and brain tumors, though most had no history of illness.

"Drake Cummings, old buddy. How the hell are you?" A portly man about 25 years his senior, who outweighed him by as many pounds, sidled alongside Drake and slapped him on the back.

"Good to see you, Max," Drake forced a smile, despite the remorse in his chest and sourness in his stomach. While they rarely agreed on political matters, Drake considered him a friend.

As the group gathered, several wolf-like beings from the Trappist region wandered by in pack formation, each shifting their bodies upright and standing on two legs as they passed through the side door.

"Do you believe this shit?" Max nudged his friend. "Aliens crawling all over this place like fire ants and nobody on the outside knows about it. Ridiculous!"

"I know what you mean," Drake agreed. "If the media got wind of this, we'd have a shit-storm on our hands."

Fredo's security team began a formation around the IPP officials. "This way," one instructed, leading them to an unmarked gray door that slid open as he approached. One by one, the delegates shuffled through.

They were led through a dark and narrow hallway, taking several twists and turns before arriving at their conference room. It was ornate with plush, red, swivel chairs surrounding a long dining table that took up almost the entire room. Silk tapestries hung from the wall and two large, teardrop-shaped crystal chandeliers hung above the table.

"Must have set these guys back a pretty penny," Max nodded at the tapestries. "Each one of them must go for $75,000 a pop."

As the delegates took their seats, a female attendant from the casino's waitstaff quickly ran around the room pouring what appeared to be wine into the crystal stemmed glasses at each seat.

"Now, this is my idea of a meeting," another joked.

"Oh, I don't drink," one woman protested, blocking her glass. "Maybe just some water?"

"It's the non-intoxicating kind, madam," the attendant explained. The woman nodded and took a polite sip. It tasted like wine...but, wasn't.

"Nice to know we're outsourcing to other planets now. And to think, we used to complain about all the jobs going to China!" yet another man joked.

From a mile away, Sabrina and Hamish watched the room from a remote viewer with growing annoyance.

"Not what one would expect from members of the International Peace Project, is it?" Hamish asked his wife.

"Indeed not," she agreed. She looked distastefully at a fat man placing his entire meaty hand over a plate of hors d'oeuvres being offered. "Don't these fools recognize how powerful we are? I control the weather. If I had wanted to, I could have wiped out this little petri dish of a planet long ago!"

"Patience, my dear," Hamish put a hand over his wife's as if to console her. "Just a few minutes more." Sabrina pulled her hand away in irritation without taking her eyes away from the viewer.

At long last, all delegates of the IPP were at the table, greedily filling up on libations and small servings of filet mignon and shrimp bites.

Drake quickly surveyed the room, as if memorizing it and everyone in it. Satisfied, he nodded to one of the attendants. Drake stood while Max was waxing eloquently about which planets had the best soil for starting a vineyard. "Excuse me, Max, I need to step out. Be back in a moment." Max nodded and gnawed on a bit of shrimp. For a split second, he thought about asking his friend to go with him, but that wasn't part of the deal. And, who knows what the repercussions of that might be? The attendant stepped away from the door, allowing Drake to pass.

His palms were sweating as he made his way down the hallway. The humid air smacked him in the face as he exited the building.

Without a word, Fredo opened the door for him and they were on the road moments later.

In the distance, he heard the explosion, but didn't turn around. He couldn't. It was as if he was frozen in place. Drake could see the flames in the reflection of the rearview mirror as he realized that at least half of the casino was now gone.

"That seemed awfully large for such a small room," Drake choked to Fredo.

The sound of fire trucks and ambulances drowned out Fredo's reply, so he'd waited until they'd turned off onto a side road and were a safe distance from the main highway. Fredo tried again, "Sovereign doesn't have a need to return to the casino again, so there was no reason to leave it standing."

"You mean…but there must be thousands of people in there!" Drake felt sick to his stomach.

"Yes, they're dead. But, congratulations. You get to live. It's your lucky day."

19

NEW MOON CELEBRATION

SUNDAY EVENING. FIVE YEARS AFTER THE ASSEMBLY.

Tanager was already waiting for Lucene when she climbed out of the window. He was wearing his usual fedora and long jacket even though it was at least 85 degrees out. The sun was setting, and he stood partially hidden behind a large oak tree in the yard, just a few feet from the window. Were it not for the sudden feeling that she was being watched, she might not have noticed him at all.

But he noticed her, watching her expertly climb through the window while wearing a flowery, knee-length sundress, both with admiration at her agility and her...well, just everything. From the ground, she tugged her dress into place and smoothed her hair. She had it combed straight with a simple hair clip in the shape of a dragonfly, which pulled several locks of hair away from her face.

Lucene headed toward the driveway, beckoning him with a quick nod.

She climbed into Kermit, pulling her dress away from the door before slamming it closed, realizing only then that instead of getting in the passenger's seat, Tanager stood politely by the side of the house.

She made a laborious effort to roll down the driver's side window. "Hop in," she finally called. He glanced furtively in each direction before coming toward her, making her instantly regret having spoken so loudly.

Tanager looped around the front of the SUV. "Open," he instructed, staring at the door. The door didn't move. He tried again before looking quizzically at Lucene. "Turn key, remember?" she smirked, leaning across the passenger seat to release the lever from inside.

"Ah, yes," he recalled, pulling on the door's handle and clambering inside. "I assume 'hop in' is just a figurative term?"

"Yeah, just figurative," she confirmed. After a long and awkward silence, she felt the need to make small talk. "So, since you're new around here, I don't suppose you've ever been to a New Moon Celebration before, have you?"

"No, this would be my very first." He wrinkled his brow, puzzled.

"You have no idea what it is, do you?"

"Not in the slightest."

"But you know what a moon is, right?"

"Naturally."

"Well, a new moon is said to be symbolic of new beginnings. Plus, this one is extra special because it will become the blue harvest moon."

"Why is that special? Does your moon actually turn blue?"

"Not exactly. It sometimes gives the illusion of turning blue, and...well...a blue moon is so rare, hence the expression, 'once in a blue moon.' " She searched his blank expression for recognition. "Never mind," she continued. "It's when there's a second full moon within a single month. On top of that, the harvest is symbolic of reaping the rewards of all a person's hard work. So, this celebration is where we ask for all the blessings we want related to all the goals we have set throughout the year up until now. We start at the new moon and let it build all the way until the moon is full."

"Fascinating. Who do you ask?"

"Well...God...the Universe...your higher self on a different plane...pretty much whatever you believe in."

"And what do you believe in, Lucene?"

Lucene paused for a moment. "Good question," she stared at the road uncomfortably and continued driving.

"Where is this celebration taking place?"

"Ah," Lucene answered. "There's an open field behind the sanctuary where I work. The minister, Reverend Isabella, will open the ceremony by having me and a couple other helpers pass out wish paper and pens for participants to write down their wishes. We then collect them for her. She'll lead a meditation where we focus on what we wrote. The papers go into a burning bowl, anointed with oils. The bowl is set on fire, and Reverend Isabella uses a feather to fan the flames up to the heavens."

"But what if a person's God of choice is an Earth spirit living in the ground. How will the prayers reach them?"

"It's symbolic," Lucene re-iterated. "Besides, the ashes are then sprinkled over the field, so I'm sure Earth spirits are included."

Tanager nodded. That answer was deemed acceptable.

"And, now I have another question for you," Lucene glanced in Tanager's direction.

"Yes?"

"What's with the fedora and the jacket all the time? Are you in disguise?"

"Apparently not." He looked down at his garb. It hadn't escaped his attention that he didn't quite mesh with his new surroundings, but hadn't quite figured out how to remedy the situation just yet.

"Well, if you're trying to be less conspicuous, you would have done better to wear shorts and a t-shirt. To kind of blend in."

"Then, I probably shouldn't confess that I'm wearing a crisp, armed shirt with fancy pants under my coat."

"Armed shirt with fancy pants?" Lucene laughed. "Oh, I think you mean a long-sleeved shirt with dress slacks. Aren't you hot?"

"Sweltering."

"Tell you what," Lucene offered. "Let's stop in 'the Closet' at the sanctuary before we hit the ceremony. We're early and have a few minutes to spare. We have a large assortment of clothes in varied sizes that people have donated. I'm certain we can dredge something up for you to help you fit in." She pulled into the parking lot as Tanager deciphered 'dredge' in the context of the conversation. "Follow me," she instructed, leading the way to the back of the sanctuary.

The Closet, as it turned out, was a small, faux wood-paneled room. Two sides of it were lined with clothes racks, men's clothing on one side, women's on the other. The wall closest to the door held simple shelving filled with shoes, separated by their intended gender and further segmented by size. Next to the open door, two curtains hung in concealing circles. The center of the room, however, was not nearly so well organized. A long table sat with a variety of ties, hats, scarves, and even a few pieces of woven and metal jewelry.

Tanager surveyed the room with interest. Lucene sensed his question. "It's for people who need everyday clothes or clothes for a job interview but can't afford it. How about this?" Lucene held up a Hawaiian shirt, peppered with palm trees.

"That seems very...obvious...to me," Tanager answered carefully.

"Nah, people will just think you're a tourist."

Tanager's eyes suddenly lit up as he spotted a gray fishing hat with a piece of aqua ornamental bait stitched to the side. He tried it on, happily.

"Oh, that's definitely you," Reverend Isabella popped her head into the room. She was stunning with a blue-green, multi-hued, full-length robe and beaded headdress.

Lucene and Tanager looked up, somewhat startled at the interruption.

"Lucene, tell me, who is your new friend?" She peered at him closely. "Or, should I say, old friend?"

"Reverend Isabella," Lucene replied quickly. "This is a friend of mine from New York, Tanager. Tanager, this is Reverend Isabella. She founded this sanctuary and is the head minister."

Isabella resisted a laugh as Tanager tipped his fishing hat to her. She put out a hand and, to Lucene's relief, Tanager shook it instead of kissing it. "It's nice to meet you." She couldn't help but notice that his hat was completely out of place with the rest of his attire.

"Tanager is here on business and completely forgot to pack casual wear. We thought perhaps he could pick out a couple of pieces here, and in exchange, he could donate one of his suits to the sanctuary."

"Given the cost of your threads," Isabella eyed him again. "I'd say the sanctuary is getting the better end of the deal. I'm sure it will make someone in need very happy."

"I sincerely hope it does," Tanager answered. Until that moment, he hadn't considered that by swapping clothes, he might actually be helping an Earthling. The thought made him smile.

"It's not much," she pointed to one of the curtains, "but you can change there. I hope you will join us for the ceremony."

"We'll be there," Lucene confirmed. "I'll be out front to help in about 15 minutes, if that's okay with you."

"Perfect," Isabella winked, before she seemed to, quite literally, float out of the room.

Within no time, Tanager had settled on one pair of shorts, one pair of cargo pants, two casual shirts, one sun cap and, although he really didn't need it, one fishing hat. He opted to wear the cargo pants, a Hawaiian shirt and a "Salt Life" cap. Lucene managed to talk him out of the fishing hat, explaining that it might be out of place for this event. He kept it anyway.

In exchange, he left his dress shirt, slacks, suit jacket and trench coat folded neatly on the center table. "Is it okay if I keep the fedora? I've grown somewhat attached to it."

"Of course," Lucene smiled. She had grown rather fond of him wearing it. "I promise you that what you have left is more than enough."

"Once I return home, I will ask Ivan to donate the rest of my clothing as well."

"That is very thoughtful of you." Lucene tilted her head and smiled at him with admiration. Remembering herself, "We'd better get going. Why don't I drop the rest of your things in the car first?"

Lucene planned on depositing Tanager at a nearby lawn chair while she helped Reverend Isabella, but in true Tanager fashion, he had to be of service. She handed him some crinkled wish paper, which he distributed to attendees strewn out across the field, some in chairs and others on blankets. She followed up with pencils.

"Hey, I like your shirt," a man commented to Tanager, who looked down and beamed proudly at the man. "I used to have one just like it, until the missus made me get rid of it," he nodded toward his wife. Her faced flushed with embarrassment as she elbowed her husband in the ribs.

"He has too many, and I must say it suits you better than it did him." Her husband grunted. Tanager didn't put the connection together and simply tipped his cap to her as a thank you. With that, they continued their task.

"Well, fancy meeting you here!" a boisterous voice came at them from behind, startling Lucene. There, Roman hovered over them, dressed in his usual, all-black, goth-like jeans and t-shirt. He grinned at her in a way that made her uncomfortable.

What exactly did he know about her that she didn't already know about herself?

"Roman, it is nice to see you again," Tanager shook his hand in earnest. Lucene found it interesting. Her tendency was to distrust until proven otherwise; whereas, Tanager, on the other hand, seemed completely neutral, a blank slate until someone showed their worth, or lack of it.

"A fine celebration, isn't it?" Roman spewed enthusiasm. "The only thing that would make it better is if my lovely Fatima were here."

Lucene searched his face for insincerity through his flowery words. She found none.

Moments later, Reverend Isabella addressed the crowd. All fell silent and settled in for one of her meditations. Lucene motioned for Tanager to take a seat beside her on a blanket that was offered by a family sitting nearby. "We brought extra, just in case," they smiled.

Lucene instinctively sat cross-legged on the ground, resting her palms lightly in her lap, left over right and closing her eyes. Tanager could feel her energy shift immediately...surprising. He assumed the same pose, his left knee lightly touching her right, and the familiar energy between them was back again. Lucene opened one eye to glance at her knee, just to make sure they were actually touching... they were. After the dinner last night, she had to be sure. Tanager smiled lightly to himself.

Roman knelt behind them, sitting on his heels and holding his arms out with palms raised and thumb and forefinger pressed into a mudra. Several people looked on with interest, but mostly to wonder how he planned to hold his arms up for that long, and then sank back into their own meditation.

Reverend Isabella began with a protection prayer, blessing the land and all those who were on it, asking that all learn to walk gently on Mother Earth. Lucene's mind sank. Images floated up from her subconscious, along with the words, "experimentation" and "preserves." Suddenly, she was back in New York, watching as the IPP summit went up in smoke. More images surfaced, flooding in faster than she could filter them. She opened her mouth, about to let out a scream.

Tanager wrapped an arm around her and touched the palm of his hand to the side of her face, pulling her toward him. Roman watched with interest, expecting him to kiss her. Instead, he did something very odd. He pressed his forehead to hers, and in a moment, she calmed down. She couldn't bring herself to open her eyes. Tanager knowingly pulled away and returned to the meditation.

Some time later, Reverend Isabella summoned people to come up, in groups, to drop their wish paper into the fire. Lucene took that as her cue, jumping up to help guide small groups, making sure small children didn't get too close to the flames. Roman gave her a knowing look as he tossed his paper into the fire, except that she still didn't know what it was she was supposed to know.

After the ceremony, people began to gather up their belongings and head home. Tanager was pulled away momentarily by Reverend Isabella who asked for his assistance in gathering ceremony materials. He obliged without question.

As Lucene moved to help them, Roman took her by the elbow. "Walk with me for a moment, won't you?"

Confused, Lucene fell into step beside him, taking two paces to his single, long stride. She looked up at him, questioningly. "I know you like him," he said, not looking at her.

"Who?" He nodded over his shoulder. "Oh, you mean Tanager... well, I suppose he's alright."

"Just be careful. He's not who you think he is."

"What do you mean?"

"I mean, I think he is a traitor and is secretly working for them."

"Who's *them*?" She asked, more confused than ever.

"The Royals," he stopped, nodding, as if this should have meaning to her.

"I literally have no idea what you're talking about." She stared him in the eyes as if demanding meaning. Roman was taken aback. She really didn't remember.

"He's dangerous," his expression turned dark. "I thought he was here to help our planet...as I...I mean, as others who came here before us were; but I am concerned that the stories are true."

"And, what stories would those be, Roman?" Lucene bristled a little at the accusation.

"His only interest is in helping the Royals wipe out civilization as we know it and re-populate the Earth...and he needs you to do it."

20

MR. SPARKS

I t took little time for Lucene to find him. Somehow, she'd settled on the most unobtrusive boat along the docks, watching as a frazzled little man climbed aboard, seemingly having a conversation with himself.

"Jim Sparks?" Lucene asked.

"Uh, y-y-yeah," the man answered, trying to arrange his dirty, unkempt hair without much luck. He looked around nervously, giving his unshaven chin a scratch. "Do I know y-y-you?"

"I don't think so, but I'm not sure. My name is Lu—"

Jim's eyes grew wide as he spotted the tree-like patterns on Lucene's uncovered arms. "C-c climb aboard...q-q-quickly." Jim motioned for her to hurry. Lucene obeyed, even though all common sense would have told her getting into a strange man's boat was a bad idea. She'd already done a lot of uncommon sense things lately. Why should this be any different? From across the marina, a pear-shaped woman with frizzy, red, curly hair glared at her from her tiny houseboat, her eyes peering suspiciously over the romance novel she was reading. Jim waved to her in reassurance.

"Hmph," the woman muttered, returning to her book.

"Surprised to see y-y-ou, Lucene. Er, make yourself c-c-comfortable," he offered, once she was inside.

Lucene looked around the boat, littered with pieces of unwashed, tattered clothing on the seats, a few dishes and utensils with food still stuck to them on the dinette, and a smell worse than Red Tide. The man, himself, would have passed for homeless had she not, in fact, been standing in his home.

Lucene politely lifted an unwashed t-shirt from a chair with her forefinger and thumb, gently placing it to one side, and half-sat on the edge of the seat, conscious that she may need to check herself for lice after the visit. Jim leaned against the pantry door, apologetically.

"Sorry," he apologized. "I haven't had time to c-c-clean yet this week...been a little busy." The tiny sailboat looked as if more than a week had gone by since it had received a little tender loving care... more like 52 weeks.

"Mr. Sparks," Lucene was confused. "You seem to know *me*. Do I know *you*?"

"Good, good...good question," he stammered. He ran his hands through hair and then tapped his fingers together as he searched for the right words.

"How should I put this," he tapped his head. "They're gonna k-k-kill you." He finally blurted out. Lucene was taken aback. Once again, she was getting a 'danger' alert. She knew she should have been afraid of this stranger, but he gave off a similar recognizable energy as Tanager and Cepheus, albeit much weaker and more... frazzled, somehow. She continued with caution.

"Wait. What? Who?" Lucene searched his face for meaning. He held his head. "Who is going to kill me?"

"My head hurts," Jim responded.

Instinctively, Lucene went to him. Jim flinched slightly as Lucene touched three fingers to his head. For a moment, she could feel his pain and his fear. *The Royals,* she heard him think. Jim wiped a few painful tears from his eyes, using the hem of his t-shirt. He reached into his pocket and pulled out a prescription bottle and popped a pill, chewing it up, crumpling his face at the apparent bitterness.

"I'm sorry you're in pain. But you must tell me, how are the Royals involved in this?" she asked, backing away.

"Ah, you got that," he nodded. "We always knew you were special."

"About the Royals?" she asked again.

"A nasty bunch," he shook his head. "They c-c-came here eons ago to repopulate Earth—and other places—by setting up their nurseries. 'Cept things didn't go as planned, and now they want to k-k-kill everybody and try again."

"Everybody, or just me?" Lucene persisted. She knew the Royals were banned from the IPP because of shady practices, but this part was new.

"Well, you're special. They want what you have...gee, my head hurts. They want what you have...what I have...had. They tried to take it from me, but I wouldn't give it to them. But you..." His eyes grew wide. "You're more than special. C-c-an't let them get you."

Lucene began to see images in her head, bright lights, sounds, pain, surgeries—many, many surgeries. She began to scream.

"No, no..." Jim clasped his dirty hands over her mouth. "Mustn't do that." He looked around nervously. She mentally shut a red door with the sounds, sights and pain trapped behind it.

"Everything okay in there?" the red-haired woman croaked, peering her head down from the top deck of the sailboat, suspiciously. With no way to get from her houseboat to Jim's sailboat at such speed, it could only be assumed that she'd been listening in for some time.

"Y-y-yeah," Jim called to her. "Thanks, Ginny. My...er...niece saw a roach and got sc-c-cared."

"Don't doubt that. Your place is filthy!" She coughed. What she did doubt, however, was that Lucene was his niece.

"Y-y-you c-c-can go now, Ginny!" Jim called up to her, visibly annoyed.

"Hmmph," she said again and began shuffling toward the exit ramp. She decided that she had no interest in meeting, what she presumed, was the "other" woman anyway. "If you want me, you know where to find me!" she called. Under her breath, she swore, "Niece, my ass!"

"Y-y-you should go," Jim told Lucene. "It isn't safe. Ginny's a sweet gal with a big mouth."

"Just one more thing…do you know a fellow by the name of Roman? He's very tall with dark hair and a light complexion. He claims to be…one of us," she said, carefully.

Mr. Sparks shook his head fervently. "Nah, I never heard that name before…not ever. I'd be c-c-c-areful if I was you."

"Thank you, Mr. Sparks. And, I hope your head feels better."

A weird calm overcame the man. "Thanks, it already does. Always knew y-y-you were special."

"Hang on," Lucene paused. "Let me at least give you an address where you can find me. Perhaps we can meet again soon. I have a friend who I believe might be able to help you…with your headaches."

"Naw," he shook his head. "Don't give me your address. Okay, maybe." He nodded. "Y-y-yeah. No…no." He debated with himself for the next minute, nodding and then shaking his head.

"Do you have a piece of paper, by chance?" She interrupted him, looking around with uncertainty.

"Jest think it, and I'll see if I c-c-can retrieve it."

Just think it? She was getting used to her connection with Tanager, but hadn't considered its wider application, and she certainly wasn't trained on how to use it yet.

"I'll try," she nodded, thinking the address as hard as she could. Mr. Sparks winced a little, and then gave up with a sigh. "I'm sorry, Mr. Sparks. I'm not sure how to direct my thoughts like that."

"It's ok-k-kay. Y-y-y-ou'll git it back soon." He leaned in. "Y-y-y-ou jest whisper the address to me. I'll remember."

Lucene wasn't terribly sure about that, but she obeyed. "900 Prosperous Lane. It's..."

"That's enough," Mr. Sparks waved his hand. "I know where y-y-you are."

Lucene nodded. "I'll be going now." As she began to climb the stairs, he stopped her.

"Oh, y-y-yeah. Y-y-y-ou might want to watch out for mermaids and blue butterflies too. They c-c-claim to be here to help; but, I'm none too sure about them." Lucene gave a confused nod and quickly made her exit.

Monday Afternoon

Jim Sparks was quite shaken by Lucene's visit earlier in the day. He instinctively reached for his pain medication and chewed an extra pill. He retreated to his bed: a small mattress located in a cubby hole toward the back of the boat. As he felt the boat listlessly drifting back and forth, up and down, he remembered his homeland. So much time had passed since he left Erde that he struggled with certain details. But there were some things he could remember vividly...its lush green landscapes, unspoiled waters...and their language. He loved that their native tongue was so melodic. Neighbors from visiting planets always commented that they didn't have to speak the language in order to understand its sentiment. And, if exposed to it long enough, they were able to easily speak it—even without formal training. He'd spoken next to nothing but English since he'd arrived on Earth. Jim smiled blissfully to himself as he floated off to sleep, mumbling a few blessings to himself in his old language.

He didn't hear that someone had boarded the boat and was making their way toward him. In his mind, he was already elsewhere.

21

MR. CUSHING AND THE MERMAID

"**Y**ou've been a bad boy, Mr. Cushing." Drake Cushing's gaze shifted downward toward his sneakers. There, just beyond the dock where he stood, the greenish-blue torso of a woman waded in the marina, her lower half obscured beneath the water's surface. Her indigo hair was cropped short and matted against her head. Her face had natural streams of blue-and-gray, flowing stripes across it making her the perfect camouflage if she had been standing in front of the Northern Lights, and tiny gills could be detected on each side of her neck. Everything else about her features looked perfectly human from this vantage point, and she did nothing to hide her breasts as she bobbed up and down in the water.

"Odessa, how lovely to see you," Drake flashed her his toothiest grin, the fake one he always used to imply friendliness when he didn't really mean it. He continued his walk along the dock. She swam alongside him, a splash of fins thrashing behind her. He pretended not to notice. He had an appointment to keep. Finally, Odessa grew impatient and splashed him with her tail, just enough to wet his jeans, but preserve his shirt and suit jacket. "What can I do for you this morning?" Drake scowled, stopping abruptly and wiping a water droplet from his eye.

"There's a nasty rumor going around that you're double-dealing, Mr. Cushing." Odessa smiled flirtatiously, waving her arms back and forth to keep her afloat. "My superiors don't like it."

Odessa was the reason people still believed in mermaids. She wasn't one but looked every bit the part. In reality, she was an informant for the Vitruvians from Section 2 and was supposed to report any and all suspicious activity that might affect the wellbeing of her people. As with all Vitruvians, she had the ability to shift into different forms, sometimes human-like, but more often what Earthlings would describe as "animals." She discovered she was partial to the water and spent most of her time as close to the marina as possible, only coming on land when her job required it.

"I don't know what you've heard, but I can assure you, Odessa, my intentions are honorable." He squatted down to look her in the eyes, but not before surveying his surroundings. While it may have been becoming slightly more acceptable for species from other planets to take up residence on Earth when on special government assignment, it certainly wasn't common, and it certainly wasn't appreciated. "I'm simply fulfilling my role as Chief Negotiator between your people and the Royals, as both parties have asked of me. Please don't interfere."

"When have I ever interfered, Mr. Cushing?" Odessa pouted, her feelings hurt. "I have no allegiance to anyone whatsoever...I'm just doing my job."

"Well, you can tell the Vitruvians that everything is going according to plan."

"Morphinae might disagree with you."

"And how is our little blue butterfly these days?" Drake did nothing to hide his contempt.

"That's a fine way to talk about someone who saved your life."

"You know something?" Drake ignored the comment. "Your people have a strange way of getting what they want. They won't overtly kill anyone, but if the Royals decide to decimate the human population, well, that's just fine. Everyone will divide the spoils and the Vitruvians walk away with the self-righteous illusion that they are a peaceful people."

"Tsk tsk," Odessa clucked at him. "And here I thought you'd understand, being American and all. We put our people first. Sure, we'll defend ourselves should the Royals prove to be less than honorable; but we do our best to mind our own business."

"Like what you're doing now, you mean?" He motioned his hand wildly into the air. "Look, I prefer not to be seen in public talking to a mermaid."

"I'm not a mermaid!" Odessa squealed. She quickly softened her expression, however, when she saw Drake's amused expression. She had fallen right into his trap.

"Odessa, it's been a pleasure," Drake lied. "But tell the Vitruvians they have nothing to worry about. The deal is going down according to plan." With that, he waved a hand in dismissal and stood. Odessa made a gesture with her face that was probably derogatory on her planet, but one that was completely lost on him. She did a few backstrokes before disappearing beneath the water.

Drake pulled a handkerchief from the back pocket of his jeans and wiped his brow. It was getting easier with each attempt, but he still found this whole business nerve-wracking. After a few cursory glances around him, he made his way just past a tiny white houseboat in the marina. He took a seat on a nearby bench, as planned, and pulled out his cell phone to send a simple text. "I'm here."

Moments later, Mr. Sparks' Ginny showed up, disguised with a scarf around her head and thick sunglasses. Her frizzled red hair poked out from under the scarf.

"Hi Ginny," a neighboring boater waved as she walked by. She began to wave back before remembering that she was supposed to be in disguise. Ginny quickly ducked her head, grabbing her scarf with both hands under her chin and tugging it tightly. Drake watched with a curious expression, as she walked past the bench where he sat, looked over her shoulder and kept going. She made it to a lamppost several feet away before she turned and shuffled back over to him.

"You Cushing?" She whispered gruffly.

"I am." Drake flashed her a grin. "You must be the lovely Ginny."

She let out a hoarse laugh, followed by a cough. She sat down next to Drake, who instinctively slid away from her as he caught of whiff of heavy cigarette smoke. His eyes began to water slightly before he once again made use of his handkerchief.

"Now, you promise me that Jim's gonna be okay, right?"

"Of course, Ginny. I'm so glad you phoned me. The family has been worried sick."

"I kinda had a feeling it might be something like this," she shook her head. "Poor, Jim. He's a sweet man, but a little touched in the head…ooh, sorry. I didn't mean that."

"It's quite alright," Drake reassured her. "Mental illness can be so unpredictable. He up and disappeared one day, and if it weren't for you, we wouldn't have found him. Now, which boat is his?" Ginny cleared her throat, awkwardly. Drake nodded, understanding. "Of course," he pulled a folded cashier's check from his shirt pocket. "Three thousand dollars as a finder's fee and our family's gratitude."

Ginny's eyes lit up like a dog spotting a squirrel. She took it gingerly, trying not to appear too eager. "I wouldn't even ask for it. It's just that I can really use the money right now."

"I completely understand."

"And, he'll be okay?"

"I assure you, Ginny, Jim is going to get the best care from top doctors. When he does, I have no doubt he'll be back to visit you. I hear he's a little sweet on you," Drake teased, nudging her arm.

"Aw, g'on," Ginny's cheeks turned red. She tucked the check in her bra strap under her blouse. "Not too sure 'bout that. Had a young thing stop by earlier." Her eyes lit up. "Hey, he claimed she was his niece, but that can't be right, can it? Seein' how the family's still looking for him?"

"That is curious," Drake agreed, trying to suppress his own curiosity. "Did you happen to meet this...niece?"

"Naw, he tried to keep me away...probably some young floozy. "

"Could you describe her for me?"

"Well..." Ginny tapped the cashier's check, subconsciously. Drake took the hint.

"I don't have much," he informed her, reaching for his wallet. "But I could give you an additional $100 cash for your troubles." He pulled out a crisp bill.

"Aw," Ginny snatched the bill from his fingertips and tucked it behind the other, unoccupied bra strap. "I wouldn't ask for it, 'cept... you know. I'm a little light on cash these days."

"Times are hard, all around," Drake frowned, sympathetically. "I'm grateful for your help."

"Well," she thought for a moment. "Her hair was kinda short and brown."

"Yes?"

"Mmm...couldn't see her eyes, but she had a normal-ish shaped face."

"Yes?" Drake grew impatient."

"Wore jeans and a green t-shirt...nothing unusual about that."

"Anything else?" Drake clenched his teeth.

"Oh," her eyes suddenly lit up. "There was one thing!"

"Yes?"

"She had these weird tattoos on her arms. Looked like tree branches." Drake's surprised micro-expression was lost on Ginny. He quickly recovered.

"You didn't happen to catch her name, by chance, did you?"

"Well, it was hard to get with Jim's stuttering, but it sounded like 'Lucy.' "

"You've been very helpful, Ginny, thank you." Drake stood. "If you remember anything else, you know how to reach me. I promise to pay you for your efforts."

Suddenly, her eyes lit up. "Ooh! I remember she lives off Prosperous Lane." Ginny hugged herself proudly and leaned back on the bench. "They didn't think I could hear, but I have ears as sharp as an owl's. Say, who do you think she was?"

"No idea," Drake answered. "But I will certainly report it to the family. Could be a drug dealer. Who knows?"

"Probably that," Ginny furrowed her lips.

"Now, where can I find Mr. Sparks?"

"It's the tattered white sailboat over there, next to my houseboat. Mine's the one with the yellow flowerpot on the deck."

"Thank you, Ginny," he answered, watching as she struggled to stand. "To avoid Jim getting embarrassed, would you mind keeping our talk to yourself?"

"Nobody will hear a peep out of me, I swear," Ginny promised, eyes wide.

"Well, that's just fine. Good day, Ginny."

"G'day, Mr. Cushing."

22

SANCTUARY

MONDAY EVENING. FIVE YEARS AFTER THE ASSEMBLY.

B etween Mr. Sparks telling her that the Royals were trying to kill her, an unusual visit from Tanager and Cepheus who, for all she knew, *could* have been the Royals, and Fatima's new alien romance, she needed to clear her head. She made her way to the Singing River Sanctuary, but not before leaving a note in Ivan's mailbox to meet her in the serenity garden at the church as soon as possible, but not to tell anyone where he was going and who he was going to see. She signed it, "Kermit's mom" in the hopes that he would, for once, actually check his mail on time and, that he would realize it was she who made the request.

A series of ivy-draped trellises surrounded the gardens with a fountain composed of planets orbiting the sun. At its base was a circle of people, animals, and mythical creatures standing together in unity collecting water that flowed from each of the planets into the pool of water at the bottom. Around the fountain were four stone benches etched with names: Stillness, Quietude, Tranquility and Peace. Branching out from the center were four shell pathways. Between each was a variety of native plants: Beautyberry, Fire Bushes, Oyster plants and Muhly grass.

Lucene sat on the Quietude bench, in hopes that it would calm her racing mind. She assessed what she knew so far. In a matter of days, she had met four strange men, all of whom seemed out of place with their surroundings and, based on their behavior and wild claims, possibly psychotic. One claimed she, herself, was born from alien parents. And all four seemed to think she was special, and, as such, was in great danger.

She knew she had irrational fears: being tracked or controlled via phones, car computers, laptops and other GPS systems. Red doors scared the Bejesus out of her, and it didn't matter if they were attached to a house, a car, or something else. She had wild gaps in her memory and, if she were being honest with herself, the real reason that she didn't tell Fatima about her life in New York wasn't so much about privacy as it was that she simply didn't have the full picture. She remembered pieces of it: the car accident, certain days working at the UC, the awesome falafel food truck near Times Square. Furthermore, if she were being even *more* honest with herself, she could swear that the tree-like tattoos on her arm were starting to change shape.

"Lucene, I didn't expect to see you today, particularly after staying late to help out with the celebration on Sunday." Lucene lurched a moment in her seat, before realizing who it was. Today, Isabella wore her long white hair in tight braids with a large-brimmed straw hat covering her head. For once, instead of her usual flowing attire, she was actually wearing green linen pants with a matching button-down shirt. In her hands, she carried pruning shears, gloves and a bucket.

"Hi, Reverend Isabella," Lucene greeted her quietly. Maybe Quietude was working.

"Lucene, I've told you before. You don't need to call me 'Reverend' outside of ceremony. Isabella is just fine." She sat on the Peace bench and crossed her legs, revealing tan sandals with laces that crisscrossed up to her calves. "If I may inquire, what brings you here today, on your day off?"

"Well..." Lucene thought for a moment. "Fatima's family is in town, and they have very, well, boisterous personalities."

"Yes, I can see that." Reverend Isabella smiled.

"I thought, since the sanctuary rooms are not in use at the moment...perhaps I could stay in one of them for a few days. You could take it out of my pay, of course."

"Of course, you are welcome to sleep here as long as you need. I have no intention of taking it out of what little I pay you as it is," she laughed. "If anything, your staying here will give me some relief if we have walk-ins needing refuge."

"Thank you, Isabella," Lucene responded, sincerely.

Isabella rose to go, but before she did, she looked down at Lucene and said, "However, in the future, it is completely acceptable to answer a question with, 'I would rather not say.' There's no need to fabricate a story." Lucene blushed and nodded. Isabella continued, "Let me try this again. If I may inquire, what brings you here today on your day off?" Her violet eyes looked straight into Lucene's.

"Uh...I'd rather not...say?"

"Exactly," Reverend Isabella answered, and started down one of the pathways, carefully lifting her feet to avoid bits of broken shell from collecting in her sandals. "The kitchen is open to you should you need to store anything in the refrigerator or make yourself something for dinner. I lock up at 9 p.m., but you can let yourself in and out with your key at any time."

"Thank you, Isabella." Lucene stared into the fountain. "You are wonderful."

"Yes," Isabella smiled. "I know I am, as are we all."

Lucene had just about given up on Ivan showing when she suddenly spotted a mop of red hair cutting through the dark and heard the shuffling of feet from around the corner. She gave him a wave but remained quiet. Timed lights resembling multi-colored fire-flies lit up the bushes as the sun went down.

"Aye, Lucene," Ivan gave an awkward wave as he approached. "Turns out I can enter a church without getting struck by lightning," he laughed at his own joke, but then coughed when he caught sight of Lucene's lightning-stricken arms. "Er, sorry. That went different in me head."

Lucene smiled. "It's okay, Ivan. I get the joke."

Ivan stood at the fountain and scratched under his chin. "So, uh, I got yer note."

Lucene nodded. After waiting through a long pause for a question that didn't come, she continued.

"I'm really worried, and I wasn't sure who to talk to."

"Whew!" Ivan let out a sigh. "I'm so glad ye said that. I've been worried, too." He kicked the base of the fountain with his toe absentmindedly before catching Lucene's questioning look. He pulled his foot back and blushed. He really didn't know how to behave in churches, or anywhere where social norms were expected to be kept.

"You have?" Lucene asked.

"Aye! This Roman fella shows up outa nowhere and tries to hooch up to Fatima. I don't trust him, I tell ya."

"Ivan, that's not at all what I'm talking about."

"It's not?" He tugged at his earlobe. "Then, what?"

"How well do you know Tanager and Cepheus?" she asked.

"Well, Tanager I only jest met, but Cepheus and I have been corresponding for over a year now."

"Corresponding?"

"Aye. In an online technology board."

"But, how long have you known him…in person?"

Ivan calculated on his fingers and looked upward as if trying to remember. "Since…er, Friday evening."

"So…three nights ago, the same night Cepheus wigged out and showed up in my bedroom trying to steal my cat."

"Aye. I thought that was weird me-self, but Tanager explained it to me."

"And that explanation would be?"

"He went through a bad trauma...lost his wife and kids, and that jest broke him. Random triggers set him off and he can't seem to adjust his human-like state with his lizard one...poor fella."

"And it doesn't concern you, having him in your house in such a fragile state?"

"Nah. Everybody's been through something." Somehow, that answer seemed very reasonable to Ivan, but not at all acceptable to Lucene. Surprising, given her random outbursts and aversions to red doors and computers.

There was another long silence. Ivan stared into the fountain, almost mesmerized, as if he were trying to figure out the mechanics of how it worked.

"They think I'm an alien, you know?" Lucene said, matter-of-factly.

"Hmm..." Ivan answered, and after a pause added, "That makes sense."

"It does?"

"Aye. You're as eccentric as the lot of 'em, so it stands to reason yer having trouble adjusting to life on this planet. Did it never occur to you that maybe ye didn't belong here? Originally, I mean. Of course, ye belong here, but—," he stumbled over his words.

"I get it," Lucene held up her hand. "And, I guess so. I knew I didn't quite fit in but..., why would someone want to kill me?" She looked at the ground, contemplating this.

"Say what now? Kill ye?"

"I went to meet a Mr. Sparks after Roman mentioned to Fatima that he needed to speak with him about research."

"I knew it would git back to that guy. I tell ye, I don't trust him!"

"Ivan, focus!" Lucene commanded.

"Sorry."

"The point is, this Mr. Sparks was obviously traumatized. He said he'd been tortured, and if I had to guess, there's more to Cepheus's story than Tanager led on. I think he was tortured as well."

"Tortured, by who?"

"The Royals."

"Who the hell are they?"

Lucene tapped the side of her head. "I feel as if I should know... from my time working with the IPP, but I can't remember."

"Ye worked for the IPP," Ivan stated, not questioned. "Seems there's a lot we don't know about ye, eh?" Lucene did not respond. "But why would someone want to hurt ye? Ye seem pretty harmless to me."

"I don't know, but I can't risk putting Fatima in danger. The sanctuary rooms here are empty at the moment. I figure I can hide here for a few days until I sort things out."

"Who's gonna look after ye though...ye should call the police."

"And tell them what? That I may be an unregistered alien, but I'm not sure. And, oh, by the way, people I don't know are out to get me?"

"Hmm, well. When ye put it like that..." Ivan thought a moment. "Ye should confide in Tanager and Cepheus. So far, they seem to know more about ye than ye know about yerself." He nodded, as if that settled it. Lucene paused for a moment.

"Okay," she agreed.

"Really?" Ivan was surprised. "I didn't expect ye to agree with me so readily. I didn't think ye trusted them."

"I don't," Lucene confessed. "Well, not entirely, I don't."

"Then, why would you do it?"

"Because I trust you, Ivan." Ivan blushed a little. "Can you please let them know I'm here, and definitely let Fatima know that I'll be gone for a couple of days, but don't tell her where."

"Aye. I don't know where Tanager is at the moment, but I will let Cepheus know. I'll also give a knock on Fatima's door."

"Thanks, Ivan. You're a good friend." She gave him a hug.

Ivan blushed again as he bear-hugged her back. "Well, ye just stay safe."

With that, Ivan made his exit, being careful that no one was watching him. At least, he *thought* no one was watching.

After Ivan left, Lucene quickly unlocked the back door to the church and, just as quickly, locked it behind her. She made her way down a narrow hallway, passing a small bathroom and pausing at the kitchen to grab the turkey and Swiss cheese sandwich she had stored in one of the large industrial refrigerators. She grabbed the sandwich, tucked an aluminum bottle of water under one arm and made her way toward the main congregation arena.

From her vantage point, she was greeted by a nearly ceiling-high stone wall in the shape of a half moon, ornately colored by a mural depicting scenes from the natural world. There were strategically placed wall fountains dripping into a narrow pool that wrapped around the wall. The only break in the wall was a compact passageway with a small cobblestone path that led to the seating area and lectern.

Lucene passed along the pathway, marked at each side by two tall areca palms and towering stone-like seats that descended into the floor. When viewed from the front entrance, the room looked more like a sunken indoor Grecian garden with a five-tier coliseum seating area that formed a half-moon around a small, octagon-shaped platform. The slightly raised platform was encased by four tall cream-colored columns and was accessible by two small steps at one side.

"A most unusual church you've got here, Lucy," Drake observed, standing in front of the main double doors holding what appeared to be a Canterbury picnic basket.

Lucene almost dropped her dinner, peering closely at Drake in case she'd made a mistake. After all, she hadn't seen the man in over five years, not since the assembly.

"I like what you've done with your hair," he motioned toward his own neck to reference her short pixie cut. "Though, I think you look better with long blonde hair, not that you asked. Just a personal preference."

"What are you doing here?" Lucene was confused. A knot in her stomach began to form, but she couldn't tell whether it was apprehension or just nerves. After all, he was her longest-standing crush and, to her annoyance, she still found him attractive.

"Is that the way you greet your old boss?" He smiled. She didn't react. "Fair enough," he nodded. "The truth is, I'm worried about you."

"Why?" she answered.

"Because you are in danger." She winced and began to protest. "It's okay, I know. I came to Florida because of an emergency meeting with the IPP. We're trying to prevent the Erdlings from abducting humans and taking them back to Section 3. What I didn't realize at the time was that this human was…is…you." Lucene didn't answer and didn't move. "Could we sit and talk for a moment?"

"Sure," she answered finally, motioning to a seat in the coliseum.

"A most unusual church" Drake repeated absently, gazing at the seats surrounding him.

"Oh, this is no ordinary church," Lucene explained, as if it needed explanation.

"I can see that," Drake agreed, tapping one of the seats with his foot, surprised that it felt as if it had some give to it.

Lucene spoke. "Bioplastic seats made to look like stone but far easier to work with and much more comfortable. Give it a try." Drake set the basket down, stepped up to the first row and took a seat. Surprised that he sank ever so slightly, as he did. He leaned back and stretched his feet out. "See?" Lucene beamed with pride, "next generation memory foam seat cushions and backs."

"Interesting," was all he said. Lucene handed him the basket, her sandwich and water container before climbing up to take a seat next to him, leaving a space between them. "What have you got there," he asked, referencing the sandwich.

"It's a clean meat turkey sandwich," she opened the container. "Want half?"

"Clean..." He was confused.

"Clean meat," she explained. "It's grown from the cells of animals, but no animals are harmed in the making of it. Isabella frowns on actual meat in her sanctuary."

"Uh, what's her feelings on cheese and wine?" he asked, taking half of the sandwich.

"Is it cruelty free, organic cheese?"

"Said so on the label."

"Then, she is a fan of both."

"Excellent." Drake lifted the flaps on the basket. "This is five years overdue, I think," he smiled at her. Lucene's cheeks flooded with pink. "I hope a New Zealand red Zin is okay with you?"

"Maybe just one glass," Lucene conceded. "I've got to keep my wits about me."

Drake poured two glasses and offered Lucene one. "Thanks," she said. The weird sourness in her stomach returned. Stupid nerves.

"A toast," Drake announced, holding up his glass. "It's taken us five years to finally enjoy a drink together," he joked. Lucene politely tapped his glass, not sure how to take the comment. After all, he had never in the past, suggested that an after-work drink was an option. Perhaps because he was her boss at the time?

"Earth to Lucy," Drake snapped his fingers in her face. She flinched in surprise.

"Sorry, I was just wondering what you know about these people who are after me, how you found me, and how you plan to help."

He took a bite of his sandwich. "Tastes like turkey," he exclaimed, happily.

"Well, what did you expect a turkey sandwich to taste like?"

"The way you described it...tofu."

"Surprise," she joked.

He reached back into the basket and drew out a small ready-made plate of diced gruyere and sliced gouda. She plucked a slice of gruyere and took a bite. Drake set the plate down.

"None for you?" she asked.

"Truth be told, lactose intolerant. But you enjoy it. Now, about your questions, do you remember our last conversation before you... eh...disappeared?"

"Not sure," Lucene confessed. "My memory's been a little foggy lately."

"At the time, I told you that there were forces at work, three, to be exact. The Earth, as we know it, is changing, and there needs to be an intervention. Ringing any bells?"

Lucene ate another bite of cheese. "What kind of intervention?"

"We humans are killing our own kind, destroying the planet, and creating our own famine and disease in the process," he continued, ignoring the question. "Really, if left to our own devices, we will be the only species in history to make *ourselves* go extinct! Isn't that insane?"

"Sounds...like it." Lucene cautiously responded. She gnawed at another piece of cheese slowly, feeling a little sluggish. "What three forces are you talking about?"

"Have you been approached by someone named Cepheus Baruch offering to take you back to Erde in Section 1 for your protection?" Lucene stopped chewing. "I can tell from your facial expression, that I am correct. You may not remember him from the last Assembly you attended, but I can assure you, he cannot be trusted."

"Why not?"

"Why not?!" Drake seemed perturbed by the very question and sucked in his breath for a moment. "For one thing, because they have been abducting humans for years under the guise of creating safe havens for us. When, in reality, all they've been doing is human experimentation for their own research."

"That's one," Lucene took a sip of wine, groggily.

"Then, there are the Vitruvians from Section 2. They claim non-interference and will do nothing to help protect us against ourselves. But their so-called renegade band of 'Balance-Keepers' are all about balance when the chips are in their favor. Their idea of 'out of balance' really means, 'what's not in our best interest.' "

"That's two." Lucene went back for what was now her third slice of cheese, not realizing that she'd allowed her half of the turkey sandwich to fall to the floor.

"The Royals. They are what we humans should have become, evolved in every way, physically and intellectually."

"The ones trying to kill me?"

"Kill you?!" Drake laughed. "My silly, naive, Lucy. They are the only ones trying to actually help you."

"How?"

He peered at her closely, gently removing her wine glass from her grasp before she dropped it on the floor. "By fixing you."

"Fixing me?"

"Yes," he whispered, "Don't you get it? Your poor family was a product of Section 1's experiments. Surely you sense that...pardon me for being indelicate...you're not quite right in the head."

Lucene nodded, groggily and yawned. "How are they planning to fix me?"

"By helping you use your slightly altered brain in an intellectually superior way."

"But what about emotionally and spiritually?" Lucene was going for sarcasm, but still wasn't sure where those words came from, since she never considered herself as possessing deep empathy nor a spiritual nature.

"A species cannot flourish being touch-feely. There are too many predators out there just waiting to wipe us out. We're finally seeing evidence of that now. And as far as spiritually, why pray to a god when you can become one?"

Lucene wasn't sure how she suddenly went from silly and naive to a god. She also wasn't certain when the room started revolving. "So, what would you, in your infinite wisdom, recommend?"

"There are negotiations in place with planets from nearby solar systems to help us restore our planet. Since many representatives from these neighboring friends have taken up residence in Florida, we decided to hold the meeting here."

For once, Darke paused to gauge Lucene's reaction. Finally, she answered. "There's just one problem with all of this," she finally blurted out.

"What's that?" Drake clenched his jaw.

"My damaged brain doesn't believe you," Lucene slurred her words as her mouth went numb. She spit a piece of chewed cheese into her napkin, since swallowing it was not an option, and let out a cough.

Drake started laughing. "Easy there," he caught her by the shoulders. "I'm surprised by your constitution, though, I guess I shouldn't be. Between the sleeping meds I added to the wine and the cheese, you've guzzled and eaten enough to down a horse."

Lucene tried to form an unseemly response, but the words wouldn't come.

"Okay, she's ready," Drake announced. Two human-sized red salamanders emerged from the shadows with a gurney in tow, and one easily lifted a drowsy Lucene to her feet. She put up a pitiful attempt at resisting, but her legs were turning to jelly. "Imagine my surprise," he told her, as they laid her on the gurney and began strapping her into place, "when I learned that Lucy Jones' parents were listed in the alien International Registry that you so nicely procured for me back in New York." Lucene, vaguely conscious, recalled the files he'd asked her to find that day in his office five years ago.

"My parents?" Lucene fought to remain awake.

"But not you." He looked down at her. "You weren't listed because you were born here. By the time I'd made the connection, you had already run away. Do you know how many Lucy Jones there are in this country, let alone the world? It took forever to find you.

And to think," he said finally, before everything faded to black. "You were right under my nose for three years."

Drake nodded for the guards to take her away as he carefully packed up the picnic basket, pausing only to take a bite of his sandwich. "Clean meat," he laughed. "Who would have thought?"

"Who are you?" Isabella demanded at the surprise guest in her sanctuary.

Drake turned to see the striking dark-skinned woman with snow-white hair standing in the doorway. It was at that moment she caught a glimpse of a gurney and two red salamanders disappearing down the back hallway pushing something. She couldn't quite see what it was.

"I was just leaving," Drake replied, reaching into his pocket and pulling out a small pistol. He shot Isabella through the chest before she could react. She fell to the floor in a heap. He raised his arm and set its sights for a head shot.

"Mr. Cushing." One of the guards came running back in. "Ambassador Hamish and Ambassador Sabrina are on the line. They want to know if you have the girl, and when they can collect her. They are rather insistent."

He looked at the lifeless body on the floor. Blood was beginning to pool from under her shirt and spill out onto the floor.

"Okay." He put his gun away and dropped his sandwich on the floor, trampling on it on his way out. After all, he'd be long gone before anyone could match any prints or DNA to him.

23

SPARE PARTS

MONDAY EVENING. FIVE YEARS AFTER THE ASSEMBLY.

" **C** epheus, we've got a situation here, and I need yerr h—"
Ivan stopped mid-sentence as he witnessed his friend perched on his work table pulling an assortment of washers, wing nuts, screws and the old pair of pliers out of containers that were lined up on shelves or hanging on the wall...neatly labeled, he noted to himself with disappointment. He had planned on filling Cepheus in about his talk with Lucene at the sanctuary moments ago, but this episode clearly needed his immediate attention. Cepheus paused to analyze a small brass gear before tucking it in the jacket pocket of his long black coat.

"Ye okay, buddy?" Ivan asked, at which time, Cepheus hissed at him, accidentally hitting his head on a hanging mason jar light that shined over the workstation. He didn't seem to notice.

Cepheus, still hunkering over the table like a wild animal eating prey it had caught, continued to tear through tools and accessories, exhibiting an odd sense of pure joy at each trinket he discovered. Ivan, not usually given to unnecessary worry, watched his friend with a mix of concern and odd fascination.

"I want this shiny grabber," Cepheus announced, holding up a small adjustable wrench, proud of his find.

"Sure thing," Ivan answered. "Whatever ye need."

Cepheus nodded, as if that answer was expected and acceptable. At that moment, he hopped off the table and darted out the back door.

"Where are ye—" Ivan began, following Cepheus out of the shed and down the trail in the dark, stopping at a large tree stump—the remains of an Oak that had fallen during the last major storm. Ivan repurposed it as his favorite "think" spot, often sitting there for an eternity until he'd solved a major problem.

He watched as his friend reached his hand into a small hole that an animal had made along its side, uncertain whether that "animal" had been Cepheus. "Don't know that I'd reach in there, could be brown recluses and—"

He was hissed at again and fell silent as Cepheus carefully tucked his new treasures safely into the hole like an oversized ferret. He then grabbed a handful of dirt and haphazardly tossed it over the hole in a poor attempt to cover it back up.

Without acknowledging Ivan, he darted back to the shed. Ivan pulled out a pocket flashlight and followed him back, more slowly this time, as the darkness seemed to fall rather rapidly over the sky.

As he approached the shed, he saw car lights in the distance. He recognized them as Fatima's. *One disaster at a time,* he thought. He would phone her after he'd gotten Cepheus under control. It was then that he remembered the medicine that Tanager had given him should Cepheus have an episode.

He ran back in the shed. Cepheus had moved onto the engine that they'd been working on and began to plug and unplug wires.

"No, no, no!" Ivan swatted his friend's hands away. "Don't do that!" Cepheus's eyes grew wide as he instinctively shoved Ivan away. He was deceptively strong for a thin and wiry frame, and his push sent Ivan reeling overtop of a custom motorcycle he'd built, sending him crashing to the concrete with the bike on top of him, enough to pin him painfully to the ground, but not enough to puncture any organs he might need in the future. Fortunately, he'd had enough mishaps to remember to tuck his chin, so his head missed smacking against the floor. There was a pause before the pain in his spine connected to his mouth. "Ow," he whined.

Like a cat who'd been shooed away from the pantry, Cepheus promptly went back to exploring the workstation again, oblivious to Ivan's discomfort or that he'd caused it.

Just then, Ivan's cell phone rang. With some difficulty, he managed to slide a hand under the bike and into his pocket to retrieve it.

24

ODESSA AND TANAGER

Tanager may have arrived here with some misconceptions about current Earth attire, lingo and customs, but he was observant and a quick study. Plus, he had Lucene to guide him. By the time he'd reached the marina, he was wearing a pair of bone-colored weekender shorts, a coral, mesh-lined fishing shirt and river sandals. His curly locks were stuffed under the "Salt Life" cap he took from the Closet. Sadly, since his borrowed threads belonged to a much taller and bulkier man, nothing fit quite right. Conversely, the sandals were Ivan's, and at least one size too small. Consequently, he still stuck out.

He searched the water using night vision binoculars, but so far, the only things he spotted were clumps of eelgrass, several needle-fish and assorted marine debris.

"Well, would you look at that getup," a voice from the water called. Tanager lowered his binoculars, only to find that Odessa was at the edge of the dock, right at his feet. "Looking for me?"

"As a matter of fact, I was," Tanager answered, seriously. Odessa floated on her back, with her breasts bobbing up and down like two buoys in the water. Tanager politely looked away. "Could you float a little...lower? That's very distracting."

"Get you a little hot and bothered, does it?"

"Hot? No. But it does bother me...a little." Odessa smiled and lowered herself in the water, treading so that only her head and shoulders were visible.

"Thank you."

"Didn't do it for you," Odessa smirked. My nipples were getting a little chilly." Tanager remained silent. "So, what brings you here? Did you miss me?" She winked.

"It is always nice to see you..."

"Oh my God, you are such a bore!" Odessa whined. "Always nice to see you," she mocked. "Blah blah blah. Tanager, if you're ever to truly understand Earth culture, you're going to need to learn how to be far less Goddamned polite!"

"I will take it under advisement, thank you," he replied as she rolled her eyes. "We're running out of time," he admonished. "I need you to tell me where the Royals are, and if they have located our Earth-born Data Collector yet."

"Hold the phone. *You* may be running out of time. Whereas, *I* on the other hand, have all the time in the world." Tanager let the phone reference go for now, with a mental note to research the expression later.

"Odessa, I know you love this world. So do we. But if Sabrina and Hamish fulfill their mission, this Earth will be recycled. And, I promise you, it won't come back as something you will love, and it won't be a place where anyone outside of the Royals will be invited." Odessa seemed to be considering this for a moment, her face crumpling in what could only be described as despair. "All living beings on this Earth will die, and this will only be the beginning."

"But I cannot interfere." For the first time ever, Odessa seemed to be choking back something that felt like a sincere emotion. "I can only report what I observe and deliver messages as instructed."

"Then, surely you can tell me..."

"To *my* people, not yours."

Tanager tapped the tip of his sandal on the dock and hung his head, willing a brilliant idea to pop into it. In what instance would her people allow her to divulge such important information? Suddenly, he looked up. "Morphinae is a Vitruvian, is...ze...not?" Tanager struggled with Earth's gender-neutral pronouns, finding language here incredibly difficult. *Was it ze and zir?* He decided on the masculine pronouns, since male was Morphinae's most common form. Odessa became indignant. "Morphinae is a renegade...a maverick. He is a Balance-Keeper, but who the hell knows how he measures what balance is?"

"Can you tell Morphinae what you know?"

"I suppose. But what would be the point of that?"

"Will you call on Morphinae, please? I know he will listen to you. Tell Morphinae, and then maybe I can convince him to tell me what I need to know."

"And why would I do that?" Odessa asked, seeking validation.

"Because I know that this is your home more than Section 2 ever was."

Odessa thought for a moment, and then tilted back her head, letting out what could only be referred to as a siren call...a melodic sound that can be adjusted to reach only certain frequencies. To Tanager, and to many, it was a beautiful sound. On Earth, however, it seemed that only animals had the ability to hear and appreciate it.

It took several minutes, but eventually, Morphinae floated in as a butterfly and transformed into his masculine self.

"Well, don't you look handsome?" Odessa flirted.

"I chose this form when I saw whose company you were keeping," Morphinae flashed a glance at Tanager. "I sense he is uncomfortable with the female form."

"Is that true, Tanager?" Odessa winked. "Do women make you uncomfortable?"

"Please, Odessa, there is no time." Tanager answered. Odessa shrugged. A small fishing boat could be seen approaching the dock. "This might not be the best place to talk. Is there someplace more private we can go?"

"Absolutely." Odessa winked. With that, she used her arms to hoist herself onto the dock as her fins transformed into legs. And yes, she was completely naked. "Follow me," she said, unabashed. A moment later, she turned and held her finger to her lips for silence before shapeshifting into a blue-green butterfly. She nodded for Morphinae to do the same. Tanager, with no such capabilities, merely struggled to follow their errant path. Eventually, the three had relocated to a small storage unit inside a large abandoned warehouse. The two Vitruvians resumed their former appearances. This time, however, Odessa was wearing a strange grass-like skirt. Tanager eyed it curiously.

"Oh, it's attached," she confirmed. "You can touch it if you want," she licked her lips. Tanager's face flushed.

"I don't have time for…" Morphinae began to complain.

"Fine. Fine. Fine." Odessa sighed. She pointed an upturned palm toward Tanager. "Speak," she commanded.

Just as Tanager was about to explain to Morphinae why he was summoned, voices could be heard echoing in the distance…but very much in the same warehouse as they were.

Odessa's eyes grew wide in mock amazement, as if to say, "Well, would you look at that?"

The voices belonged to none other than Hamish and Sabrina. And they were talking…not quietly…about Lucene. The three listened with interest.

"Do you really believe he has her?" Hamish asked, tiredly.

"If he doesn't, he will very soon. I'm out of patience, and we need to get out of here tonight, before the entire SWAT team arrives…or, whatever it is they are calling them these days."

"I suppose it didn't help that you blew up a casino," Hamish responded, nonchalantly.

"Shut up, you idiot," she pointed a clawed finger at her husband's throat. "I don't need a lecture from you about how bad my temper is, and you shouldn't anger me in my..." She caught herself. "You shouldn't anger me."

"But where are they leaving from?" Tanager whispered. Odessa pressed her fingers to Tanager's mouth and shook his head as a sign to be quiet. Just then, Tanager's watch gave off a warning chime, along with an accompanying red light.

"What was that?" Sabrina looked up.

"Nice going," Odessa whispered, and she and Morphinae transformed back into butterflies and headed for the rafters. Tanager frantically silenced his watch and hid behind what looked like a few cobweb-covered bourbon barrels...and hoped for the best.

Moments later, Hamish replied, "I'm sure it's nothing, but we should take cover, just in case."

'Cover' turned out to be the very storage unit where Tanager was hiding. "I cannot believe we've been reduced to hiding like vermin," Sabrina complained. They were just about to shut the door when Odessa appeared, this time wearing a blue-green suit that was clearly another shapeshifting maneuver. It appeared as if she actually were wearing clothes.

"Knock, knock." She smiled, standing at the entryway. "Sorry if I startled you just now, Sovereigns."

"What do *you* want?" Sabrina clutched her clothing as if trying to hide her embarrassment.

"My superiors were just alerting me to confirm that your meeting with them will commence as scheduled tomorrow?"

"Yes, of course," Sabrina nodded.

"Excellent," Odessa turned to go.

"How did she know we were here?" Sabrina asked her husband.

"She's one of the observers. No doubt she notices everything. Good thing we're leaving tonight."

Tanager remained motionless until he was fairly certain they had left. Still, he knew that running would appear suspicious. Instead, after darting out of the storage room, he sauntered over to the docks as if he owned the place. It was only when at a safe distance that he picked up speed. The alert he received meant that Cepheus was undergoing trauma again. But what kind, he couldn't determine.

25

NEWS STORY

MONDAY EVENING. FIVE YEARS AFTER THE ASSEMBLY.

F atima and Roman were at the cottage, snuggled on the living room couch under a blanket, with two glasses of wine and an assorted cheese plate and grapes sitting on the end table. Occasionally, Roman would reach for a grape and offer it to Fatima who playfully let him feed it to her.

Roman clicked the remote and the TV sprang to life. He was about to switch to movie streaming when a "breaking news story" graphic popped up on the screen. What followed was a location shot of a small church with crime tape wrapped around the building and investigators shooting photos and taking notes.

"Hold on," Fatima stopped him. "That's Lucene's church. Turn that up!" she commanded. He obeyed, and the two watched a young reporter give details about the scene behind her.

"This just in! We've learned that Reverend Isabella Simone of the Singing River Sanctuary in Parrish has been shot. She was rushed to a nearby hospital where she is in stable condition. No word yet as to what happened. We'll bring you continuing coverage on this developing story."

"Oh, my gosh," Fatima whined. "Lucene spends a lot of time

there, even when she's not working. I hope she wasn't there!" Fatima unwrapped herself from the blanket and leapt to her feet.

"Can you call her cell phone?" Roman sat up, concerned.

"No, she doesn't carry one."

"Who on this planet doesn't carry a cell phone?" Roman was shocked.

"*She* doesn't. She says they're too easy to track. We have to call the police."

"And more breaking news..." the television interrupted again. The news anchor had a momentary look of glee at her good fortune, being there for not one, but two, important stories. She quickly recovered, touching her ear as if receiving information from an ear mic. "We've just learned that a man was found dead on his boat at the Port Hammond marina. He's been identified as 53-year-old Jim Sparks. Further details are being withheld as his death has been ruled as suspicious."

Fatima's face turned pale. Roman tossed the blanket aside and stood. "It's not what you think," Roman explained waving his hands as he spoke.

"Jim Sparks," she whispered. "Dead."

"I know, but that had nothing to do with me. I'm as shocked as you are." For once, the trusting Fatima appeared unconvinced.

"We have to call the police," she backed away, slowly. When she'd reached the kitchen, she bolted for the door. She'd gotten as far as unlatching it and turning the knob.

"Stop!" Roman commanded. "Or, I'll shoot." Fatima paused, glancing over her shoulder, her heart rate beginning to escalate. Roman stood in the living room, a gun pointed at her chest. "Please, close the door."

Fatima obeyed.

"I didn't kill Jim Sparks," he claimed.

"I'm having a hard time believing you when you have a gun pointed at me," Fatima's eyes welled up. Her hands were shaking.

Roman instinctively moved toward her to comfort her before catching himself.

"If they found Jim Sparks, they can find me. We need to leave. It isn't safe here."

"Again...gun," she pointed out.

He slowly pointed the gun toward the ceiling, holding it with two hands at the ready. "I was afraid you'd run away. If they find you first, they will torture you to get to me."

"Who are *they*?" Fatima whined.

"I'll explain on the way. Just get your cat and I'll tell you where to drive us."

"My cat," she repeated, confused. "You mean, car?"

"No, cat. There's a good chance we won't be coming back for a while. I'm pretty sure you don't want to leave him behind. Now, I'm going to put the gun down if you promise not to run away."

Suddenly, Fatima choked out a laugh.

"What's so funny?" he wanted to know.

"Put the gun down, silly. I'll get Bagheera." She made her way toward Lucene's bedroom—the cat's favorite hangout. "I don't know of any murderer who'd be concerned about killing me but saving my cat."

26

REVELATION

"We need to call the police, not hide out in your apartment," Fatima tugged her arm free from Roman's grasp as he pulled her inside and shut the door. She set her large, paisley, beach bag on the carpet, and Bagheera leapt to his freedom, instantly beginning to sniff around his new surroundings.

"No police," Roman barked back, running to the living room window and peaking around the red blackout drapes to make sure they weren't followed. "I've already told you; they'd like nothing more than to see all of my kind destroyed."

"Well, we can't just stay here and do noth—" Fatima stopped, mid-sentence as her eyes fell on the far wall in the next room, partially revealed through the open bedroom door. Roman glanced over her shoulder. As he caught wind of what she saw, he rushed to the door to close it, but she'd already made her way inside. "What is this?" She stared, mesmerized by the wall-to-wall photographs and notes strung all over it like a giant collage—photographs of her going to work, of Lucene and Tanager dancing, of Fatima talking to Ivan in the yard, a calendar noting arrival and departure times, and a US map with thumbtacks all over it.

"It's part of my research," Roman explained hastily, slipping past Fatima and guiding her out of the room, closing the door behind them.

"But there are pictures of...me...on that wall," Fatima's voice trembled softly as her eyes began to well up. She slumped against the wall and put her hand to her heart. "Is that all I am...research?"

Roman's spirit crumbled as he choked back tears. "Of course not, my love." He rushed to hug her, only to discover her struggling to stand. He wrapped his long arms around her plump waist, supporting her as they made their way across the room where she sank into the couch.

"I'm okay. I'm okay," Fatima waved a hand to dismiss him. "Just need to catch my breath." She was surprised by the episode, as she hadn't had one since...she tried to remember. It had to have been about five years, not since Lucene had come to live with her. That much she knew.

"Meeting you was a happy accident," Roman gushed, pulling her attention back. "You saved me, Far." He knelt in front of her, enfolding her hands into his.

Fatima tensed up, pulling her hands away as Roman searched her eyes, questioningly. "Far? Is that supposed to be some sort of nick-name for me?"

"But—." He backed away slowly, mouthing the words 'Fatima' then 'Far,' as if trying to figure something out. There was a space in his memory that was blank, and he struggled desperately to remember as one might struggle to remember a once-vivid dream. He backed into the living room wall, sliding down it like a rag doll until he had come to his knees. Wrapping his arms around his legs, he laid his head in his lap and began rocking like a small, scared child. "Far!" he cried as he rocked. "How could I forget you?"

Fatima struggled to her feet, looking helplessly from side-to-side, wondering which disaster to deal with first, her missing friend or the broken man at her feet. Who could she call for help? More impor-tantly...*who* could she call who would actually believe her?

Remembering her fallen purse, she rushed to it, fumbling nervously for her phone. She hit a speed dial number, waiting impatiently, eyeing the fallen man on the floor who was still very much in his own world.

"Alo, Fatima," Ivan answered, his voice sounding strange.

"H...Hi," Fatima choked back. "Ivan, I need your help."

"What's wrong?" Ivan voiced concern. "Are ye hurt?"

"No, it's Roman." Fatima swore she could feel Ivan cringe on the other end of the phone line. "He's had a breakdown and is acting strange."

"Seems to be goin' 'round," Ivan answered. "Got me hands full with a similar situation me self." Fatima could hear strange rustling sounds over the phone.

"Is everybody going crazy? Never mind...it gets worse. Lucene's in trouble."

"I know that, but how do you?"

"Wait...what?"

"I just spoke with her at the church...Crap, I wasn't supposed to tell you that!"

"What? When?"

"I dunno, maybe about 30 minutes or so. Why?"

Fatima let out several uncharacteristic expletives. "Well, you must have just missed the shooting."

"What?!"

"Never mind, Lucene's not there. At least, I don't think she is. I don't know where she is. Just get here and we'll figure it out."

"Aye, where are you now?" Ivan asked.

"I'm at Roman's apartment." Another cringe. Fatima rambled off the building number and street. Ivan made a mental note of it, repeating it in his head to make it stick.

"Ye may want to wait out front, if he's acting kookie."

"No, I'm okay, and I think we should lay low. Please be careful and...thank you." Ivan felt a little pang of feeling in the center of his chest, near his heart...just a little.

"Aye...be there in a jiff." There was doubt in his voice.

Ivan did his best to use his upper body to push the bike off of him, succeeding only in moving the handlebars so that one was now poking into his rib cage. It was at that moment that Cepheus reached into one of the drawers and pulled out a plastic syringe.

"Oh, shit," Ivan mumbled. "Man...wait!" Too late. Cepheus had already run back outside, presumably to the tree trunk to hide his latest find. Ivan waited for what seemed like an eternity, but Cepheus eventually came back.

"Cepheus, ol' friend. I need you to git over here and help me." Cepheus ignored him. Ivan felt a numbness start to overtake the lower half of his body as the weight of the bike began cutting off circulation. "Cepheus," he tried again, a little louder, but hopefully not loud enough to inspire another violent reaction. "Lucene and Fatima need us." Cepheus, who had been pawing through a box of metal fasteners, suddenly looked up."

"Lucene...in trouble?" Ivan could almost see a gray cloud over his friend's head, as if a storm were beginning to clear and sunlight was about to come through. "I thought she was dead."

"Why would you think that?" Ivan's eyes grew wide, wondering if he'd somehow been involved with Lucene's current disappearance. "Never mind, I need you to focus. Put down the toys and help me!"

"Of course." Cepheus said, quietly, stepping down off the table with catlike grace and brushing off his dark pants, as if to brush off cobwebs. Suddenly, realizing his friend was pinned under the motorcycle, he quickly reached down and lifted it off him with one hand. With the other, he offered his hand and hoisted Ivan awkwardly to his feet.

"Thanks, man." Ivan struggled for a moment to stand upright and took a few cautious steps to make sure everything was still in working order.

"Are you okay?" Cepheus asked. "I hope I didn't do anything...inappropriate."

"Ye were a hot mess, ye were," Ivan blurted out. Diplomacy was not his strong suit. "But that doesn't matter right now. We've got to get going, and fast. Follow me."

The two rushed to Ivan's van, nicknamed the "mongrel" because of its unique build and functionality. It sat in the covered car port next to the driveway. Cepheus instinctively climbed in the back while Ivan settled into the driver's seat up front. Ivan wasted no time in backing down the drive and heading out. As they passed Fatima's house, there was a roaring explosion as the cottage burst into flames. Remnants from the explosion floated around the mongrel. Startled, both Ivan and Cepheus jumped in their seats. A moment later, there were two more explosions. Peering in the rearview mirror, Ivan saw both his and Fatima's home and his workshop on fire. Instinctively, he hit the gas pedal and didn't look back again. Ivan's heart raced when it sank in that had they wasted even half a minute more, they would be dead.

"Tell me the truth, Cepheus. I won't be mad..."

"It was not me, my friend." Cepheus answered, reading his thoughts. His mind now returning to clarity for the first time without requiring medication. "It was they."

"They, who?" Ivan asked over his shoulder, as he turned the corner and headed toward the highway.

"The Royals."

There was a loud knock at the door. Fatima quickly eyed the peephole, seeing a thick red beard staring back at her. She opened the door and Ivan and Cepheus rushed in.

"Yer not hurt, are ya?" Ivan took Fatima by the shoulders, concerned.

"No, I'm fine. It's him I'm worried about." She gave a confused once-over at the lanky man who accompanied her neighbor. "Your eyes are very yellow," she said, almost transfixed.

"And your hair," Cepheus answered in a deep voice, "is very purple."

"It's good that we're both so observant," Fatima whispered back in something between a joke and surprise. Ivan wrapped an arm around her, concerned.

"He's not from around here," Ivan said.

"So, I gathered," Fatima whispered back, sinking into Ivan's chest for support.

Cepheus went over to the crumpled man, cautiously. He sank down next to Roman, who picked his head up and looked at Cepheus, his eyes suddenly widening with recognition. "You are one of them?" He wiped his tears with his sleeve. Fatima and Ivan watched the scene with a mixture of amazement and concern.

"I am," Cepheus answered. "You've been searching for us for quite some time, haven't you?" Roman nodded. Bagheera came out from behind the curtain where he had been hiding and began rubbing up against Cepheus's leg. He reached out to scratch behind the cat's ear, but did not turn his attention from Roman. Cepheus hung his head for a moment, as if listening to something, and then nodded back in understanding. "Was he sick for very long?"

"Two years," Roman sobbed, looking at Fatima as if to apologize. Fatima smiled back, weakly, a mix of understanding and disappointment. "I heard about the Data Collectors during the televised report of the newly formed IPP many years ago, when Section 1 first revealed their presence on Earth. I thought that if they cared that much about the planet, and had the technology to help us..."

"That we might have had the resources to save your beloved?" Cepheus acknowledged.

"Yes," Roman answered. "Maybe even take us back with you? To your planet?" Roman looked at Fatima pleadingly. "I didn't remember any of this until now. I swear to you, lovely Fatima, I didn't intend to hurt you."

"I know," Fatima pulled away from Ivan and rushed to Roman's side, kneeling down and touching a hand to his shoulder. "Who was he?" Ivan pretended not to care.

"He was a monk, originally from the outermost region of Macar. It's billions of lightyears from here. His people lived on a small planet—very primitive. They relied on their sovereign for every-thing: food, shelter, healing, protection. And then, Far was born."

Roman went on to explain that when Far was a boy, he demon-strated the unique power of transporting himself over great distances to avoid danger. He was also a prophet, and that made their sovereign uncomfortable. Far was nothing but a skinny, frail little thing with blonde hair and pale green eyes. "There was nothing intimidating about him, and yet—"

"They tried to kill him," Fatima filled the gap. Roman nodded.

"Yes. His family told him to run…to run to the farthest place he could. That's how he found his way to Earth. I met him thirteen years ago, when he was an adult."

"Kinda funny, when you think about it," Fatima wiped a tear from her eye. "You tried to suppress your pain so much that you ended up dating a fat woman with lavender hair and gray eyes…the absolute opposite of Far." She laughed a little, though she wasn't really happy.

"Oh, sweet Fatima," Roman touched her hand. "You are beautiful and wonderful. And, I do have love for you. I just…forgot…every-thing for a while. I'm so sorry."

"Oye," Ivan's eyes widened, being pulled away from the story. "We needs to warn Tanager 'bout not coming back to the house!"

"What happened to the house?" Fatima asked.

"The Royals happened," Ivan answered, still not completely certain who they were.

There was another knock at the door.

"Where is Cepheus?" Tanager demanded, storming in, syringe in hand, as Ivan opened the door, quickly shutting it after him. Seeing Cepheus, Tanager immediately rushed to his friend's side, leaning down and holding the syringe to Cepheus's neck. Ivan grabbed his arm and shook his head.

"He doesn't need it," he nodded to Cepheus. Having left Roman to Fatima's care, Cepheus was now sitting cross-legged on the floor, eyes closed as if in deep meditation.

"You mean he recovered? On his own?" Ivan nodded again. Tanager let out a relieved smile, mixed with hope.

"How?" Fatima began, pausing a moment to take in Tanager's new wardrobe.

"Tracking device," Tanager explained impatiently. "Cepheus, while my mentor and the brightest man I know, is still under Watch. Unfortunately, I'm not as intuitive as he, so..."

"So you..."

"Know him," he finished her sentence, pointing. "Yes."

"Will all of you please begin speakin' English? Yer making me head hurt," Ivan complained. "What in the hell is 'under watch'?"

"Where is Lucene?" Tanager demanded, finally taking a moment to survey the room.

"We don't know," Fatima answered. "She was last seen at the church where she works, but there was a shooting and she is missing."

Tanager's face turned white and he held back the tremors he felt in his hands and heart. He turned back to Cepheus. "I know where the Royals are. They're hiding in an abandoned warehouse at the marina. Can you sense if Lucene is near there?" Cepheus lifted his chin slightly, to acknowledge the question, but did not open his eyes.

"Why would he know where she is?" Fatima questioned, pointing to the yellow-eyed Cepheus on the floor.

"Because he's her mentor," Tanager answered. "She doesn't remember, but he trained her as a small child."

This didn't seem to clarify things for her.

"He's psychic," Tanager said. That seemed the easiest explanation. Fatima nodded. Tanager lamented the fact that he was supposed to have a similar vibration as Lucene, and yet he couldn't connect with her. Truth be told, neither one of them had been trained properly.

"You mean, I was right?" Roman looked hopeful. "She's the one?"

"The one," Tanager agreed.

"One what?" Fatima asked.

"She's not from here, and she's very…special."

"You mean she's an," Fatima couldn't believe she was saying this, "*alien*?"

"Yes, and she's not safe here. We need to take her home."

"But this is her home!" Fatima's chest began to rise, as Ivan motioned with his hands to lower her voice, pointing to Cepheus. She turned to Ivan, "So, we're just all okay with this?"

"I was wrong, Fatima," Roman struggled to his feet. "My mind wasn't right. They're not experimenting on humans. They are attempting to genetically modify Data Collectors to accurately gather and report information back home. Somehow, that got switched up in my head."

"Genetically modify!" Fatima was incredulous. "How is that better?"

"Fatima, please." Tanager pointed to Cepheus again. "First we need to find her."

Fatima nodded and bit her lip.

The group waited in silence for what seemed like hours. In reality, it was closer to 20 minutes.

Cepheus's eyes popped open. "I know where she is."

27

THE RED DOOR

"We've been so stupid," Hamish exclaimed, rubbing his forehead tiredly. "For the longest time, we assumed that if we simply learned the special gene-splicing cocktail added to the Data Collector's DNA, we could replicate the process and transmute our own Royal army."

Lucene struggled with the restraints that had her strapped to the hospital gurney. "I don't know what you're talking about," Lucene panicked. "You've got the wrong girl."

Lucene let out a yelp as an attendant, dressed in a long gray lab coat, thrust a needle haphazardly into Lucene's arm.

"Don't lie to us, you stupid creature." Sabrina stuck her face right above Lucene's, spitting a little as she spoke.

"Don't you know who you are, my dear?" Hamish asked in a deceptively calm and collected voice. "What you are capable of?"

As Lucene stared at the harsh fluorescent lights above her head, the world around her began to fade.

"Begin the process," Hamish ordered to the two female attendants in the room. "We haven't much time."

Lucene dreamed as she'd never dreamed before. She found herself floating back to the house she lived in when her parents were still alive. She was five, and it was one of many training sessions that they would have together.

Her father sat across from her on the floor, his legs folded under him, cross-legged. His eyes were closed, in a state of deep meditation. Lucene did her best to mimic his movements. She rested her hands solemnly in her lap as she also sat cross-legged with her eyes closed. She had no innate flexibility, and her thighs popped up off the floor like winged butterflies. She felt jittery and found it difficult to sit still.

"Stop fidgeting, Lucene, and concentrate," her father said gently.

Lucene let out a frustrated sigh and tried again. Her brow furrowed in deep concentration.

From across the room, Lucene's mother watched with interest. She sat at a high-top table in the kitchen, nervously folding and unfolding the same dinner napkins over and over.

Both Lucene and her father sat there for some minutes before his eyes popped open with excitement.

"A green elephant," he proclaimed.

Lucene smiled proudly. "Yes!" she answered, thinking back to a plush toy her dad had won for her at the state fair a few months back. "A green elephant!"

"Very good, Lucene. Your powers of transmitting messages are —"

"You thought I was going to picture a yellow sunflower in my head." Lucene giggled just thinking about the giant sunflower mural on the wall in her bedroom. It made her happy every time she saw it.

"But—" her father began.

"And mom is worried that they will soon discover who I am and take me away." Her face fell. Dora stopped folding and shot her husband a concerned look. He simply nodded.

"Very good, Lucene. But how did you manage to both transmit an image while also receiving what I was thinking, and what your mother was thinking, at the same time."

"I'm not sure," Lucene furrowed her brows once again. "I was thinking really hard about the green elephant, when it turned into a sunflower. You were handing a flower to me. Then, I saw strange looking lizard people trying to take me away. Mommy stared through the window. She wanted to help, but she couldn't move. They popped into my head so fast, that I didn't have time to stop them."

Lucene's mother came into the room to join them, sitting down next to her, running a hand through the girl's long hair. "Yes, that's right, Lucene. And what should you do if you ever see those lizard people?"

Lucene didn't even have to pause and take a deep breath. Without thinking, she answered, "Run."

Lucene awoke with a throbbing headache that made her sick to her stomach. Bright lights blinded her as they flashed repeatedly in her face. Sounds reverberated in her ears as if someone had turned up the volume on every radio station on the planet, causing a cacophony of words, music and background noise. Random smells bombarded her olfactory system, and her tongue was heavy with the taste of metal. Her skin itched with the feeling of crawling bugs, though she was unable to sit up or move her arms or legs to swat them away. Her neck ached, and she realized that her head was somehow pinned against the gurney, too, making it impossible to get the kink out of her neck. Her pulse quickened, and she desperately fought the urge to do what one of the loud voices was urging her to do.

"Go ahead, scream," Sabrina admonished, bitterly.

From just a few miles away, a deep voice cut through the chaos. *Lucene, can you hear me?*

Cepheus? Lucene could barely hear him among the other noises. *If that's you, please send help!*

Focus on my voice, his thoughts transmitted. *Filter everything else out except for my voice.*

I don't know how, she thought.

Yes, you do, Cepheus responded. *Close your eyes if you need to. Remember your training. Now, more than ever, you must remember.*

Lucene clenched her eyelids tightly together as she flashed back to the training her parents had given her, from the time since she could first remember to the day the lightning struck and her parents were taken away forever. That was nearly five years of almost daily lessons in mentally sending and receiving messages, of picking up what others were sensing and feeling: humans, animals, plants, anything that lived and breathed. The memories flooded back with squall-like force. In addition to all the other sensations, it was almost unbearable. *I can't, too much noise!* Lucene's face and arms pulsed with heat as if they were on fire.

Focus on just my voice, Cepheus ordered, more forcefully now. *Silence everything else.*

Dizzy and on the verge of passing out, Lucene's world suddenly went quiet. She sucked in a deep breath. *Okay,* she answered, simply.

Very good, Cepheus answered. *Keep breathing...inhale in... exhale out.* This was familiar to Lucene, not just from working with her parents. His voice and very presence were familiar though. How? She returned her attention to the task at hand.

From outside her consciousness, Sabrina snapped, "What happened? What's wrong with her?" She nudged Lucene's arm, but got no response. It sounded to Lucene as if Sabrina were far away, speaking from the other end of a tunnel.

"Probably the same thing that happened to all the others, including our son," Hamish's lazy voice answered. "You've driven them mad."

"But she's supposed to be the 'gifted' one, born of two Data Collectors with the perfect DNA structure." She pushed one of Lucene's eyelids open quizzically and peered into the motionless hazel eye. "Do you think we can still take DNA samples even if she dies?"

From inside her mind, Lucene awaited more instructions.

Now, Cepheus continued. *I need you to imagine that someone has opened a window and there's a breeze gently blowing in. With it is a scent. What do you smell?*

She imagined the window; she could almost feel the breeze. Somehow, Lucene expected to smell one of Fatima's apple cinnamon pies baking in the oven or the scent of fresh cut flowers from the garden, but she didn't. Surprised, she transmitted, *I smell brackish water, disinfectant, and something loamy.*

Excellent, Lucene, Cepheus praised. *Now, keep your eyes closed, and imagine there's a radio in the room. Someone has just switched it on and has tuned into a single channel. Only let one channel in. Have you got it?*

Yes.

What do you hear?

I hear a woman with a grating voice. Sabrina. Her name is Sabrina. Lucene could feel the tension and fear emanating from Cepheus's energy. *Who is she?* Noises began to overtake her mind once more: cars, horns, voices, music, as if all the stations were on at once.

It does not matter. Stay focused. Filter the noises that do not matter. Only let the most important ones in.

I hear gulls, and water hitting the side of a dock...and the sounds of a motorized boat in the distance...I think I'm at the docks, Cepheus. Except...

Except what?

The birds are next to me. But all of the other sounds are below me. I think I am in the air.

We're coming for you, Lucene. Stay calm and remember, you are in control of what experiences you let in.

In that quiet space, Lucene was suddenly aware of a series of doors in front of her. A few opened on their own, letting in a swarm of sights, smells, tastes and sounds. In her mind's eye, she slammed them closed. She even closed the window and turned off the radio. In the silence, she asked herself, *Which door will tell me why Cepheus is so familiar to me?* Through the darkness, a red door appeared. She walked over and stopped cold. Her face felt flushed and her palms sweaty. She took a deep breath, then opened the door. Suddenly, she was transported back in time, and found herself sitting in the back seat of the family's SUV during a storm. Her mother peered nervously over her shoulder from the front passenger side as her father's hands gripped the steering wheel. She felt terror. She was crying out to someone for help. Who? *Cepheus.*

The memories returned, and it became clear how she knew him, why his voice was so familiar when he stood to speak at the IPP convention several years ago and when he first appeared in her home. He was her mentor. Her parents had taught her basic meditation and intuitive proficiencies, but she needed more than that. Beyond sending and receiving messages from a single source, she received insight from her entire surroundings and was even able to, in some small way, manipulate the experiences of those around her. This caused them concern, and they turned to TARA for guidance. Because of her potential power, they paired her with Cepheus, a well-respected scholar and skilled empath. It was hoped that she would grow to be capable of transmitting data about her surroundings back to Erde more regularly, and use her skills to make Earth a better place. Her parents would ensure that she was morally grounded and would not use her power in a dangerous manner.

How on Earth could I have forgotten all that? She wondered. Ah…she knew the answer. The lightning strike, losing her parents that evening, and the fear of being in danger, the perfect cocktail for forgetting. Then take into account being thrust into the foster care system and shuffled from one home to the next, it's no wonder this got locked away deep inside her...until today.

From the far corners of her consciousness, Lucene heard a knock at the door. Being careful to only open one door at a time, she shut the red door in her mind and waited. A dark gray door appeared.

"What do you want?" Sabrina's voice demanded in the distance.

Lucene mentally opened the door to see who was on the other side.

"They're closing in. It's time to move."

Drake. Even with her eyes closed, she could visualize the young man sauntering through the door to where she lay, confident in all circumstances. The only difference between her vision and reality was that she could actually see herself, lying on the gurney, pale and helpless. He peered down at her with disinterest, and yet, there was something else that went deeper. Regret?

"Well, who's fault is that?" Sabrina snapped.

"You can't have everything, Your Majesty," Drake sucked in his breath. "You can't blow up a casino holding all the remaining IPP members on Earth and expect there *not* to be an investigation."

"Fine," Sabrina waved her long fingers at the attendant. "Wrap her up. She's going with us."

"It won't work," Lucene whispered, her eyes snapping open. Sabrina peered down at her in surprise.

"What won't work, my dear?" Hamish asked, almost sorrowfully.

"Even if you figure out the recipe, it won't work on you."

"Why the hell not?" Sabrina pushed Hamish out of the way. "Is it species-specific?"

"Nope," Lucene answered groggily. "You have to have empathy, and you have to train it regularly. You are impatient, impulsive and lack even basic sympathy for others."

Sabrina's eyes turned yellow and her claylike nails began to rapidly grow as she transformed into her lizard state. "You stupid—" she raised an arm. Hamish caught it.

"Please, my darling," he reasoned. "If you destroy her in anger, then we've lost. She can't teach us empathy if she's dead."

Lucene was on a roll, as knowledge came pouring in and flowed right back out again. "You can't explain it verbally," she emphasized 'verbally' and smacked her lips together. "You communicate with your heart and your thoughts, in that order, over great distances."

"Can those messages be intercepted?" Sabrina demanded as they began rolling the gurney toward an upright pod-like structure— presumably a protective shell so that Lucene would "keep" for the long journey. They pulled the strap off her head and neck in preparation.

"Only if you're on the same frequency," Lucene groggily rolled her head to one side, happy that it now swung freely from side to side.

"And what frequency is that?" Sabrina spat.

"Love," Lucene answered. "That's why messages go back and forth between the Data Collectors and TARA without anyone notic-ing." Lucene smiled. "It's so simple when you think about it. The Peace-Keepers are like none other. Plans for restoration and peace right under your noses, but you couldn't sense it." Lucene snorted and began laughing drunkenly.

Once again, Sabrina raised an arm. Once again, Hamish intercepted.

"Earthlings are nothing but germs in a petri dish that I can wipe out by sending one tsunami. And what did Peace-Keepers learn about war and self-defense?" she bragged. "Nothing! That's why they were so easy to destroy, one by one. Couldn't even withstand a simple interrogation without dying or going insane." Sabrina paused for a moment, peering so close to Lucene that she could smell the lizard's acidic breath.

"Neither could your son," Lucene replied softly.

"What?"

"Cepheus. He's your son, isn't he? He was a Royal but he couldn't withstand your torture either, could he?"

"That wasn't my fault," a brief look of something like remorse crossed her face. "I hadn't realized that living among the Peace-Keepers for all of those years would have turned him into putty."

"Sovereigns," a soldier addressed them as he burst into the room. "Pardon my intrusion, but I believe we have visitors who could impede our departure. Do we destroy or imprison?"

"Kill them," Sabrina announced. "What good are Earthlings to us?"

"Not Earthlings," he answered. "Your son."

"Let me handle this, my dear," Hamish replied calmly. "You must prepare for departure."

"And trust you to do what needs to be done?" Sabrina barked. "Not on my life."

28

THE RESCUE

NOW. FIVE YEARS AFTER THE ASSEMBLY.

"Let me come with you," Roman implored. He wiped his eyes with the sleeve of his ruffled shirt and stood. "I've spent several years researching the Data Collectors, the IPP and TARA. I probably know more about how the Royals operate than anyone."

"Then you know how powerful they are," Tanager reasoned.

As the group prepared to leave, Fatima quickly scooped Bagheera up. He protested as she placed him abruptly back into her carpetbag. "Sorry, kitty," she apologized, zipping it enough to prevent his escape and hanging it on her arm. "Hey," she called to the team, who were already following Tanager's lead out the door. "Don't you think we need to do something about *that* first?" She pushed the door to Roman's bedroom open, where his flowchart of images and information were clearly visible.

Ivan swallowed with some difficulty, bothered both by what he saw, and that Fatima clearly knew what was behind the bedroom door. He pushed that out of his mind for the time being.

"Not to worry, my fair Fatima," Roman was restored to his old bravado. "I have had to relocate quickly before." He ran into the room, took a long rope at the edge of the diagram in hand and pulled.

The team watched with interest. Three seconds later, the entire diagram was up in flames.

"Let's go," he instructed, taking Fatima by the arm and motioning others toward the door.

"But," Fatima protested. "Fire?"

"Flame retardant walls. It will cause a lot of smoke and may cause someone to call the fire department, but it will fizzle out in a few minutes. I disabled the smoke alarms in here for that reason. But we need to leave. Now."

With that, Tanager ran out of the room with the team close at his heels as they made their way out the door and down the back staircase leading outside.

"Respectfully," Tanager pulled Roman and Ivan aside, "I suggest you use your knowledge to assist Ivan."

Ivan's ears perked at the mention of his name. "Aye," he answered. "The vessel?"

"Exactly," Tanager nodded, reaching his car, which was parked down a side lane behind the Mongrel, its front tires on the curb and its back end hanging precariously in the street. "We need to be prepared to head out as soon as Cepheus and I retrieve Lucene." To Fatima, he advised, "You should go home. You'll be safer there."

"What home?" Fatima snorted, unwilling to be dismissed. "I've been led to believe that I no longer have one."

Tanager looked surprised. "What do you mean? What happened?"

"The Royals happened," Ivan grumbled, still not entirely sure who they were. "They blew up their home and mine." Ivan rested a hand on Fatima's shoulder. "Perhaps you'd be safest with us."

Tanager nodded. "But, be careful. If you see anything suspicious, run. Between the IPP, the military, and the Royals, I have no idea who might try to intercept you." Had Tanager known that nearly all of the IPP members—minus Drake Cummings—had been killed in an explosion in the part of a casino that no one even knew existed, he may have felt a slightly less sense of urgency, but only slight.

"At the very least, I can stand guard," Fatima offered as she, Roman and Ivan headed toward the Mongrel. She followed Ivan's lead, as he motioned for them to climb in the back and strap themselves in.

As Cepheus got in alongside Tanager in their little blue car, a few pedestrians stopped to gape at his appearance. He pulled his hood a little further over his face before they remembered that it was impolite to stare.

"Are you certain you are ready for this, my friend?" Tanager was concerned.

"Yes, it's time I faced them."

"Where are we headed?" Roman asked after they'd driven out of town and were now venturing down several overgrown and isolated streets in the middle of nowhere.

"To a preserve..." Ivan began.

"Never mind, don't say it aloud," Roman admonished, hastily. "Can't be sure who's listening."

Under normal circumstances, Fatima would have assumed it was part of Roman's delusions. But now, there was a possibility that he was right.

Ivan continued down one path after another, moving further and further from civilization. Roman wasn't even sure some of where Ivan was driving was technically roads, but the Mongrel seemed to pass over the terrain with ease. It may have been his imagination, but he could have sworn the truck was adjusting in height and width so that its body remained just above any water and tall grass, and slipped easily between cypress trees.

"We're here," Ivan finally said as he managed to park his vehicle at the center of the marsh where they now sat. He reached under his seat and pulled out knee-high rubber hip boots. "Check under your seats. You've got some, too."

Sure enough, under each seat was a pair of one-size-fits-all boots.

"Why do you have so many of these in your car," Fatima wanted to know.

"Used to run eco-tourism trips some time ago," he explained.

"Really?" Fatima was surprised. "You've been my neighbor practically forever. How did I not know this?"

"There's lots ye don't know about me," he answered seriously. Opening the driver's seat door, he hung one foot out at a time as he slipped them into the boots before sloshing his way, calf-deep in water, toward the back. "There's just one problem about our current situation," he said.

"Only one?" Fatima chortled.

"What's the problem," Roman asked.

"These Royals, whoever they may be, blew up me lab. We'll have to get by with the tools I've got here." He opened the double doors where Roman and Fatima were stationed. They'd unfastened their seat belts and were already hastily pulling on spare boots that they'd found under the seats. It was a choice between those and flippers, and the boots seemed more appropriate.

"Anything else we can use to help us?" Roman inquired.

"Well, I've got this 3-D printed micro car repair kit that might be useful."

Cepheus and Tanager drove toward the docks. "I was just here," Tanager lamented.

"Was it my fault? Did you have to come after me because of an episode?" Cepheus felt ashamed.

"Not exactly. Er…do you remember having an episode?"

"I remember not being myself, and then something bringing me back. Perhaps if I had not gone away, you would have found her sooner."

"I'm certain it would have made no difference. After all, it was you who located her, and I don't have your powers of reception," Tanager offered, graciously.

Once they arrived, Tanager stopped their vehicle. He and Cepheus jumped out not bothering to confirm that it was in park or that the engine had been turned off.

The two headed toward the abandoned warehouse at the end of the marina. "When I heard the Royals, they hadn't located Lucene yet." Tanager continued, "I can't say what happened between the time I left and now, but I know for certain that I wouldn't have been equipped to face them without your help."

Cepheus detected movement, and signaled Tanager to be quiet. On the building's ground level, demolished soot and stone lay all around them along with broken wooden beams and debris. A single lightbulb cast a dim shadow over the area, doing little to help with visibility. The warehouse appeared empty this time around. Cepheus paused for a moment to listen.

"You might want to try the roof," a voice called from beneath the docks. Odessa swam up to one of the nearby pilings. "But you didn't hear it from me."

"Thank you," Tanager seemed surprised at her continued support, given her resolve to never interfere.

"Don't thank me," Odessa called before swimming off. "I don't want to see Earth destroyed. It's my home, too." With that, she made a swanlike dive and vanished beneath the water.

Tanager turned to find Cepheus already scaling the walls of the warehouse like a brown anole. He realized that he'd have to find another way up. Running back inside, he scoured the ground floor until he found an old stairwell. As quickly as he could, be began the long climb to the roof, cursing the fact that he hadn't spent more time on the treadmill.

Preferring to travel the old-fashioned way, the Royals' vessel sat on the roof in preparation for its launch into space. To the common observer, however, it would not appear to be a spacecraft they witnessed before them, but a rooftop green space. A small green patch of grass protruded from the metal rooftop which, when viewed from a distance, appeared to be no more than an environmentally friendly mound. The irony was not lost on Cepheus, who leapt gracefully from the ledge onto the roof. The irony, of course, was that the Royals would risk destroying all of Earth's natural resources in order to take control.

Hamish sensed his arrival before he saw him. "Cepheus," Hamish said, instinctively aware that the anole had slipped beside him. Hamish stood overlooking the horizon, clad in a three-piece gray suit with a blood-red tie and black patent leather shoes, looking as human as possible. In the back of his mind, Cepheus wondered exactly who they planned to meet, since they were planning their departure from Earth and the garments were completely unsuitable for travel. Were they stopping somewhere along the way?

Just behind him, Sabrina stood, regally decked out in a bright red, sequined dress and heels with long, matching colored fingernails. On her wrist, she wore a large, round watch. "Fredo, you've got two minutes to get here or we leave without you," she screamed into the watch's receiver. "And, you can rot on this mangy planet!"

"Cepheus," she acknowledged, turning her attention to the caped man before her. She pinched his face in her hands to get a closer look. "Finally!" He resisted the urge to snap her fingers, choosing, instead, to gently break his oblong face free from her eagle-like grasp. "But, you're too late to help us now. We already have the girl. You're useless to us."

Hamish opened his mouth to protest, looking at his son, sheepishly.

At that moment, Fredo emerged from the stairwell, dragging Tanager behind him like a rag doll. "Found this in the stairwell," he grunted, tossing Tanager to the ground before crossing his tree-trunk arms in front of him, exposing the talons on each hand.

Animal-like scratch marks were visible across Tanager's neck and face. Cepheus went to rescue his friend, but Hamish stopped him. "You're too late. There's nothing you can do once the poison has reached his heart. Which, by the look of it, already has." Tanager's complexion turned a sallow yellow as the veins in his neck gradually became an intense blue. His eyes began to glaze over.

"What are you?" Sabrina asked the crumpled man on the ground, "An Earth-loving Peace-Keeper?" Then, her eyes grew wide in recognition. "Wait! Don't tell me this is Tanager, the other famous foundling responsible for training the precious Data Collectors? Some leader you are...were." She spat on the ground beside him. "Fredo, let's go," she weighted her foot alongside the green patch and reached her hand down as if to grab a handful of grass. Instead, her fingers wrapped around a lever. She lifted back the hatch and began to descend into the craft with Tanager's assailant at her heels like an overgrown puppy. "Finish this, Hamish," she commanded, "or I will."

"You have to let Lucene go," Cepheus told his father, calmly, as soon as his mother and Fredo had gone. He fought back all emotions and came from a hollow space where feelings refused to live.

"I'm afraid it's not entirely up to me, son. You know as well as I do that I'm just a figurehead and that neither of us have the power that Sabrina seems to think we do. We answer to a higher source, and that source thinks that that girl is very important to us."

Cepheus nodded for a moment, gazing off into the distance. He wasn't planning his next move, he was tuning in. It was then that he realized Lucene was already on board and they were ready to depart.

"Then, you leave me no choice," Cepheus grabbed his father by the collar with both hands and attempted to hoist him off the roof and into the water below. His father fell haphazardly over the ledge before his instincts kicked in, and he caught himself on the wall with suction-like hands, his feet scrambling to kick off his shoes, to afford him a better grip. Cepheus lost no time. He deftly climbed into the ship's hatch, setting the lift to descend at full speed once inside, anticipating another battle below. He knew his father would survive the fall but hadn't expected him to recover so quickly. Unfortunately for him, he didn't have it in his heart to kill, even now. Equally unfortunate is that his parents had no such qualms.

As expected, Fredo pulled him from the lift before it touched the floor. With a tremendous swing of his arm, the bodyguard tossed Cepheus violently into a metal wall, recoiled his arm and moved to strike a second time. Cepheus dragged himself to his feet, sidestepping the attack, and planted a blow to the side of the salamander's absurdly large head. Fredo barely flinched. He swung his battering ram arm widely, knocking Cepheus to the ground. His target's head slammed against the wall for a second time. Using what little training he could remember, Cepheus swept his leg across Fredo's knees, toppling the soldier. The red salamander landed face-first on the ground with his arms in front of him bracing his fall, artfully ending up in what could best be described as the pushup position—a skill he'd learned in the military for following up a fall to avoid broken knees and ankles. Fredo leapt to his feet with a triumphant smile in time to see that Cepheus was gone; he'd already made his way to the bridge. "Lucene, where are you?" he called, now close enough to be within earshot.

There was a muffled cry down the hall. He followed it, finding Lucene still strapped to a gurney and Sabrina pressing her hands across her mouth to stifle her scream. Even with limited mobility, Lucene had one remaining option. She bit...hard. Sabrina let out a scream. "You little..." Her poison-tipped fingernails descended as she prepared to lash Lucene's throat. Cepheus grabbed her arm and dislocated it in one move. Sabrina wailed in pain and paused to relocate it as Fredo grabbed Cepheus from behind in a bear hug. As Cepheus struggled, he pushed his feet off the gurney, which toppled sideways, taking a strapped in Lucene with it. The side of her face hit the cool surface of the floor sending pain shooting through her skull. There she remained, lying sideways, hanging painfully off the gurney from the shackles that bound her to it. Fredo's grip across

Cepheus's chest grew tighter and the wiry man struggled to breathe. His knees weakened as he became increasingly lightheaded. Fredo tossed the man back and forth, his legs flopping like a fish out of water, making it impossible for him to even kick his assailant in self-defense. Cepheus finally stopped struggling, both to catch his breath and to hopefully gain his freedom.

Suddenly, Fredo stopped, loosening his grip on Cepheus, who fell in a heap to the floor, gratefully swallowing the air around him. A trickle of blood dribbled from Fredo's mouth as he landed with thud on top of Cepheus. Once again, Cepheus, his frail-looking frame beaten, had gotten the wind knocked out of him. He squirmed out from under the massive Fredo. It was only then that he noticed an oversized fingernail protruding from Fredo's back. Hamish, in full reptilian form, stood solemnly at the beast's feet, sucking at his bloody finger, his suit tattered around him as his tail swung in agitation from side to side.

"What have you done?" Sabrina clasped her injured arm. "What have you done!" She fell to her knees, sobbing over Fredo's body.

Hamish stepped around them, removing a key from his jacket pocket and unlatching the shackles from Lucene's arms, legs and chest. He helped her slowly to her feet, trying not to bleed on her. She held onto his arm for support. Cepheus struggled to his feet and rushed to her side, eyeing his father questioningly.

"I'm sorry, my son. I was angry and felt betrayed when you left us. But what we did to you..." he said looking into Cepheus's yellow eyes and seeing a man perpetually stuck between the transformation of being half human and half lizard, one demolished by the loss of his family. "There is no excuse for what we did to you."

"You idiot!" screamed Sabrina, still sobbing over her lost Fredo. She raised her good arm and barked into her watch. "Emergency backup needed immediately, no restraint! I repeat—"

Hamish grabbed Sabrina's arm with one hand. He wrapped the other around her neck and shoved her into the wall. "Hush, my darling." To Cepheus, he admonished. "Best to go now, my son."

Cepheus bowed his head slightly, and guided Lucene back to the lift. He heard a loud choking noise, followed by silence. Hamish was saying something to those on the other end of receiver, something to the effect of, "False alarm, stand down." But he couldn't be sure. He didn't look back.

At the surface, Lucene spotted the tall blue figure of a woman with yarn-like hair standing over Tanager's body. "No!" she cried, breaking free from Cepheus's grasp and running over to kneel beside Tanager.

"He appears to be dead," Morphinae pronounced, without feeling. Having grown tired of his male and butterfly forms, Morphinae had now transmuted into a female figure.

"You are the blue butterfly Mr. Sparks talked about." Lucene wiped back tears. It was a statement, not a question.

"Yes," Morphinae cocked her head to one side, curiously.

"Can you save him?" Lucene asked.

"Perhaps." Morphinae regarded Tanager as if weighing the possibility. "But I don't understand why you need me."

"Will you help us?" Cepheus knelt on one knee and wrapped a protective arm around Lucene. "She's not ready yet, and I'm not powerful enough."

"I can only retain balance, and balance here appears to have been restored."

"The way you restored balance when you saved a young boy's life once? A boy who would come to not deserve it," Lucene spouted angrily, her eyes red from tears. Morphinae was taken aback and felt a pang of something. What was it? Guilt?

"Be careful," Cepheus warned. But Lucene could not be silenced.

"A boy whose influence led to thousands of people being killed, and a world that is now in danger of being destroyed, repurposed and repopulated out of greed. That same boy whose actions inevitably led to a very well-meaning and kind man lying dead at your feet. If you do not save this man, you have upset the balance. The universe needs more of the loving kindness that this man has to offer."

The gnawing in Morphinae's stomach grew stronger. It was a rare feeling, indeed. Morphinae relented, leaning over Tanager's stiff body, she touched a hand to his heart. His body jumped as if receiving a jolt from a defibrillator and returned to stillness. Morphinae tried again. Once again, his body jumped, but nothing more.

"We are too late," Cepheus mourned. He began twitching as his eyes began to roll back into his head.

"No, no, no," Lucene commanded. "Stay with me, Cepheus. You have to help me." He hugged her shoulders tighter and nodded, pulling himself back into the present. "I refuse to believe that we are too late," Lucene touched a hand to Tanager's heart. "Once more, please."

"Okay." Morphinae obliged, putting her hand on top of Lucene's. Instinctively, Cepheus did the same. "Come back to us," Lucene implored. She felt energy flow through her arms like a gentle wave of water, magnified by the combined intensions and energy of those around her. The branch-like strands of lightning that decorated her arms began to glow.

Tanager gasped for breath and color flooded his face. His chest heaved as he sucked in oxygen. Without thinking, Lucene grabbed his hand in hers, and held on tightly. Tanager turned his gaze toward hers and joked, "Well, she certainly is a charmer, isn't she?"

"Oh no," Lucene sniffed back, playing along. "I don't practice magic, only science." She leaned over and pressed her forehead to his for a moment before catching herself and backing away.

Tanager raised his gaze toward Morphinae. "Thank you, my friend."

"You don't need to thank me," Morphinae responded, coldly. "I am here only to restore and maintain balance, nothing more. I don't have any friends."

"Understood," Tanager acquiesced. "But should your position on such things change in the near future, we are here for you and indebted to you."

Morphinae nodded awkwardly, before rising up into the air as if attached to strings. Suddenly, her wings unfolded as she transformed herself into a little blue butterfly and fluttered away.

Cepheus helped Tanager to his feet. "We must go, quickly." The three helped each other to the stairwell as if they were a house of cards, each one holding the other up. They made a less-than quick descent, but finally reached the docks.

"You three look worse than a dried-up horseshoe crab on the beach after mating season." Odessa wrapped her arms around one of the dock's pilings, and swished her tail back and forth playfully, enjoying the show.

"Wonderful, I'm being insulted by a talking ship's figurehead," Lucene retorted. Just one month prior, she might have been taken aback by Odessa's mermaid-like appearance. But little surprised her these days.

"We might owe Odessa our gratitude for sending reinforcements," Tanager responded gracefully. The three moved as quickly as a water turtle toward their car.

"You mean, Morphinae? Nah, I had nothing to do with that." Odessa swam along beside them. "My job is only to report my findings to the Vitruvians. What they do with that information is entirely up to them."

"Of course," Tanager acknowledged, but did not stop.

"If you're heading out now," Odessa offered. "I might suggest an alternate form of transportation."

The three stopped. "What do you mean?" Cepheus asked quietly.

"You three are already a spectacle. Driving around in an easily identifiable car with angry Royals and the people they betrayed nipping at your heels might not be the way to go."

"What do you suggest?" Cepheus leaned in quietly, ignoring Odessa's obvious attempt to flash her breasts at him for attention. She did a few backstrokes, with her upper torso glistening under a strategically placed dock light.

"You might consider traveling by sea instead of land. I can't help you, of course, that would be interfering. However, if you happen to follow me without my knowing, well that cannot be helped, now can it?"

"How is it that you know where we're going?" Tanager asked, suspiciously.

"I know everything," she winked at him. "For example, if you happen to take that boat over there..." She motioned toward the dilapidated fishing boat that used to belong to Mr. Sparks, which was now wrapped in police tape. "How can I stop you? It doesn't appear to be in use at the moment. Cops have gone home for the evening, and I don't expect them to be back until first light."

Tanager lengthened his frame, standing tall with renewed energy. "Excellent." Then he turned to Cepheus and Lucene, still wearing his ridiculous fishing outfit. "Do either of you know how to sail a boat?"

"I can manage," Lucene acknowledged. "What say we follow the mermaid without her knowing it."

Odessa splashed beside them, annoyed. "I'm not a mermaid," she complained, letting out a sigh. "Off I go, unaware."

Hamish stepped over his wife's body, and then Fredo's with a surprising lack of feeling. He would figure out an excuse and how to dispose of the bodies later. For now, he knew it was time to leave.

Suddenly, something grabbed his ankle. He looked down to see Fredo staring up at him with wide black eyes. Hamish was just about to take his other heel and drive it into the salamander's face.

"Wait," Fredo gasped. "My Sovereign."

Hamish paused. It was the first time Fredo had addressed him as such, where he felt he actually meant it. It sounded almost like...respect.

"What do you have to say to me?" Hamish's tired face dropped into a deeper grimace.

"I understand if you want to kill me,"

"Well, then we agree on something," he lifted his foot.

"The baby," he gasped, coughing up blood.

"What baby?" Hamish's eyes suddenly grew wide. "You mean... Sabrina is...was...pregnant?"

"Yes," Fredo whispered.

Hamish turned to look at his wife's lifeless body on the floor.

"How is it that you knew this before me?" Terror crossed the salamander's face.

"It's not my baby, is it?" He pressed his heel into Fredo's throat. "Is...it?" *That explained Sabrina's urgency to make a baby,* Hamish thought to himself. *It was just a cover.*

"No," Fredo choked, defeated. He knew there was no chance of saving the child now–his child. It was his first and only feeling of humanity, and an emotion that felt like sorrow crept into his soul.

Hamish's first instinct was to leave them both—and the baby—to die. His thoughts returned to Cepheus. She had taken him from them. It was her fault. Now, there were no heirs to take his place. *Unless...*

Hamish picked up the receiver again. "Disregard previous orders," he feigned panic. "Send medical and military aid immediately! My dear Sabrina and I have just been attacked. So has my Royal guard. "

He leaned over Fredo's body. "Now," he grit his teeth. "If you want me to let you live, you need to hurt me enough to be convincing. Go ahead, take a swipe at me."

Fredo, his blood, spilling out over the floor and beginning to lose consciousness, obeyed, raising an arm up weakly. Hamish had to lean in so Fredo could reach. The salamander took a large swipe across Hamish's face. The Royal let out a yelp as blood trickled from his left eye.

Backup could be heard from the space craft's upper level as aid rushed to descend to their station. Moments before they arrived, Hamish gave one last order to Fredo, "You are never to speak of this incident—ever again."

29

THE GRAND ESCAPE

NOW. FIVE YEARS AFTER THE ASSEMBLY.

"This is the end of the line," Odessa called. "I can't take you any further. But I suspect you know the way from here."

They docked their boat at the water's edge with little concern about securing it and climbed onto a narrow stretch of sandy shore not much wider than three feet before being engulfed by towering tupelo trees.

"Thank you, Odessa," Tanager's voice was warm and grateful.

"Didn't do it for you," she replied as she swam away. "This is my home, too."

Cepheus sniffed the air momentarily. "This way," he instructed. Tanager and Lucene struggled to keep up with Cepheus as he seemed to move his body in putty-like fashion, wiggling between low-lying overgrown foliage. It was when he reached the freshwater swamp and began nimbly dancing across cypress knees and clinging to trees without ever actually sticking a toe in the water, that his two followers stopped to assess their situation. Cepheus disappeared soon after.

It was then that they heard low voices in the distance.

"Hang on, I've got ye covered," Ivan suddenly appeared, sloshing through the water carrying two additional sets of hip boots and a caving helmet. "Put these on. I've got cottonmouths in here."

Tanager obeyed but looked confused.

"Venomous snakes," Lucene explained, putting on the lit helmet before also accepting the boots. "You don't need to be poisoned twice in one day."

"It's just up a ways." Ivan motioned.

After suiting up and following Ivan's lead, it wasn't long before the Mongrel was in view, floating effortlessly above the water. It was what lay beyond it that caused Lucene to suck in her breath. Her helmet light caught a glimpse of something protruding from the center of the swamp. It was a tall, moss-covered dome with branches sticking out of it from all directions. It blended with its surroundings with the exception of its placement. Somehow, she recognized what it was.

At that moment, the branches moved as a hatch at the top opened and Cepheus climbed out. There was little surprise on Lucene's part that he had found his way inside the craft with such speed. "Quickly, my friend," he called to Ivan.

Ivan sloshed on as fast as possible, artfully grabbing tree limbs attached to the outside of the space craft and making his way to the top. He was not as nimble as his taller, more slender friend, but it was clear he was comfortable climbing. He followed Cepheus down the hatch, inside.

"It isn't much," Tanager apologized, turning to Lucene from their watery, ground-level view, "but it is more modern than what you on Earth are used to—a bit more space and a few more comforts. Plus, we have the option of being in hibernation for at least part of the trip."

"And, how long did you say this trip would be?" Lucene asked, standing knee-deep in water.

"If Ivan was successful in creating a virtual engine to link to our actual engine, then we may be able to make it home in half the time it took us to get here, about six months."

"This is a lot to take in," Lucene was pale.

"It may provide solace to know that if your current space agency attempted the same trip, it would take them approximately 115 years to reach our planet, given their present technology."

"A little solace." Lucene agreed.

Tanager touched her shoulder, and that familiar, comforting energy flowed through her. "I understand your feelings. Unfortunately, you are not safe here. We are your best option for survival."

"And if I hate it there, can I come back?"

"I wish I could make that promise, but I cannot guarantee we have the resources to do so, not without risking more lives and spending an enormous amount of money to do it." He was empathetic to the deep, conflicting emotions that Lucene was feeling: sadness, doubt, fear, excitement and hope all rolled into one. "You haven't been alive here for some time now. You've been hiding for years without knowing why. What I can promise you is that the quality of life, your life, will be better with us. If we can safely get you home."

"You keep saying 'home' as if it's mine. But this is the only home I've ever known."

"And how has this home treated you?"

"Well, I have my friends: Fatima, and Ivan and Isabella." Tanager cringed at the mention of Isabella, though he wasn't sure why.

"Hey! Over here," Fatima waved from the side of the craft. Her large frame looked mouse-size by comparison. Roman was beside her and reached to steady her as she threatened to lose her footing.

At that moment, a helicopter could be heard in the distance.

"I don't mean to alarm ye," Ivan popped his head out from the top of the craft. "But, that's nah good." He was referring, of course, to the helicopter, which undoubtedly carried armed military personnel. "They don't take too kindly to aliens randomly stopping by and blowing houses up!" The irony of a team of soldiers waging war at the loss of members of the Intergalactic Peace Project was lost on them as the explosion, suspiciously, did not reach the news. "Best if we talk inside," he climbed to the top of the craft. "Roman, can you help Fatima climb aboard, and then the others?"

Roman, who had slipped back into a quiet funk of depression mixed with shame, found renewed energy at the thought of possible redemption, and of being useful. He offered his arm to Fatima. "May I?" he asked, sheepishly. Fatima gently took his arm, a funny scene given that they were sloshing in murky water and not about to waltz on a marble dance floor, as his gesture suggested. She began to climb the side of the craft and was more agile than Ivan had anticipated. "Jest go fer the handles that look like rounded branches. They are secure to hold onto and step on," he offered. Roman held his hand at Fatima's back, and once realizing she was a nimble climber, began to follow her.

"I used to use the rock-climbing wall at my gym all the time, back in the day," Fatima called to Roman, proudly.

"I can see that. Good going," Roman forced a smile.

"Shall we?" Tanager suggested, lifting an upturned hand toward the craft as an invitation. "This isn't a trap. You don't have to go with us if you don't want to."

"I know," Lucene looked into his eyes. She knew he wasn't lying to her. "You go first."

"But," Tanager was well versed in old customs that called for the male allowing the woman to take the lead.

"You almost died today, Tanager," Lucene reasoned. "Even with left-over sedatives in my system, I maintain that I could sooner catch you if you lose footing than the other way around."

Tanager hated to admit that she was right. "I will follow your suggestion, not because I am unable, but because time is of the essence."

Lucene giggled.

"What is funny?" Tanager asked.

"'Time is of the essence,'" she laughed. "The only slang you know from this side of the planet is nearly a century old."

"Really? They don't say that anymore?" He glanced over his shoulder as he climbed.

"Hardly ever," she assured him.

The entrance to the vessel was centrally located, planting the group, who had now formed a small circle around the ladder leading upward, right at the main control room. Fatima, Roman and Lucene looked around in wonder. Thick bucket seats with harnesses, four on each side of the craft, lined the walls facing outward. It almost appeared as if a human-sized suit were built into each one, just waiting to wrap around anyone who sat in them. Two had steering panels in front of them, while the others had an assortment of navigational gear. Additional display panels lined the walls above and below them, all within reach, even when seated. While the chairs faced light green metal walls at present, uneven paneling suggested that they opened up to reveal windows to the outside world. Ivan and Cepheus wasted no time. They had to finish testing the system, with Cepheus taking a seat at one of the controls and Ivan disappearing through a hatch in the floor leading to the engine room. Moments later, he and Cepheus were communicating over an intercom, barking commands back and forth.

"There is a surprising amount of greenery in here," Roman noticed. Hanging from the walls were a variety of air plants and vines.

"Yes, we find it helps keep us calm, even during stressful situations," Tanager answered. "They also help purify the air, and many of them are actually edible." To demonstrate, Tanager plucked a white flower from one of the vines and took a bite. He then picked a second one and offered it to Roman, who took a hesitant bite. Roman wrinkled his forehead in anticipation, but then relaxed. "Tastes like honey," he proclaimed, rather happily.

From where they stood, they could see the corners of four slightly partitioned-off rooms, with only one having a visible door. One corner appeared to be the sleep station; another, a small efficiency kitchen and dining station; the third, a fitness and bath area; and the fourth seemed more hidden away.

"What's through there?" Lucene asked.

"It's our study and meditation room," Tanager answered. "Let me show you."

"This is like the coolest tiny house I've ever seen!" Fatima nodded excitedly. "With real estate being at a premium, I think it's fabulous that you made space for a meditation room."

"While we use it ourselves, we constructed this one with Lucene in mind. It is the vessel's largest room, aside from the engine room." Tanager motioned for them to follow. He slid a wood-covered metal door to one side. Lucene felt herself emotionally pulled inside. It had the faint smell of wild ferns with soft lighting and a domed ceiling that gave the illusion of a sunrise or sunset, depending on what time of day you were in the room. "It adjusts the scene throughout the day so that we feel less confined on our journey. It also helps us keep ourselves adjusted to the days as we travel."

"Extraordinary," was all that Roman could say.

There were deep couches forming a circle, sitting on top of a soft grass floor. The walls were forest-like, giving the illusion of being outside, surrounded by trees, with the sounds of birds and cicadas in the distance. In one corner, a small waterfall began trickling quietly, on cue with people entering the room.

"Wait," Fatima pursed her lips, "don't you have to wear clunky space suits all the time and float around uncomfortably all the way home?"

"We have lightweight emergency suits in the event of unexpected climates or internal malfunctions," Tanager answered. "But for the most part, we are able to maintain an internal gravitational system and oxygen supply much like Earth. We are typically able to wear whatever garb we choose."

Lucene, who had been looking up at their internal sky the entire time, mesmerized, said to Tanager, "Okay."

"Okay, what?" Fatima asked.

"Okay," Lucene looked at Tanager, and he heard her thoughts. *I will go with you.* His facial expression was one of relief.

"I think that means she's agreed to go with them, my darl— Fatima," Roman answered, catching himself before calling her 'darling.'"

"Yeeeeesssss!!!" Ivan could be heard exclaiming from across the vessel.

"While I share in your excitement," Cepheus called back. We must leave now. I can feel them closing in."

Sure enough, from one of his monitors, he could tell the helicopters were getting closer, which meant the trucks and sea crafts could not be far behind. One monitor was also beginning to pick up voices in the distance.

"Gather, quickly," Tanager commanded. The group obeyed, circling up, once again in the center of the vessel.

"We have enough provisions and space for whomever wishes to join us, but you have to decide now."

"Fatima," Lucene implored. "You should come with us. They can fix your heart."

Fatima's eyes welled up. "I can't go," she almost whispered. "My family is here."

"But the military and police will never leave you alone," Roman warned. "It won't be long before they discover your connection to the Data Collectors, and they will arrest you for interrogation."

"But I have nothing to hide," Fatima answered. "Once they return home, what secrets will I have?"

"Unfortunately, they might not see it that way," Roman warned.

"Er," Ivan stepped up. "That's if they find us. I happen to own this land, all 125 acres of this preserve, and another 200 acres on the other coast. I can help Fatima hide, if necessary, and reunite her with her family at a time when it is safe."

Roman felt a faint pang of possessive jealousy, but pushed it aside as he knew he had no right to it. "I'm not sure it will ever be safe, but I support your decision, if you decide to stay."

"Thank you," Fatima answered. "I will stay. And, I trust Ivan to keep us safe."

Ivan's face lit up with the pride of a small child who just rode his bike without training wheels. "Aye, I will do me best."

"I assume that means that you will be staying, Ivan?"

"Aye," he nodded, simultaneously with Cepheus as if they'd already had this discussion. "I have technology that needs to get in the right hands in order for us to have a chance at surviving in this multiverse. We are far too behind."

"Yes," Cepheus acknowledged. "And remember, it came from you."

"Aye," Ivan nodded. "I feel funny taking credit, but I understand why."

"And you?" Cepheus put a hand on Roman's shoulder.

"You know I would give anything to come with you," Roman teared up. "For me to heal and maybe even to find Far someday."

"You are welcome with us, friend," Tanager reassured him.

"We need to git," Ivan announced. He gave Cepheus a bear hug, which caught him off guard for a moment, before he wrapped his arms gently around his friend in a return hug. "Ye too, bring it in," he hugged Tanager, who awkwardly hugged him back. It wasn't as if they didn't show physical affection on his planet, he just wasn't used to Earthlings being forthright about it. He followed suit, giving Roman a hesitant half-hug, half pat on the back. Roman did the same in return.

"You're okay," Ivan decided. Roman smiled weakly back.

"Thanks," he replied.

Finally, it was Lucene's turn. "I will miss you, Ivan." Lucene's eyes welled up as she embraced him fiercely.

"Right back atcha," he answered, circling his arms around her small frame.

Fatima followed Ivan's lead, hugging each of them, one at a time. At last, Fatima faced Lucene, both now crying feverishly. "I'm gonna miss you so much," Fatima cried. "You're my best friend. And, I should tell you I still think you're crazy for going, but I understand why you would. Just be careful, okay?"

"I'm going to miss you, too," Lucene wailed back as the two women wrapped arms around one another. "But I will be okay, and I will find a way to contact you. I promise." Fatima released her and nodded.

Suddenly, Lucene gasped. "Oh my god, what about Bagheera?"

"Safely in the Mongrel, don't worry. I wouldn't let anything happen to our fur baby." Lucene let out a sigh of relief.

"We need to go now," Ivan took Fatima's arm gently. The four remaining crew members watched as Ivan and Fatima climbed up the stairs and through the hatch. "Cepheus, I'll signal ye when we're a safe distance from the vessel."

Cepheus nodded. "Stay safe, my friend."

Once they had exited, Tanager moved quickly. "Please take your seats and pull on the lever to the right of your chair. Don't be alarmed. The suits embedded in the seats will wrap around you and conform to your shape. The harnesses should then trigger automatically." He motioned to them to take specific seats on the opposite side of the control room, with he and Cepheus on the other. The two obeyed, and Lucene and Roman were soon strapped in place and feeling as if layered in bubble wrap with a thin window to the world where oxygen flowed. "I won't have time to give further instructions until we're out of this atmosphere," he yelled so they could hear him through the suits, testing their harnesses to make sure they were secure. "For now, treat this like a roller coaster in one of your theme parks. Keep your head upright, your back against the seat and hold onto your armrests. It will be a bit intense at first, but the pressure won't last long. Once we are clear, I will give the okay to get up and move around."

With that, he strapped in beside Cepheus and turned on their audio gear. He took a deep breath.

"Are you ready, my friend?" Cepheus asked.

"Ready," Tanager confirmed.

As if on cue, a message came in over the ship's speakers. It was Ivan "We're clear! Go now and be safe!"

Ivan and Fatima were now in the Mongrel, traveling through the swamps at a low speed to avoid detection. "Even if they can see us," Ivan reasoned, "they won't have the vehicles to get into these close spaces." He maneuvered the vehicle through the swamp grass and trees, and Fatima could have sworn that the Mongrel was ever so slightly changing shape to match the terrain.

"Where are we headed?" Fatima asked.

"Well, once we exit the preserve, we need to ditch this vehicle. Which reminds me,"

"Yes?"

"Is yer car reliable enough to get us to the other coast?"

"My car? Of course, it is. You of all people should know since you're the only one who repairs it, silly," Fatima laughed. "But I don't see how it can help us. We left it back at Roman's apartment, remember?"

"Well, I have a wee confession."

"Ivan, what did you do?"

"Well, ye remember at dinner when I showed ye that little present I made for you?"

"Not at all," Fatima confessed.

Ivan let out a sigh. "Never mind. Can ye reach inside yer bag and fetch me yer phone?"

"Sure." Fatima reached behind the seat to retrieve it.

"Now, just follow my instructions exactly." Ivan began rambling off demands that began with, "Hit the numbers 1 and 5 while pressing and releasing the power button 3 times," and eventually ended with, "Okay, now re-start your phone and tell me what you see."

Fatima restarted the phone. "I see a map with a little blue dot on it. The dot is moving."

"Where is the dot headed?"

"Looks like it's headed toward the highway, not too far from here."

"Yeeeessss!" Ivan shouted. "Keep an eye on where that little dot goes, okay?"

"Sure. Why?"

"We've summoned yer car. With any luck, it will meet us somewhere where we can easily retrieve it."

"Seriously?" Fatima looked over Ivan, wearing his torn jeans, faded shirt and hip boots. He hadn't even bothered to take his spelunking helmet off. "You are full of surprises, Ivan."

"Aye," he smiled. "Looks can be deceiving. Didn't know I was such a great catch, didja?"

"So, I'm discovering." Fatima sank back into her seat. "Did you say we were going to some land you own on the other coast? Do you really have over 200 acres?"

"Well, it's more like 700 acres, in total." Fatima's eyes grew wide. "Figured I'd buy as much land as I could while I had the money to help prevent more developments and habitat loss."

Moments later, she heard a shuffling from the back of the Mongrel. Bagheera had long ago found his way out of the carpetbag and had been curled up in corner in the back of the vehicle. "I suppose we should pick up a sandbox somewhere soon."

The realization hit them both at the same time. "Too late," Ivan wrinkled his nose as the scent of cat urine wafted to the front of the vehicle.

"I suppose we had that coming," Fatima reasoned. "Stuffing the poor boy in the bag."

"Aye," Ivan's entire faced cringed at the aroma.

Just then, Fatima's phone began to ring. "It's my mom. She must have heard the news and is freaking out."

"Don't answer, and don't touch anything on yer phone, not until we git yer car."

"But she'll just keep calling. And, if I don't answer, soon, *everybody* in my family will be on high alert."

"As soon as we get to the other coast, we'll find a way to get a message to them. I promise."

Fatima nodded, and sank back in her seat.

30

DRAKE AND MORPHINAE

TUESDAY EVENING. ONE DAY AFTER THE ESCAPE.

T hings hadn't gone at all the way Drake had planned. He sat in a club chair in the corner of his hotel suite staring at the floor. A wall-mounted reading light hung over him as he poured himself yet another scotch. It was well after midnight, but he was still dressed in a dark blue suit with a matching tie and a crisp white shirt underneath from an earlier meeting with the Royals. He hadn't even bothered to take his leather shoes off. Behind him, the waves of the Gulf could be heard crashing against the shore, along with the faint sound of beachcombers drunkenly singing "Margaritaville" and laughing as if no one had thought of that before.

At 12:09 a.m., there was a knock at the balcony door. Not the front door, mind you, but the balcony door which was three stories from the ground level.

"Come in, Morphinae," Drake grunted.

Morphinae entered the room quietly via the balcony, and Drake did not even question how he managed the lock. This evening, Morphinae was dressed exactly as he remembered him as a boy: torn jeans, a blue crochet face and with button eyes.

"Do you know why I am here?" Morphinae asked, standing over the man.

"Why don't you tell me," Drake answered roughly, downing the last of his drink and looking up at Morphinae.

"I upset the balance when I saved you that day. I have to make amends."

"Killing me won't make amends," Drake laughed nervously. "Do you know how many people have been murdered or injured as a result of my actions?"

"Three thousand two hundred forty-eight," Morphinae said, blinking.

Drake hung his head. "Can you grant a man one final drink before taking your revenge?"

"Of course," Morphinae granted. "But I am only a Balance-Keeper. I seek no revenge."

"Right," Drake poured himself as tall a serving as his glass would allow and held up the bottle to offer Morphinae some as well. Morphinae shook his head, declining.

"If it helps, I will not kill you in any worse manner than the fate you would have suffered if you had drowned. In fact, if you prefer, I can drown you in the—"

"It's probably best if you don't tell me, and make it as quick as possible," Drake held up his hand.

"Of course. I will try not to make you suffer."

"Why are you being so nice to me?" Drake questioned. "I don't deserve it."

"I hold myself accountable as much as I do you," Morphinae explained. "After all, had I not saved you, none of this would have happened. I feel as much remorse as I sense that you too now feel."

"I tried not to care." Drake gulped his scotch. "I tried to be the hard businessman and consummate professional. But then I turned over the nicest employee, nicest woman, I have ever known to some of the worst people on the planet, strike that, in the universe." He brushed away what looked like a tear. "And in the end, I couldn't go with them, couldn't bear to watch what they might do to her. I am weak."

Morphinae nodded. "I understand. I am not prone to feelings, and yet I was moved too when she was almost taken by the Royals."

"Almost?" Drake gazed a drunken head up, with interest.

"Yes, the Peace-Keepers from TARA intervened just in time."

"Excellent. That's great," Drake answered, thinking. "Where is Lucene now?"

"She's with them, why does it matter?" Morphinae nodded, noting that Drake was nearly finished with his drink.

"Well, you are technically a Vitruvian, are you not?"

"Yes, but I am also a Balance-Keeper. We follow a special law. You know this."

"But, wouldn't it help you make amends for your actions if you and I worked together to bring Lucene to your people instead? I mean, who better to ensure that her powers are used in the fairest way possible than the Virtruvians? The bleeding-heart Peace-Keepers on Erde wouldn't even begin to know what do with that kind of power."

Morphinae's face dropped into a frown of disappointment and Drake could almost see a shadow pass before his eyes. He set down his empty glass. With no further hesitation, Morphinae spoke, "It's time."

31

ISABELLA AND THE LONGHORN BEETLE

TUESDAY EVENING. ONE DAY AFTER THE ESCAPE.

"How are you feeling, Reverend Isabella?" the nurse asked the woman lying in a hospital bed in a private room. She was no longer being given oxygen, but an IV was still supplying her with necessary pain killers and healing remedies. Unlike the stark white walls and rampant smell of disinfectant in the old style of hospital care, this one had nature-green walls and sea-colored tile floors. The faint blend of cinnamon and clove could be detected in the air. There was a light drumming music playing over a portable sound system in the room.

"I am well, my dear Miranda." Isabella smiled at the young nurse. She thought to tell her she needn't call her "Reverend" outside of ceremony but decided against it. Knowing Miranda, she would continue to do so anyway, and chastise herself every time she forgot. So, she remained silent. "I was shot the other evening in my own sanctuary, and yet I am still alive to talk about it. I'm guessing the Universe isn't finished with me just yet."

Miranda smiled at her minister in gratitude. "Of course, it isn't," she answered. "We need you." With that, the nurse left, and Isabella settled in for a short meditation. As she began drifting off to the quiet sounds of the drums, she noticed something.

"Well, hello there," she glanced at the large yellow and black Longhorn beetle that was resting calmly on her arm. "I didn't see you until just now. A beetle is a sign of transformation. Will you now be taking me to a different realm?" The beetle gave no response, but instead of brushing it away, Isabella simply laid back and smiled, sinking into her meditation.

Oh, no, Odessa thought happily as she calmly rested on the older woman's arm. *You are right about transformation. But your friend Miranda is also correct. This world needs you.* She smiled in anticipation. *We are going to have so much fun together!*

ABOUT THE AUTHOR

Danielle Palli

Danielle Palli is a writer, business owner, multimedia specialist, mindfulness coach, and podcast producer and co-host. She lives in Southwest Florida with her husband and far too many pets. She also finds joy in nature, travel, theater and the arts, and is known for singing and dancing around the living room at any hour of the day or night. Also, you can convince her to attend almost any event if you promise her that she can wear a themed costume. Learn more at www.birdlandmediaworks.com.

CPSIA information can be obtained
at www.ICGtesting.com
Printed in the USA
FSHW020958110122
87382FS

9 780989 989381